The Hanging Place

Nick Louth is a million-copy bestselling thriller author, and an award-winning journalist. After graduating from the London School of Economics, Nick was a foreign correspondent for Reuters, working in New York, Amsterdam, London and Hong Kong. He has written for the *Financial Times*, *Investors Chronicle*, *Money Observer* and *MSN*. His debut thriller, *Bite*, was a Kindle No. 1 bestseller and has been translated into six languages. The DCI Craig Gillard series and DI Jan Talantire series are published by Canelo, and in audio by WF Howes. He is married and lives in Lincolnshire.

Also by Nick Louth

Bite
Heartbreaker
Mirror Mirror
Trapped

DCI Craig Gillard Crime Thrillers

The Body in the Marsh
The Body on the Shore
The Body in the Mist
The Body in the Snow
The Body Under the Bridge
The Body on the Island
The Bodies at Westgrave Hall
The Body on the Moor
The Body Beneath the Willows
The Body in the Stairwell
The Body in the Shadows
The Body in Nightingale Park

Detective Jan Talantire

The Two Deaths of Ruth Lyle
The Last Ride
The Dark Edge
The Deep End
The Hanging Place

THE HANGING PLACE

NICK LOUTH

canelo

Penguin Random House

First published in the United Kingdom in 2026 by

Canelo Crime, an imprint of
Canelo Digital Publishing Limited,
20 Vauxhall Bridge Road,
London SW1V 2SA
United Kingdom

A Penguin Random House Company
The authorised representative in the EEA is Dorling Kindersley Verlag GmbH.
Arnulfstr. 124, 80636 Munich, Germany

A CIP catalogue record for this book is available from the British Library.

ISBN 978 1 80436 891 6

Cover design by Andrew Smith

Cover images © Shutterstock.com

Printed and bound in Great Britain by Clays Ltd, Elcograf S.p.A.

Look for more great books at
www.canelo.co | www.dk.com

For Louise, as always

Chapter One

Detective Inspector Jan Talantire was heading at speed from Barnstaple CID into Exmoor National Park, her familiar destination, on call yet again to the police and crime commissioner. It was a beautiful May morning, and she was driving with the windows open along flower-filled lanes with high hedges. She turned her unmarked Skoda into the wooded lane, under mature horse chestnuts, whose unfurling leaves and candelabra-like blooms left a beautiful scent.

It was a good hour-and-a-bit drive from the north-west Devon coast to the village of Little Bychecombe, deep in the heart of Exmoor where the Honourable Lionel Hall-Hartington had built his Sleepy Monk cheese brand. Not so much a farm as a hefty industrial estate, with a thousand head of dairy cattle, a couple of thousand sheep, an enormous creamery and several warehouse-sized sheds used for maturing cheese. All this was not quite in keeping with the rural ethos of the Exmoor National Park that contained it, but then this was a man who could pull strings in all the right places.

Talantire drove past the high stone gates of Bychecombe Manor, their fifteen-foot pillars topped by sandstone griffons, heading towards the service road that led to the farm proper. She took in the Jacobean manor house itself, with a magnificent façade, crenellated rooftop and gorgeous pilasters, set amid fabulous gardens and built on the site of earlier military fortifications going back at least to the Norman era. The Hall-Hartington family dominated the village, almost all of which was on lease to the estate, which Lionel had inherited from his late wife. To the untrained eye, it was picture postcard perfect, with neat cottages and a triangular village green, protected from untidy parking by whitewashed stone posts connected by hefty iron chains. The pub, a Georgian honeystone delight called the Griffon, was an upmarket fine dining establishment, where even the starters had two-digit prices. Like the chintzy tearoom next door, it was owned by the estate. Talantire had heard that there was a growing resentment within the village against the Hall-Hartingtons, where the conditions of the lease prescribed the colour and style of exterior decoration – including the maintenance and care of the front gardens, which were to be laid out with traditional English country flowers. One anonymous local resident had been quoted in the local paper describing the rules as a kind of modern-day serfdom, particularly the strongly encouraged 'voluntary' participation in the annual ragwort pulling festival over the August bank holiday to eradicate the pervasive and poisonous weed from the estate's pastureland. Nevertheless, the expansion of the farm had provided dozens of jobs to local people and ensured that the village continued its run of winning regional 'best kept' prizes at least every other year.

As Talantire turned right into the service road to the farm, she noted the electrically operated metal gates controlled by pole-mounted cameras. She had heard the Honourable Lionel boasting about how they use the same number plate recognition system as airport car parks. She also knew that the wily thieves who targeted sprawling farms like this one were not so easily stopped. The service road became an avenue of horse chestnuts with parkland on either side, and the cattle were enjoying the fresh pastures.

Talantire parked between a pair of huge warehouses, adding her rather tatty grey Skoda to a row of more upmarket vehicles, from Range Rovers down to the original old-fashioned green Land Rover, and a single police patrol car. A balding mid-forties individual in overalls came out to see her. His name was embroidered over the breast pocket, below the name of Sleepy Monk Creamery: Bassin. Talantire recalled he was from Slovenia.

'Ms Talantire, please come this way.' She followed him into a large nineteenth-century barn, which had been converted into an office. Four employees were sitting around on chairs and desks, while a PC called Carl Smith asked them questions. They all looked up as she walked in.

PC Smith greeted her and said, 'I'm really glad you're here because I've been getting it in the ear from the commissioner.'

'He's been going absolutely fucking berserk,' offered Bassin with a slight smile.

'Well, we can't show favouritism, Constable,' she said.

'It's been a pretty clever theft, ma'am,' PC Smith said. He indicated a CCTV screen. Bassin took over, playing some night-time footage.

'The two bastards came in on electric scooters,' Bassin said. The screen showed two hooded individuals, both slim and young-looking, speeding one behind the other past a camera, which clearly had an infrared lens. The timer showed 2:17 a.m. 'They must've carried them down

3

the footpath from Great Bychecombe, because the first time we see them is at the back of the old barn. It's the next building to the equipment storage.' He flicked from one camera to the next, showing that they knew exactly where to go. 'As you can see here, they forced off the padlock.'

It was less than a minute later when the two quad bikes were seen roaring out of the shed, with electric scooters strapped across the back.

'They must have known where the keys were kept,' Talantire said. 'To be out that fast.'

'No. The key cabinet wasn't touched,' said one of the men.

'It has an alarm,' Bassin added.

'I told them they should use quad clamps,' PC Smith said.

'It's a waste of time,' Bassin said. 'It really slows us down every morning to have to take them off, and yet we've seen clips of thieves using angle grinders to cut through them in less than a minute.'

'Do you have trackers?' Talantire asked him.

'Yes.' It came as a chorus from all the men.

Talantire, having recently been to a rural crime forum, was aware that criminal gangs in some cases had been able to either locate the devices and remove them or mask the signal by covering most of the machine in silver foil.

'You see, the thing is,' Bassin said, 'that we had a quad bike stolen two years ago, and that's why we put in the metal gates on the service road. With all the new galvanized kissing gates on the public footpaths, there is no other route out that is wide enough for a quad bike. We built up the hedges, reinforced the fences and everything.'

'So how did they get out?'

'They got out at the top of Buttercombe into National Trust woodland,' said another of the men – Bob Slater, according to his overalls. He was in his fifties, with a few strands of greying hair slicked down over his scalp.

'How?' she asked.

'Well, let me show you,' Bassin said. He led them all out of the building and up a muddy track, with quad bike tracks clearly in evidence in the thick, chocolatey mud. The track led to a meadow, which had been churned up by identical tyre tracks. They took the steep 300-yard walk to the top of the field, which was bounded by mature hedges of hazel, field maple and blackthorn, a good ten feet high. Before the hedge was a weed-filled ditch. The track ran straight up to the edge of the ditch and simply vanished.

It looked baffling.

'They must've put planks across the ditch,' Slater said. 'These big old stems have been cut, the hedge above removed and then put back again neatly,' he said, pointing low down to the neat cuts through four-inch-thick field maple.

'That would have taken them a while surely, and someone would have heard the noise at that time of night,' Talantire said.

'They probably did it several days before,' Bassin said. 'Cut it in advance, trim down any tangles that would impede the quick removal, then on the day a couple of guys on the other side would pull them away as the quad bikes approached. Then remove the planks and replace the hedge plants. Bingo.'

'It's brilliant,' Talantire conceded.

'These people aren't local idiots, you know,' Slater said. 'They're organised, and it's only because of who his nibs is that you lot are actually round here. When Pennycoat Farm was done last year, no one came for a month – and even then it was a PCSO.' He indicated with a thumb over his shoulder.

Well, blame the commissioner, Talantire thought. *He is the man who controls the resources.* She realised she couldn't say that in front of this group of people. Of course, she recalled that putting a stop to the epidemic of rural crime was part of the Honourable Lionel's pitch to be elected as commissioner three years ago. And now, ironically, it was his own farm that had been targeted yet again. The effrontery of the criminals was astonishing, thumbing their noses at the most senior police official in the county.

Slater and one of the other farmhands removed a section of the hedge so that Talantire could step through into the woodland beyond. It wasn't hard to follow the quad bike tracks, which led a hundred yards or so towards a track, then headed off the half mile towards a B road. Where the track joined the road, there was some evidence of vehicles having parked on the soft verge, but the quad bike tracks entirely disappeared as soon as the first bit of asphalt was reached. The nearest ANPR cameras were miles away, but she supposed they would have to look at them nonetheless. The commissioner would expect nothing less.

PC Smith had already taken statements from most of the employees, and Talantire looked through them. Bassin had mentioned that a week previously, he had spotted a small commercial quad copter drone flying low over the farm and passing through the central courtyard where the equipment was kept. He had reported it to Hall-Hartington, who ordered him to shoot it down with a shotgun. However, by the time he had taken the weapon from the locked gun cabinet and loaded it, the drone had disappeared.

Talantire viewed this as potentially important information. The drone would be the perfect way of reconnoitring for a crime of this nature. Rural crime may have sounded like a backwater in policing terms, and certainly didn't have its fair share of resources, but the thieves were clearly savvy and clued up on the latest technology.

–

Back at Barnstaple CID, Talantire stood with digital evidence officer Primrose Chen as she logged onto the tracking software that was embedded on the quad bikes. She typed in the serial numbers of the two vehicles and hit seek. Nothing came up. She clicked through to the historical tab and saw the trace as they were driven up towards the edge of the farm at Buttercombe and through the National Trust woodland. The traces ended at the B road.

'They were probably driven into a lorry at this point,' Talantire said.

'It seems like a professional job to me,' Primrose said.

'I agree. Perhaps a reconnaissance by drone followed up by a night-time raid. There was very little chance of them being caught. Still, I don't think Bagpuss will see it that way.'

Primrose grinned from beneath her hijab. Having overheard the commissioner's wife's pet name for her husband, he was rarely referred to in any other way by the police who had to respond to his every whim. And it was certainly true that the commissioner's flat and rather florid face bore some resemblance to the cartoon cat.

'We do have some leads that we can follow,' Talantire said. 'Two quad bikes were stolen from the farm a couple of years ago, and I recall that we had some CCTV footage of the culprits. Dave Nuttall was looking at it. More recently, an unattended quad bike was stolen from one of the fields and turned up for sale on Gumtree.' She called across to Nuttall, who had just finished a phone call. 'Dave, I'm following up the latest twists in the Bychecombe Manor quad bike thefts. I'm after every bit of background you have on the previous investigations.'

'Right you are,' Nuttall said. 'There's quite a bit in the files.' A reliable detective in his mid-forties, divorced and a lifelong jazz fan, he was wearing his trademark leather jacket and jeans, thick-framed glasses, dyed dark hair slicked back. In some lights he looked like a throwback Teddy Boy or 1950s rocker.

Talantire looked over his shoulder as he pulled up the relevant information. 'Derek Cloddy was the thief we caught through Gumtree. He had no significant previous convictions, so he got a suspended sentence of two years. He wasn't local, so we assume he had a co-conspirator, but he kept his mouth shut.'

'He doesn't sound quite professional enough for this latest gig,' Talantire said. 'But let's speak to him anyway. What about the CCTV of the previous theft?'

'That didn't show anything much,' Nuttall said. 'Two guys dressed in black, balaclavas, gloves.'

'Okay, let's trawl the known names in rural crime and find out who could have done it. Look at the heating oil theft list too, and the location of known Traveller families. I'll contact neighbouring police forces as far east as Wiltshire.'

The double doors to CID squeaked open behind her, and from the stiffening expression on Nuttall's face, she assumed someone senior had just arrived.

'Ah, there you are, Jan.' The commissioner's rumbling tones were quite distinctive.

'Hello, sir,' she said, turning around to face him. The Honourable Lionel Hall-Hartington was an imposing figure in his late seventies, his face a gammon hue that spoke of years of alcohol. Today, at least, he appeared to be sober. 'Shall we go to the meeting room?'

'Lead on, then,' he said, following her. 'You really must get to the bottom of these thefts. It is making me look a laughing stock.'

'We're putting a lot of resources into it, let me assure you,' she said, leading him into one of the larger glass-fronted meeting rooms so she wouldn't have to sit too close to him.

'Five damn quad bikes stolen in the last four years, and only one recovered. It's just not good enough,' he said before she had even closed the door. The commissioner eased himself into a chair with a sigh.

'We think it is a very professional job, sir, and possibly connected to the drone that was seen over the farm in previous days. There's not much to go on, given that the trackers and the vehicles seem to be masked, so let's begin by interviewing those known to be active in this type of rural crime.'

'That's all very well, but it seems rather speculative to me,' he said.

'The other possibility, which I want to raise rather tentatively with you, is that it may be an inside job or one with inside connections. Have you recently let any members of staff go? Are there any ongoing disputes between staff members that you are aware of?'

'We've let one or two go over the years, but the staff are thoroughly vetted,' he said. 'There are plenty of valuable items in the manor house, after all, which would make the theft of a quad bike seem rather small beer.'

'Really? Would you care to share that information with me?'

'Well, as you know there were some rather special Anglo-Saxon items found on the farm back in the 1980s, including the Bychecombe Brooch.'

'I hadn't heard of it,' she admitted.

'Well, the entire hoard spent the last fifteen years on loan to the Ashmolean Museum in Oxford, but we've got a few items back at the moment, and they're in the safe. I plan to have a little exhibition before they're on loan again to the Metropolitan Museum of Art in New York in July.'

'I take it this collection is very valuable?'

'It's unique, because the garnet gem used on the brooch is of a very rare green variety called demantoid, which the experts say was mined in Persia around the time of Christ. Worth millions, I suppose.'

'Is it known that it's back at Bychecombe Manor?'

'Not widely, but I think some employees know.'

–

It was two weeks later when Talantire was next in the area. She and her boyfriend Adam had arranged a Friday lunch at the Forge, a gastro pub in the neighbouring village of Great Bychecombe, just three miles from the farm. She had a day off and he had taken time away so they could steal a few hours together before the weekend.

As she pulled into the car park, she saw that Adam's car was already there. She found a space and made her way towards the back of the pub, past a series of picnic tables in an orchard filled with apple blossom. At one of the tables she spotted two glam middle-aged women, one of them in a wheelchair, laughing uproariously. She knew her. Helena de Courchevel, Mrs Hall-Harrington, the wife of the police and crime commissioner. She was smoking a cigar, the acrid smoke drifting across the garden. Helena recognised Talantire and called her over.

'Camilla, let me introduce our very own wonder woman, Jan Talantire,' she said loudly to her companion. 'This is a woman who is single-handedly taking a stand against misogyny in Devon and Cornwall Police.'

Talantire felt that she should curtsy to this elegant and imperious woman, and she was aware that many of the other groups in the garden were staring at her. 'Jan, this is my friend Dr Camilla Kerr-Wallace from London. We go back absolutely years.'

Camilla giggled and looked at Talantire. She was expensively dressed, very tanned and had the same high cheekbones and effortless grace as her companion. They were most of the way down a bottle of Prosecco. 'Are you the one chasing up the stolen quad bikes for Bagpuss?' Camilla asked.

'For my sins, yes.'

'Do you have any "hot leads"?' Helena asked in a stage whisper that could easily have carried across to everyone else sitting in the orchard. She exhaled voluminously from her cigar, and the smoke drifted across the garden.

'Nothing that I could share in such a public environment,' Talantire whispered. Over Helena's shoulder, she saw a beetroot-faced man marching over to the table from an adjoining group.

'Madam, do you mind not smoking that disgusting thing where people are eating?'

'Frankly, darling, I don't give a flying fuck,' Helena replied, her pale green eyes fixing on him. She blew out a fresh plume of smoke, which rose above her and drifted across the man's apoplectic face.

'I shall speak to the manager,' he said.

'Knock yourself out,' Helena replied, as Camilla giggled. Helena then turned to his retreating form and called out, 'When you do, get him to bring out a fresh bottle for us. There's a darling.'

Talantire backed away from the confrontation and explained that she was expected inside. Helena nodded and dismissed her with an inflected eyebrow. By the time Talantire got inside the pub, beetroot face was engaged in a heated conversation with a young man at the bar. She didn't envy him the task of tackling Helena de Courchevel. Squeezing past the two of them, she saw Adam seated at a quiet table at the far end of the pub. He stood up as she approached, and they embraced. 'I've missed you,' she said.

'Me too. I've been looking forward to this,' he said, 'and to seeing you again.'

Talantire immediately filled him in on the details of what she had seen.

'Well, it looks like they are getting a fresh bottle,' Adam said, looking over her shoulder at a waitress heading out to the garden with Prosecco.

'Let's give them a wide berth,' Talantire said.

Talantire picked up a menu and began to peruse the offerings. It was a bit more expensive than her usual pub grub, but they had something to celebrate. They had decided to move in together. At this stage it would probably be a rented home in Barnstaple, which would mean Adam leaving his place in Tiverton. If all went well, they would buy somewhere together in six months or so. Talantire's current rental place was a bit dowdy, and pooling their resources meant they could afford something with a bit of space at the back, a double garage, somewhere to put Adam's windsurfer and various other accumulated stuff. She had already spent quite a few hours on Rightmove, scoping out the possibilities. She really did not want to spend any more time living on Cornwallis Avenue, which had no longer felt safe in the last few months, when she was under surveillance. With her suspension over, she would feel confident enough to take on a mortgage for the first time in her life. With Adam, the first man she'd actually been able to trust in years, she finally felt ready for a new chapter in her life.

When the waitress approached, Talantire ordered the lamb tagine with couscous, while Adam chose a rare breed pork chop with dauphinoise potatoes. They opted for sparkling water.

An hour and a half later, as they left, Helena and her friend were still there, most of the way down the next bottle. The man who had complained had departed along with his family, and the orchard had emptied out. As they walked past the table, there was a distinctive miasma of cannabis. The ashtray Helena had used had what appeared to be the remains of a joint sitting next to the butt of the cigar. Talantire was aware that the commissioner's wife had already been given a quiet warning about the public consumption of weed. Though a cannabis derivative called Sativex was licensed by the NHS for the treatment of multiple sclerosis, the legality did not extend to the generalised consumption of the drug.

Helena spotted her and called her over. 'Jan, darling, aren't you going to introduce me to your charming young man?' She was drunk and possibly stoned too.

'This is Adam. Adam, this is Helena de Courchevel, and Camilla.'

'Glad to meet you,' Adam said.

'Have you been invited to the engagement party?' Helena asked. 'My god-daughter Sally is getting engaged, next Saturday afternoon at the Griffon, Little Bychecombe. Do come along both of you. There's an open bar.'

'That's very kind,' Talantire replied. 'But I'm working that weekend.'

'Well, Adam can come along on his own,' Helena replied. 'We're always short of handsome men, aren't we, Camilla?' Camilla cackled wickedly at this comment.

At this moment, Talantire heard a car horn in the car park and looked up to see a taxi.

'Ah, that's for us,' Helena said.

Talantire made her goodbyes and led Adam out past the taxi.

'She's quite a character,' Adam said, glancing back.

'Yes, she had a good lingering look at your bum,' Talantire teased.

'Helena must've been rather beautiful back in the day,' Adam said. 'She still has a rather graceful air about her.'

'She's his second wife, and a former model apparently. Prefers her maiden name to the hyphenated Hall-Hartington, and she doesn't like to be called Mrs. The commissioner inherited the farm on the death of his first wife, Gill, more than a decade ago. To be fair to him, he has built up the cheese business from nothing to a national brand. Not bad for the son of a forklift truck driver.'

'So how did he become the Honourable Lionel Hall-Hartington?'

'Well, so I've been told, Lionel is his middle name. He was born plain old Brian Hall. The Hartington bit came when he married into the local landowners here and agreed to hyphenate the name. The Honourable came from being the son of a lord.'

'A forklift truck-driving lord?' Adam asked with a chuckle.

'Yes. Eric Hall, his dad, was a leading light in the trade union movement in the 1960s, and he was ennobled as a life peer in the resignation honours of Harold Wilson. The story goes that he hadn't driven a forklift truck for a good twenty years by that time, although he did have a short stint as head gardener at a stately home after his formal retirement. Anyway, the son of a lord can call themselves The Honourable, and Lionel, not sharing the left-leaning politics of his late father, didn't waste any time in doing so. It might well have been an important asset in winning the hand of Gillian Hartington of Bychecombe Manor. She couldn't have children, and they adopted an East European orphan in 2002. Rustam turned out to be a bit of a wild child and lives up in London now. After Gillian's death in 2007, and with the creamery business now in the hands of professional managers, Lionel turned his hand to politics. There followed a career in Devon County Council, and then three years ago he decided to stand as the crime commissioner.'

'And there was me thinking he was from a long line of landowning gentry.'

'Not at all,' Talantire said. 'The man thoroughly rein-vented himself.'

'And crowned it all by getting a trophy spouse.'

'Well, she's clearly a bit of a handful.'

'Yes, but I bet she's fun.'

'She's old enough to be your mother,' Talantire said with a laugh. 'So, are you thinking of going to the party then?'

'Well, it does have a free bar.'

On the Saturday of the party, Talantire was called out to an assault case in South Molton, a market town halfway between Barnstaple and Tiverton and just south of the Exmoor National Park. A dispute between two neigh-bours over a boundary fence had escalated, and one elderly man had assaulted another, apparently with a pair of garden shears. Four PCs were at the scene, trying to keep order between the two families, while the shears – clearly seen by at least one witness – seemed to have disappeared. One man was being tended by paramedics at the scene. Although this really was a job for a local detective constable, there was no one available. Cover seemed a little bit thin.

She arrived at the address at one p.m. to find that the ambulance had gone, having taken the wounded man to hospital. One of the PCs had quickly secured some doorbell camera footage from one of the homes, while statements were in the course of being taken from the numerous witnesses. What no one had so far thought to do was to photograph the bloodstains on the garden fence and on the paved path adjoining it at the rear of the house. She got some evidence markers from the car, plus a DNA swab kit, and took plenty of pictures. The assailant, Bernard Cunningham, a retired solicitor aged seventy-three, was sitting in an armchair in the lounge of his house, resisting the attempts by two young female PCs to get him to voluntarily go with them to Barnstaple police station. They all looked up as Talantire entered the room.

'He doesn't want to go, ma'am,' said the shorter of the two.

'They never do,' Talantire said.

It soon became apparent that the two officers, clearly from the modern 'nicely does it' school of policing, hadn't formally arrested him and were intimidated by the legal verbiage being spouted by the man about defendants' rights. 'I had an artificial hip operation just last week,' he said. 'I was told to rest it.'

'Right, I'll take over,' Talantire said. 'Mr Cunningham, you are under arrest for aggravated assault and will be taken to Barnstaple police station where you will be charged.'

'I want to see my—'

'You are not obliged to say anything—'

'Stop being ridiculous, I was merely—'

'—but it may harm your defence if you do not mention when questioned something which you later rely on in court. Anything you do say may be given in evidence. Now please get up.'

'You can't arrest me.'

'Just watch,' Talantire said, lifting the man bodily from his seat.

'Ow, ow,' he complained about the grip she had on his elbow, trying to wriggle out of her hands. She was pleased to see that both PCs had their bodycams on, so there could be no doubt about due process being carried out.

'Do you want to be marched out in handcuffs as well, in front of all your neighbours?' Talantire asked. 'Stop struggling right now, or I'll add the charge of resisting arrest.' She grinned at the two PCs, who were watching her with admiration. The man was affected by a limp and bitterly complained about the pain in his hip. Talantire glanced at his wife, who was standing with her arms folded. 'Is this just for effect?' she asked her. 'Or does he really have this much difficulty walking?'

'Well,' she began, not making eye contact.

'If he has a stick, a crutch or a walking frame, let's have it now.'

'He hasn't got any of those,' she said.

'He certainly seemed to be fit enough to stab a neighbour with a pair of garden shears. Right, Mr Cunningham, walk to the car, please,' Talantire said. She watched as the two PCs manhandled the now quiescent assailant into a patrol car, while several neighbours stood around clapping. She called in her location and summarised the state of the case for the control room, telling them she was planning to return to CID.

'We've just had a 999 call, ma'am, from Bychecombe Manor. There's been a shooting reported.'

'What? Bychecombe Manor!'

'Yep.'

'Okay, I'll get straight onto it,' Talantire said. The time was 2:40 p.m. 'I'll take two of the PCs from here.'

The uniforms were getting the same reports on their radios that she had just had. A uniformed inspector was coming from Tiverton with two cars, and there was a

CSI unit being dispatched from Exeter. She jumped into her unmarked Skoda. PCs Emily Hathaway and Gary Finnegan followed in a patrol car. As she screeched off, heading north, she set up the hands-free and asked the control room for more details about the shooting.

'Several shots were heard from within the farm, and there is at least one dead. The caller is the housekeeper, sounds like a foreign national. There is apparently a lot of blood.'

Chapter Two

It was a less than ten minutes' drive to Little Bychecombe. The Griffon pub, on the village green, was thronged with people in their summer finery, milling about, many of them on their phones, others in tears being comforted by friends. Talantire now recalled that there would have been an engagement party in full swing. Stragglers from the party tried to stop the patrol car behind her, but her unmarked vehicle slid through the crowds easily, as she had turned off the blue lights on entering the village. She eased the vehicle between the sandstone pillars of the manor house with their guardian griffons and pulled the car to a halt on the gravel apron. Some baler twine had already been looped around the porticoed entrance as some kind of informal barrier, but there were plenty of onlookers even here. Two young men, both in suits, stood guard. Talantire noticed immediately that one of them had blood on the cuff of his jacket. As she emerged from the car, the other one came over. He looked no older than nineteen, a rugby player's body squeezed into a tight suit underneath a chubby face and curly blonde locks.

'The gaffer has been shot,' he blurted out. 'I mean Mr Hall-Hartington, he's dead, slumped in his office, watching the rugby.' He began to cry but fiercely wiped his tears on his sleeve. Talantire could smell drink on him. He gave his name as John Rice, a vehicle mechanic.

'How many people have been inside, and who are they?' she asked.

'There's me, and Digby there.' Rice pointed to the man with the bloodstained cuff. 'He's the head of IT. Then there's Soraya, the housekeeper, who raised the alarm. She's sitting inside with my aunt in the grand hall. What do we do?'

'Right, stay here, John. Don't let anybody else in. This is a crime scene, and we need to keep any forensic detail we find uncontaminated.'

Another man came over, scruffy haired, but wearing a shirt and tie.

'Were you inside?' Talantire asked.

'No,' he said.

'He just came from the party,' Rice said. 'He's Bob Slater's nephew Gavin.'

Behind her she heard sirens. She glanced across and saw three patrol cars, a riot van and an ambulance.

'Are there any other entrances to the house?' she asked the lad.

'Yeah, there's the kitchen door around the back and the scullery door – that's in the basement and goes to the walled garden. There is also a fire escape from the first floor, which is usually locked.'

Talantire heard constabulary boots at a run and turned to see a familiar face, Inspector Tony Thompson, leading a group of uniformed officers. After exchanging terse greetings, she briefed them on the various exits. 'I think we need an officer on each of them, given the crowds there are around here,' she said. Thompson dispatched several constables to the various exits outlined, before turning back to Rice.

'Who's in charge of the business at the moment? Is someone on site?' he asked.

'Almost everybody was at the engagement party, down there at the Griffon,' Rice replied. 'But there was bound to be someone in the office, given the thefts we've had.'

'I see CCTV cameras,' Talantire said, looking up at the portico, where one was visible. 'Where are they run from?'

'The farm office is in the big barn, but the big boss had a system in his office too,' Rice said.

'Right, I'm going in,' Talantire said. 'I've got a Tyvek in the car.'

'If you've got some saliva test kits, I'll get the DNA samples taken,' Thompson said.

By the time Talantire had returned to the car, opened the boot and extracted her go-bag, two more vans full of uniformed officers had arrived. She wriggled into her forensic coveralls, slipped on booties, blue nitrile gloves and a hairnet, before slipping up the hood. She had a feeling that this was going to be a case that had to be done by the book. There would inevitably be no shortage of official second-guessing in the months and years ahead, and she couldn't cut corners. Once a couple of PCs were guarding the main door, she got Rice to lead her in via the shortest route towards where the commissioner's body lay. The fewer footprints she left at the crime scene, the better. Rice led her around the back of the manor house, along a path that ran through a beautiful walled garden full of gorgeous roses, through a gate in a wooden fence, then to a yard full of industrial wheeled bins that lay between the back of the house and a stone barn. Twin metal doors in the barn bore the sign 'office'. Opposite it was the kitchen door, where a uniformed PC had just arrived with a clipboard to mark those going in.

'Is this the way you went in?' she asked Rice.

'Yes. I don't normally use the main entrance because I work in the farm as a mechanic. There's a boot room here at the back where I change. But after I saw his body, I ran out through the front in a bit of a panic. I'd heard screaming, which turned out to be Soraya.'

Talantire peered into the kitchen corridor and immediately saw a bloodstained right footprint by the door to the boot room, which was on the right. Looking more carefully, she could now discern several more crescent-shaped blood-tainted marks on the flagstone floor, again from the right foot, leading from roughly where she was standing on the external doormat and into the house.

Not out of it. In.

Whoever had left those prints already had blood on their footwear *before* entering the manor house building. She looked back to the farm office doors, then crouched at the base of them. There were clearly bloody prints here too, exiting the barn.

Talantire turned to the PC, who was making a start on his list with the cap of his biro in his mouth. 'Officer, I need three of your colleagues here straight away to stop anyone going into the office or any other entrance to the barn. Rice, show me the soles of your shoes.'

The lad lifted his polished brogues, one at a time, so she could inspect the sole. There was nothing visible, and indeed the smooth leather was quite different from the heavily treaded bloodstain she had seen on the flagstones. She shooed both men away from the path between the two buildings and, after placing plastic markers, took photographs of the gravel that led from one to the other. 'Don't let anybody else come in here, and make sure you

23

stand away from these footprints,' she said. She then rang Thompson and told him about the footprints.

'There may well be another body in the barn,' she said. 'I'm going to have a quick look there before doing the main house.'

'Jan, please wait. The assailant may still be in the building.'

'It's unlikely. The trail of blood leaves from the barn. But I'll leave the phone on speaker while I go in.'

She eased open the barn door, touching only the base of it with her gloved hand, and glanced inside. There were more footprints here – from the same foot but bloodier. They hadn't come from the ground floor office but from a metal staircase, above left. She stepped inside over the doormat and onto an untainted section of the concrete floor, so she could get a better view up the stairs. It was fairly dim inside, but she was reluctant to flick on the light switch and compromise any fingerprints. She clicked on the light on her phone.

'What's happening?' Thompson asked her.

'I'm inside, and there are more bloody footprints from upstairs. Whoever it was wiped their feet on the doormat here because the prints outside are fainter.'

'A tidy killer then?'

'Not necessarily. It could be an additional witness we haven't found yet, someone scared perhaps. Whoever he is has roughly size ten boots.' She made her way carefully up the stairs at the left-hand edge, placing plastic markers and photographing as she went. The staircase came to a half landing, and then she became aware of buzzing flies. She edged her way around and looked on the next flight up to the floor above. There was a lot of blood here, which had seeped and dripped down, and was still wet.

She made her way up another five steps, which was the most she could ascend without getting her own booties bloody. That still left her a dozen steps short of the open plan office above. She took her phone and stood on tiptoe to film a 180° video. When she inspected the footage, she gasped. A man lay obviously dead, arms flung wide, a blood-spattered typist's chair on its side. He appeared to have been dispatched with a shotgun, and it was very messy indeed. The scene she had captured showed that this was indeed the nerve centre of the farm security system. There were two dozen screens, amongst other electronic controls.

Every screen was blank.

Chapter Three

'Tony, I've got bad news,' she said, as she retreated down the stairs. 'There is a body up here, killed by shotgun, then I have a feeling that the entire security system for the farm is out. This is not some random killing, some act of temper. Whoever did this planned it carefully.'

Thompson responded by telling her the CSI team were only five minutes away and a mobile incident room was being brought in from Exeter. 'Do you want to wait until the crime scene people get here?'

'No. We're still in the golden hour, just about. I'll call you later,' she said and hung up. She knew ideally that she should change Tyvek suits now, and booties, so that there was no chance of her bringing in evidence from one crime scene to another. But she didn't have a second suit in her car, and time was short. When she emerged from the barn, she told the PC on guard that there was a body up there, and not to let anyone in.

There was no sign of Rice.

'He didn't go back inside, did he?' she asked the PC, pointing to the kitchen entrance, now draped with crime scene tape. He shook his head.

She ducked under the tape and went inside, carefully avoiding the footprints. The flagstone corridor was wide but low, with ancient beams just an inch or two above her head. She glanced into the boot room to the right, which was untidy and full of wellingtons, Barbour jackets and rain gear. She didn't go in but advanced until the kitchen doorway, which was ajar. She peered in, using her phone light to check the flagstone floor for prints. No, there didn't appear to be any. The kitchen was a huge Victorian set up with an old-fashioned range as well as several modern upright fridge freezers. A huge rustic kitchen table dominated the centre of the room, above which pots and pans and implements hung from iron racking.

She took a couple of photographs from the doorway and then continued on her journey into the house. The corridor ended in a T-junction, which on the left ascended on carpeted stairs. The flagstones continued on the right, and careful scrutiny with the phone light showed that the gory footprints continued this way too. The blood on each step was now just a small crescent on the heel no larger than a thumb. She placed a couple more markers by the marks and photographed them.

Her phone pinged with several messages, one of which was from the chief constable. She ignored it. There was plenty of time to brief him later, when she had more information. Her biggest worry was that the killer might still be in the house. If they had been unable to flee immediately after the shots, it would've been because of the stream of guests from the pub back towards the manor house upon hearing the noise. It was just one of many plausible theories.

She went five more yards along the corridor, past a modern service lift on the left. The footprints went straight on, stopping just a few yards short of a descending stone staircase. She could now hear the sound of a TV. Sports commentary coming from behind a door on the right. Hadn't Rice said that the commissioner had been watching rugby? She pulled up short, right outside the door, which was closed. Crouching down, she saw a runnel of still-wet blood from beneath the door, which reflected the light from her phone.

The handle was a big old-fashioned brass knob, and ideally prints should be taken from it. There was no way to grasp it without compromising the evidence. She didn't have any gel lifts with her, but she did take a DNA swab and photographed the handle while holding a marker next to it. After placing the swab in a plastic tube and pocketing it, she peered at the catch, which seemed fairly flimsy. Perhaps then she didn't need to touch the handle at all. She didn't want to kick the door open because she didn't know what was behind it. Looking around, she saw a side table in the corridor with a mirror above, a display of old pewter cutlery laid out on the surface.

She had an idea.

Talantire picked up the fork, which looked like the sort of thing you would stick into a turkey while carving it. She found she could wriggle it underneath the door at the edge where the catch was, and away from the blood. She stood on the shaft of the fork and then barged her shoulder against the door. It was enough to dislodge the catch, and the fork stopped it opening more than an inch. After extracting the fork, she eased the door open and peered inside.

It was a carpeted office with bookshelves, filing cabinets and a settee. Sprawled on the settee was a dead body, shot twice with a shotgun, once in the face and once in the abdomen. It was only because she was familiar with the appearance of the police and crime commissioner that she could be sure that it was indeed the Honourable Lionel

Hall-Hartington. He was dressed in a suit with a carnation in his buttonhole, and his trousers and the settee beneath him were drenched with blood.

She was about to call in the confirmation when she heard banging from somewhere else in the house. She pulled out the TV plug from the wall so she could hear more clearly. Yes, it was frantic, repeated hammering, as if someone was trapped. It was coming from downstairs. The noise was desperate, rhythmic, then ended with one colossal bang.

She made a very quick call to the control room and gave a brief summary of where she was and what she had found. 'I'd like to request backup. Get me someone else with forensic gear.'

'Are you going to wait for them, ma'am?' the male operative asked. 'It should only be a few minutes.'

'No, I think someone is trapped. I have to go now.' She pocketed the phone and walked over to the stone staircase. She could hear some mechanical whining, some kind of machinery. She looked over the banister and down the stairs. A wheelchair lay on its side, and there was blood everywhere, all over it, and on the staircase.

Helena! Talantire had been wondering where the commissioner's wife was and why she hadn't seen her at the front of the crowd gathered around the manor house. She made her way stealthily downstairs, using her torch to illuminate the way. It was possible to avoid the bloodstains by staying to the left on the stone steps. The corridor she emerged onto was clearly of the below stairs variety, with rough whitewashed walls, a lowish ceiling, and various pipes threaded through above head height. But the most striking thing was the trail of wet blood. It almost looked like a foot-wide brush had been used, or as if a body had been dragged. The bloody footprints resumed with additional gore, and there were several droplets of blood outside the main path. To the right, light came from an open doorway. The noise resumed. The blood trail didn't go in there, and Talantire risked turning on the light. It was a laundry room with old-fashioned dolly tubs, along with a double Belfast sink and some more modern units. She suddenly understood where the banging noise had come from.

A pair of industrial washing machines were going through the latter stages of their spin cycle. One of them wasn't anchored properly, and when the spinning began again, it rocked angrily from whatever uneven load was inside. It crossed her mind that the machine was big enough to accommodate a body, but checking that could wait.

She had a gory trail to follow.

Stopping occasionally to photograph the blood, and now out of the yellow plastic markers, she advanced along the corridor. Blood had pooled at an alcove on the left, and when she got to it she saw that it contained a book-case, almost the height of the corridor, filled with leather-bound volumes. The reflection of wet blood showed that somebody had grasped it. Looking carefully, she could see that the bookcase had concealed hinges on the right-hand side. Crouching down, she noticed that the lowest shelf had a wooden handle between the books. This too had blood on it. One section of the shelving had apparently not been touched, and she grasped this to move the book-case. It hinged towards her and to the right, revealing a modern safe, two feet high and two feet wide, set into the stonework behind. It had a combination lock, on which there were bloodstains.

She photographed everything, then backed away. The bloodstains on the floor did not terminate at the alcove, but continued along the corridor, past a lift. She pressed the call button and waited for the car to descend to this, the terminal floor. The narrow doors revealed a surprisingly deep space with doors at the far end. In the lift's bright interior light, no bloodstains could be seen. She let the doors close and turned back to the corridor, which after five more yards led towards yet another descending staircase. Cold, damp air drifted up from this narrow and seemingly ancient set of stone steps. The blood on these steps was still wet too, and Talantire had some difficulty navigating down them without treading on it. A horrible scenario was congealing in her mind, one that had been apparent from the moment she had seen the blood-soaked wheelchair. Someone had dragged Helena de Courchevel down this corridor and the stairs. She prepared herself for the discovery of a third body.

The steps descended, with nothing but a couple of electrical cables on the right-hand side as handholds. There was a light switch set in the wall. Talantire didn't press, but photographed it and then resumed the use of the phone light to guide her way. The chamber below was less a room and more a rough stone cave, with a vaulted ceiling, eight feet high at the apex. She felt sure she was deep under the medieval manor house, in the oldest part of the building. The chamber was roughly circular and fifteen feet across, and as she turned to look behind her, following the bloodstains past the steps she had just descended, she suddenly let out an involuntary scream.

A child-sized body hung on a wooden door, its eyes open and staring at her. A bloody knife lay on the floor at its feet.

Chapter Four

Catching her breath, she looked again. It wasn't a child, but a three-foot tall feminine doll with an outsized head of coarse gingery hair and a wizened face. It was dressed outlandishly in what looked like a school uniform, with a skirt, petticoat and Mary Jane T-bar sandals over white socks. The door it was hanging on was clearly ancient, set into the wall. It was like a church door with a pointed apex and iron-reinforced bands across it. About level with the feet of the mannequin was a big iron lock with a large rusty key sticking out of it. Talantire approached the door with trepidation, careful to avoid the blood smeared across the flagstone floor. There was a damp, cold draught coming from beneath. Talantire photographed everything, then took DNA swabs from the handle of the bloodstained knife, the key and the latch. Having secured the forensic evidence, she listened at the door. She could hear something, like the rattling of chains, and the faint, echoing sound of whimpering.

A human voice. Alive!

Talantire banged on the door and identified herself. 'Just hold on. I'm coming in to get you.'

The whimpering intensified, strangely amplified, but any words were unintelligible. She tried to lift the latch, but the door wouldn't shift. She grasped the key and prepared to try and turn it. It moved much more easily than she anticipated. This time the latch lifted and the door creaked open, inwards.

The vault within was cold, a larger version of the chamber she had just left, and was dominated by an iron windlass hung with chains, which descended into some kind of hole. From that direction came more whimpering, and two distinctive words: 'Help me...'

'I'm here,' Talantire said. The light from her phone revealed a four-foot-high circular lip encircling a well, a good ten feet across. When she peered over and down, she saw three sets of dangling chains descending far, far into the darkness beneath. She couldn't see the bottom, her phone light gave out after about fifty feet, and the sound seemed to come from a long way beyond that. It was like a hole to the centre of the Earth.

'Help me, please, please, please,' came a cry. 'Wind up the chains! I'm nearly in the water.' Talantire heard a distant slosh. She fumbled inside her Tyvek coverall and into her jacket for the lightweight LED torch that she always carried. This had a more focused beam and a much longer range than the phone light. Retrieving it, and gripping it carefully in her plastic gloves, she pointed it down the well.

She couldn't believe how far below the woman was, a tiny figure, apparently suspended by her ankles, just above the water, hundreds of feet below.

'Good God,' Talantire muttered. 'Just hang on. I'm going to get you out,' she said. But staring up at the windlass, with its wooden drum, cogs and metal chains, it wasn't clear how the machinery worked. There didn't seem to be any engine or electrical motor to haul up the chains, and if there was some kind of counterweight, she couldn't initially see it. Two huge semicircular gratings, made of rusting iron bars, stood on their flat sides against the wall of the chamber. They looked like they were made to cover the well. There had to be a winding handle, but she couldn't see it.

She punched out the control room number but couldn't get through. No wonder she hadn't been getting calls. There couldn't be any reception down here, underneath tens of feet of stone flooring.

'Are you Helena?' Talantire called out.

'Yes,' came the faint reply.

'I'm going for help. I will be back as soon as I can.'

She made her way back up the steps, along the corridor and towards the kitchen, where she ran into a CSI team, similarly dressed in Tyvek suits, booties and gloves. She recognised Venka, who said, 'Jan, we've been trying to reach you. We were worried when you didn't answer the phone.'

'There's no reception down there,' Talantire replied. 'But there is one person alive and two bodies. The commissioner you may have already found, but there's a corpse upstairs in the office of the main barn, also killed with a shotgun, and—'

'Another body?'

'Yes, we'll have to deal with that later. I need your help rescuing the commissioner's wife, Helena. Someone has dangled her hundreds of feet down a well.'

'Good grief!' A divorced former pharmacist from Southall, Ragavati Venkatagiri was based in Exeter, enjoying a second career in her fifties, and was normally unflappable. 'I was hoping we'd have the chance to go through the crime scene methodically, but—'

'There's no time!' Talantire said. 'The woman is dangling upside down by her ankles just over the water.

34

I've no idea if the chains will hold, or if she is so injured she might die. Get some uniforms to ask the staff if there are any ropes in the farm. I don't trust the way she is suspended. A cliff rescue team would be ideal, but we don't have any time. And we need lights, big powerful inspection lights.'

Venka turned around and called over one of her team, a big guy who looked like a yeti in his Tyvek suit. 'This is Chris Boxhall, a former Royal Engineer. He's got the strength and probably the nous to get the woman out.' Boxall had a large torch dangling from a harness at his waist.

'Follow me, Chris,' Talantire said. She led him carefully along the corridor, past the room where the commissioner's body lay, using her phone light to show him where to place his feet to avoid the bloodstains. She led him down the stone steps, stepping gingerly over the bloodstained wheelchair, along the next corridor, past the safe, past the lift, and down the final set of steps.

'This place is like a warren,' Boxall said, as he ducked his massive frame under the low roof and into the ante-chamber where the doll was hanging on the back of the door. 'Christ, what is that?' he said.

Talantire was just telling him to steer clear of it, when there was a panicky scream from the well. 'Help, help, I think the chain's giving way!' Helena screeched. 'My hair is dangling in the water now.'

Talantire and Boxall rushed in and played the powerful torch over the windlass and metal gears above the well. The chains wound on the wooden drum were rusty and clearly ancient, each link the length of a thumb. They clicked and oscillated in the well from the moving weight they held. The entire apparatus was suspended from two huge hooks in a massive wooden beam that spanned the roof.

'There's a brake, and it slipped,' Boxall said. 'Hang on, love, we'll soon have you out.'

Boxall found a rusty winding handle on the floor behind the grating, which connected to a slot on the rear of the drum. 'I'll take up the slack if you can wind this up,' he said to Talantire. Boxall seized the chains in both hands and wound them around his forearms as if he was in a tug of war. He braced himself against the stone lip of the well.

Talantire had to stand on the precipitous lip of the well in order to reach the handle, and as she needed both hands, laid down the phone light onto the floor. She reached up to the handle and turned it clockwise until there was no slack left.

'Right, I'm releasing the brake now,' Boxall said, pulling out a metal rod that prevented the windlass from turning. Talantire immediately felt the handle move hard against her.

'Heave!' Boxall said, hauling up an arm length of the chains from the well. This gave enough slack to Talantire to wind the windlass one whole turn. He took another arm's length of chain and hauled it in, allowing Talantire another turn. They carried on like this, gradually lifting the woman up the well for what seemed like hours. Talantire reckoned Helena was not a heavy woman, but the weight of dozens of yards of chains dragged heaviest. Even Boxall seemed to tire.

They could now see she was in blood-soaked white trousers and a spattered white blouse.

Her bloody feet and ankles were tied together by thin nylon rope and onto the chain in some large and complex knot. Boxall paused as her feet came within reach and then stumbled. Several yards of chains slid from his arms, and the handle that Talantire was winding kicked out of her hands. Helena wailed in anguish as she plunged, and the windlass handle whirred around.

Talantire had no choice: she blocked the handle on its next turn with her shoulder, and it cracked hard into her, forcing her into a crouch. She braced her entire body, pushing it up, to stop any further descent. She realised that she was setting her own bodyweight against that of Helena and the chains. She could hold it, just. But the weight was crushing. Boxall regained his balance and began to haul the chains in again, this time more cautiously, until after several more minutes, Helena had cleared the top of the well. Talantire slid the rusty brake rod back into the windlass, allowing Boxall to reach out and pull the woman across. He righted her and she clung to his arms, sobbing. Talantire moved rapidly to untie the thin cords around her legs, including a loop that went up to the belt of her trousers.

'I'm going to buy you two a big round of drinks for this, honestly I am,' Helena croaked.

Talantire gave the woman a quick once over. Helena was able to identify how many fingers Talantire held up and to follow them with her eyes as she moved them. From the open wounds on her head and legs, she had clearly been stabbed and beaten. She was unable to stand, though there didn't appear to be any obvious neck or spinal injuries.

'It might be easier if you carry her up, rather than getting a bunch of paramedics down here tramping across the crime scene,' Talantire said.

Boxall agreed. He was able to carry her in his arms slowly, while Talantire guided him over the bloodstained steps and along the numerous corridors. They emerged through the back exit to find a huge press of police officers and a team of paramedics who took over looking after Helena.

–

An hour later, Talantire was standing by the edge of the gold command van, a high-tech mobile HQ that had been brought over to coordinate the huge operation now taking place at Bychecombe Manor. A mobile incident room, a truck-mounted Portakabin, was on its way from Exeter too, but the most senior officers liked to keep aloof from the inevitable chaos of these cramped on-site detective workplaces.

Detective Chief Superintendent Drayton Ross was in charge, an officer she didn't know. He'd apparently been a big wheel in the City of London Police, covering fraud. This was clearly going to be a very different case. She hadn't yet had a chance to speak to him because he'd been on the phone to the chief constable for the last twenty minutes. She was already getting frustrated because the golden hour was now long gone, the blood in many places was dried and no overall plan was in place. Unable to find out what was going on, she returned many of the phone calls that she missed earlier. She was delighted to hear that her own team of Detective Sergeant Maddy Moran and Detective Constable Dave Nuttall had been assigned to the case.

Finally, Ross was off the phone. 'Ah, I've been looking forward to meeting you. The famous Jan Talantire.' He shook her hand warmly. He was lean, with wavy iron-grey hair and steel-framed glasses. He was wearing a smart, well-fitting suit.

'Glad to meet you. Sir, we need to move rapidly. I need to know that all the guests at the Griffon, many of whom are employees here, are having statements taken.'

'Yes, that's in hand. There is going to be a press conference tonight at six o'clock, and I will be coordinating with Moira Hallett of the press office.'

'Helena de Courchevel is our key witness, and I think she should be guarded in hospital.'

'Really?'

'Absolutely. She's the one person who must have seen the assailant. He is clearly well organised and ruthless, and he had a good knowledge of the building right down to the subterranean passageways. I think he tried to get her to open the safe. I'm working on the assumption that she was winched down into the well to force her to divulge the lock combination.'

'My goodness, that's quite a quick insight.'

'As I say, we need to move rapidly. Has a forensic pathologist been called?'

'Yes, I think the CSI woman with the unpronounceable name is looking after that side of things.'

'Venka, that's what we call her. My CID team are blue-lighting it from Barnstaple. I'm planning to have our first incident room meeting inside the manor house in an hour.'

'That's up to me, Detective Inspector. I'm not sure we've quite got our ducks in a row yet.'

Talantire was already impatient with this man from head office. 'Okay, I'll keep my meeting informal and report to yours whenever that is.'

'All right. Thank you.' He turned away to pick up another phone call.

'Don't forget the hospital guard,' Talantire called to him as he turned away.

Soraya Hinton, the housekeeper, was the only other witness. When the police arrived, she had been sitting in the lounge of the manor house with Rice's aunt Elaine. Talantire and newly arrived DS Maddy Moran found a wood-panelled drawing room where she could be interviewed in private.

The housekeeper was a tall and handsome olive-skinned woman in her mid-forties, casually dressed in jeans and a T-shirt, with her dark hair up in a ponytail. She had been too upset to speak about what she had seen until now. After beginning with some employment details and the nature of her work, Talantire moved gently onto more sensitive matters.

'Can you tell me about the first moment you knew something had happened?'

'I was in the upstairs front master bedroom vacuuming when I heard a gunshot, then another one. I turned off the Dyson but couldn't hear anything else.'

'You were certain what you heard was gunfire?'

'Yes, I'm quite familiar with the noise. They are always shooting pigeons, and you quite often hear the sound far off into the valley. But this sounded closer.'

'In the house?' Maddy suggested.

Soraya inclined her head in scepticism. 'Not those first shots, no. They were somewhere else.'

'So you weren't alarmed about this?' Talantire asked.

'No, not until the next shots.'

'And how much later was that?' Maddy asked.

'I don't know, just a few minutes I suppose. I had enough time to vacuum most of the room. The shots were really close and I was scared. Especially when I heard the scream,' Soraya said. 'It was cut short by the second blast.'

'What kind of scream was it?'

'It was a shout first, the word "no". It sounded like the boss's voice, then he screamed horribly.'

'What did you do?'

'I hid in the ensuite bathroom and locked the door. Then I realised my phone was on the linen trolley on the landing. I was too scared to fetch it at first and just went as far as the door to the bedroom. I could hear some banging and someone moving. I waited, and the sound seemed to be downstairs, getting fainter. Then I risked looking out onto the landing. I couldn't see anything, so I ran up to the trolley and retrieved my phone before returning to the ensuite, which I again locked. Then I rang the police.'

'That was the 999 call that was logged at 14:36,' Maddy said, looking down at her notes. The original call was quite garbled, so it had taken a couple of minutes of to-ing and fro-ing between the operator and Soraya to establish that there were gunshots within the house.

'How long did you wait before venturing downstairs?'

'Quite a long time. It was only once I heard sirens in the distance that I crept downstairs and saw blood in the corridor, footprints. I took one quick glance in the office, which was a horrible sight, and then retreated out of the front entrance, where I ran into John.'

'That is Mr Rice?' Maddy asked.

She nodded.

'I'm sorry to have to ask you this in detail,' Talantire said. 'But could you tell me exactly what you saw in the office?'

'It was the body of the boss,' she said, beginning to cry. 'He'd been shot.'

'How do you know it was him?' Talantire persisted.

'The clothes, the size and shape of the man, and it was his office.'

Talantire knew from having seen the body herself that it would be hard to identify him, given the horrible facial injuries, without relying on what he was wearing and where he was.

'Were you the only member of staff on duty that afternoon?'

'Yes. Tanya, who helps in the kitchen, was given the afternoon off because of the party. Mrs Stotfold, the cook, was away seeing her sister for the weekend. Pretty much everybody was at the Griffon.'

'That was very convenient from the killer's point of view,' Maddy said. 'Do you know who would have had access to the staff rotas?'

'I don't think there were any formal rotas. Helena allocated the work shifts.' Soraya sobbed and her eyes widened. 'I heard she was found down the well. How is she?'

'Very shaken up, but I don't think she's badly injured.'

Soraya put a hand to her chest. 'I'm so relieved.'

To Talantire, it looked a genuine reaction. 'How is she to work for?' she asked.

'She is good, better than many I've been employed by, and quite down to earth. We are on first name terms, and she often comes to talk to us. Still, she is quite strict in some ways. We aren't allowed to have our mobile phones with us while we work, which is how mine came to be hidden under the linen on the trolley.'

'Why doesn't she allow you phones?' Talantire asked.

'She thinks we'd waste our time on them. Of course, she is always on hers.'

Talantire wound up the interview. She had just been messaged that the Home Office forensic pathologist had finished with the body that had been found in the office. ID on the corpse identified him as Bassin Horvat. She'd met him. He was the farm manager, a Slovenian national, and had seemed to be a really nice and ordinary man.

–

Ten minutes later, back in Tyvek suits, Talantire and Maddy prepared to go into the control room in the main barn. As they tied on their plastic booties, a CSI technician emerged carrying a bloodstained chair in a huge polythene bag. This was the one that had been on its side in the control room. The two detectives made their way into the vestibule. Stepping plates allowed them to avoid treading in the wet blood as they ascended the staircase up into the control room. Venka and her staff had already photographed the control room, and there were plenty of yellow plastic evidence markers dotted around the desk and control panels.

But Talantire was focused on one thing: the CCTV control unit, which ran from a rather elderly-looking desktop computer. This had escaped most of the splatter of blood apart from one or two dots on the screen. She reached across to power it up and was relieved to discover that it worked. The screens flickered to life, giving a live view over almost every part of Bychecombe Manor estate.

The system hadn't logged itself out, and she was able to navigate the familiar software package to find the archive. There, she found that the entire set of history files had been deleted. The file management log gave the time of the deletion as 14:22 that day. That, as near as she could tell, was the time of the first gunshots. It fitted with the idea that the farm manager was murdered first, as the bloody footsteps seemed to indicate, and that Hall-Hartington was killed second.

The two detectives made their way out. Emerging from the building, they were greeted by Dave Nuttall, who'd been exploring the rest of the farm with a couple of uniformed PCs. 'We've surveyed all three big equipment barns with John Rice. There are no apparent new thefts of quad bikes, ride-on lawnmowers, chainsaws, strimmers or other easily saleable machinery. Everything seems to be accounted for.'

'That's very interesting,' Talantire said, as she stripped off her protective gear and stuffed it into a bin bag for testing. She glanced into the gold command van, whose door was open, and could see that DCS Ross was on the phone. The CSI team were still busy in the manor house and presumably would be for some hours. 'Right, let's have a quick incident room meeting,' Talantire said. 'We can use the same room where we interviewed the housekeeper.'

She helped herself to a whiteboard from out of the gold command van and found a couple of marker pens.

—

Bychecombe Manor's drawing room was an unusually exclusive incident room meeting, but for Talantire quality always beat quantity.

Maddy Moran, smartly dressed in a jacket and pleated skirt, sat on an ornate gold-painted dining chair, and rested her laptop on her knees. The detective sergeant had an uncanny insight into human behaviour, which had proven itself time and time again over the years they had worked together.

DC Dave Nuttall slouched in a leather wing chair, his worn jacket almost the same colour, with a faded denim leg resting casually over one arm. Nuttall was a savvy and hard-working detective, steeped in common sense. Not much got past him.

Talantire had invited DCS Ross and Inspector Tony Thompson, but neither were there. Thompson was still overseeing much of the crowd control required at the front of the manor but had promised to come in when he had a moment. Many of the farm employees who had been at the party at the Griffon were now wanting to come back to their homes, most of which were tied cottages at the farm, but Ross has declared the whole area to be a crime scene. He'd tasked Thompson with preventing any return within the 3,000 acre estate.

'Right, let's make this quick,' Talantire said. 'First off, this was clearly meticulously planned by someone with a good knowledge of Bychecombe Manor.' She turned to the whiteboard and wrote down the two words PLAN-NING and KNOWLEDGE.

'It smacks of being an inside job to me,' Nuttall said.

'I agree,' Maddy said. 'But clearly not the same perpet-rators who have been after the quad bikes.'

'Let's not jump to conclusions,' Talantire said. 'Yes, we have a very different M.O.' She wrote down the word VIOLENCE. 'The brutality really marks it apart from anything we've seen in rural crime. But it doesn't mean we

45

don't have, for example, somebody who was a member of the quad bike gang who used his knowledge of the place to go for something bigger altogether.'

The other detectives nodded at this.

'Interestingly, we seem only to have a single assailant within the house, subject to confirmation from CSI. I clearly saw a bloody trail from the control room within the barn right down through the house to the well. This man didn't hesitate to kill, and he was strong enough to drag the commissioner's wife from her wheelchair, many yards along the basement corridor and to the well.'

'Which indicates a really comprehensive knowledge of the history of the Manor,' Maddy said.

'Nah,' said Nuttall. 'There are probably websites where you can get that information. Ten years ago, well before his nibs was elected as crime commissioner, they were even doing tours. My ex went on it, with Susie. She was only eight, and I remember her being very excited about the supposedly bottomless well.'

Talantire had not been aware of that. She watched Nuttall's face, normally impassive, where the shadows of the great rift in his life still played across his features. He still spoke about Susie, even though she wasn't his biological daughter. She was now at university in East Anglia, and he still hoped that he might see her again one day. Nuttall had complained that his ex, Diane, had made it difficult for him to see Susie.

'Okay, that's something to bear in mind,' she said. 'But let's be clear, having visited the place as a tourist would not give you any of the knowledge of the location of the safe, nor how to shut down and delete history files for the CCTV security system. And this was done at speed, around the time of the first killing.'

'Like I said, inside job,' Nuttall said.

'Shall I get Rice and the other employees lined up for interview?' Maddy offered.

'First, I want to see the CCTV from the Griffon,' Talantire said. 'Every farm employee who was there for the duration has an alibi. They couldn't have been the killer.'

Nuttall nodded. 'That could be a really rapid way to eliminate suspects,' he conceded. 'A real productivity boost for us.'

'It's the former employees who I'd like to focus on,' Talantire said. 'The disgruntled, those who were sacked, anyone with a grudge.'

'There would be a lot of people who'd have wanted Bagpuss dead,' Maddy said. 'Seeing as he was crime commissioner.'

'I'm not sure,' Talantire responded. 'He was a figure-head and never put anybody inside personally. Those who hated him were probably close colleagues in the county council, or even in the top echelons of the police.'

'Christ, let's not go there,' Nuttall muttered.

Talantire was interrupted by a call. It was Inspector Tony Thompson. 'Hi, Jan, I'll be down in a minute. We've just finished visiting all thirty-eight cottages on the site. Most of them were locked, presumably because the occupants were at the party at the Griffon, but we haven't found any signs of a break-in or unexpected occupants. It's a pretty tight-knit community and those we did speak to haven't seen anything unusual.'

'Thank you for that, Tony,' Talantire said. 'Can you get one of your uniforms to retrieve CCTV from the Griffon itself? It's a quick way to establish who has a tenable alibi.'

'Yes, I'll do that.'

47

No sooner had she finished the call than Talantire noticed Maddy straighten herself and Nuttall shift his leg from the chair arm. Turning around to the door, she saw Detective Chief Superintendent Ross walk in, accompanied by Moira Hallett from the press office and a couple of senior uniforms she recognised from Devon and Cornwall Police HQ in Exeter. The place was called Middlemoor, and the denizens were often referred to by frontline cops as middle morons. From the perspective of the uniforms and detectives who had to deal with the Great British public, Middlemoor was far too full of those who did nothing but drive a desk; policy chiefs, bean counters and box-tickers. It was particularly galling that all these jobs seemed to be very senior and well-paid, but when budgetary times got hard it was the frontline that got cut.

'We have here a first-class team who I'm sure will be quick to get to the bottom of this case,' Ross said to his colleagues. 'This is DI Talantire, who I'm sure you will have heard of, and err...' He clicked his fingers.

'Detective Sergeant Madeleine Moran,' Maddy said.

'DC Dave Nuttall,' the detective volunteered, holding out his hand to shake Ross's. The senior officer ignored him as he turned to introduce the Exeter uniforms.

'Paul Shortland,' said the taller of the two. 'I used to work with Lionel at the county council in environmental services, when he was a councillor. This is a very bad business, isn't it?'

'Murder always is,' Talantire said. 'Would you like to identify the body for us, sir?'

Shortland cringed horribly. 'Oh, I don't know...' he said, turning to Ross for help.

'It's all right, we can wait until his wife has recovered somewhat,' Talantire said. She never had any intention of getting Shortland anywhere near the body. He looked like the kind of person who would wear marigolds to do the washing up.

'What's your role at Middlemoor, sir?' Maddy asked.

'Rural policing initiatives,' Shortland said. He had sandy hair and an aloof manner.

The other officer, detective superintendent rank from the uniform, introduced himself as Timothy Weaver. 'I specialise in forensic financial investigations.' He was a saturnine individual, in his late fifties like Shortland, with thick dark eyebrows and a thatch of jet-black hair just beginning to turn silver over the ears.

'Is there a financial angle as yet, sir?' Talantire asked Ross.

'Not as such, but we are certainly keen to have a look into his office here, at the first opportunity,' Weaver said. He looked over his shoulder as if a guided tour might be imminent.

Talantire went into her iPad and called up pictures she had taken inside Hall-Hartington's office. It looked more like an abattoir. 'I think CSI will be busy for a while before you can see it,' she said, showing them the screen. They all recoiled and Moira let out a little cry of alarm.

'I see what you mean,' Weaver said. 'We can do a fair bit remotely, using his office at Middlemoor.'

'We've set up a press conference from the ballroom,' Moira said. 'It's at six and will be fronted by the DCS here.'

'But obviously I need you to brief me well in advance,' Ross said. 'And I'll need you around if we have any detailed questions.'

'Of course,' Talantire replied. 'However, I'd really like the press kept at arm's length. Venka reckons she needs another couple of days at least on the CSI, and they don't need to be pestered with photographers while they are going in and out of their tents.'

Moira intervened: 'I'm arranging with the Griffon that their car park can be used for press vehicles. When appropriate, we can arrange for a photographer and news crew from the press pool to gain some limited access inside the house. There's no getting away from it that this will be one of the most high-profile crime stories of the year nationally. We will all be in the spotlight, so we have to do an exemplary job.'

'The national press will no doubt be digging into Lionel's background, both personally and financially. If there are any skeletons in the closet, we want to get there first,' Weaver said.

'That's admirably proactive,' Talantire replied. She had a feeling that there must be something suspected already for these desk jockeys to have been wheeled out into the field.

'So, Jan, give me your lines of enquiry,' Ross asked.

'We are keeping an open mind and have many lines of enquiry into this particularly savage and brutal crime,' she said.

'Very good, Jan, very good,' said Moira, jotting down Talantire's words.

'What I want to keep confidential is the strong circumstantial evidence that this was an inside job: the detailed knowledge of the location of the safe, the ability to rapidly delete CCTV footage, and a thorough understanding of the layout of the manor house right down to its medieval basement. All forensic indications so far are of a single male assailant.'

'So quickly?' Shortland said, clearly impressed.

'He wasn't particularly careful. There are bloody boot prints all over the place, a single trail from the CCTV control room in the barn, through the back door of the manor house, and past the commissioner's office on the ground floor. After shooting the commissioner, we think the assailant threw his wheelchair-bound wife down the stairs and then dragged her body through the basement and into the well chamber. We think she was tortured to reveal the combination lock for the safe, but either didn't know or wouldn't give it, and was then suspended down the well from chains.'

'Good God,' Ross breathed.

'I myself rescued her with the help of a capable CSI technician called Boxall,' she continued. 'Between you and me, I think we are looking for a very clever, very well-organised psychopath,' she said.

'It would definitely be too early to go out with that approach,' Moira said, still making notes.

'I agree. But we've got to catch him. We can be absolutely sure that he won't hesitate to kill again.' Talantire's phone buzzed and she looked at it. 'Excellent, we have the CCTV from the Griffon. It's already been uploaded to GoodSAM. If you'll excuse me, gentlemen, I have to take this.'

'What's GoodSAM?' Shortland was heard to whisper to Ross.

'It's a video sharing platform, run by a charity, a bit like Crimestoppers,' Nuttall said, eyeing the senior officer dubiously. 'It's been around a few years. I'm sure it is used by your officers in rural policing too,' he added mischievously.

'Thank you,' Shortland said. He moved away, clearly embarrassed. Nuttall and Maddy rolled their eyes at each other. Shortland embodied the criticisms that every frontline officer had of top brass: out of touch and overpaid.

Chapter Five

The top brass left, and while Talantire and Nuttall looked through the footage on fast forward, Maddy went out to find John Rice. She found him talking to a uniformed constable and brought him inside to help them identify the individuals.

The two main cameras gave a panoramic view inside the bar and outside on the terrace. Talantire counted roughly a hundred people, split between the two locations. Rice quickly identified half a dozen male farm employees and their wives and girlfriends. The happy couple at the centre of the festivities were Sally Cropper, who was in charge of the sheep, and Liam Bennett, who worked in the Sleepy Monk marketing office in Exeter. He wasn't able to identify all those who were older, but they were clearly family members from the way they interacted with the younger revellers. Drinks were brought to tables, hugs exchanged, backs slapped. It looked joyous and innocent, but poignant in the light of subsequent events.

Talantire fast forwarded to 14:20 p.m., roughly the time of the first shotgun blast. There was no sound on the footage, but on the outside camera it was noticeable that a few individuals looked up in the direction of the farm at a certain point. Whatever they'd heard didn't seem to be unusual or loud enough to interrupt the socialising for more than a few seconds. Nevertheless, she made an edit note on the tape at that point, 14:21 p.m. If the clocks on the two CCTV systems at the pub and inside the farm were accurate, it had taken the assailant less than a minute from shooting Bassin Horvat dead to deleting the farm footage at 14:22.

Fast work, indeed. Especially if some kind of password was required to access the system.

'John,' she asked Rice, 'are you authorised to use the CCTV system on the farm?'

'No, I've never done it. But Digby knew.'

Talantire recalled the dark-haired lad who had been with Rice at the entrance to the manor when she arrived. 'What is his surname?'

'Robinson. Digby Robinson.'

Talantire rang Tony Thompson and asked him to bring in the young man. While she had been looking at the main two cameras, Nuttall had been scrutinising the pub's car park and kitchen cameras – one of which gave a view across the drive up to Bychecombe Manor.

'Take a look at this,' he said to Talantire. She peered over his shoulder at his iPad and saw a black Yamaha moped with a white-helmeted rider leaving the farm drive at 14:46. A good technician would be able to get a close-up that showed the number plate.

'Any idea who this is, John?'

The young man scratched his head and finally said, 'No.'

–

This was all they had time to do before the news conference, which was absolutely crammed with journalists and reporters, some of whom had rushed down from London. DCS Drayton Ross introduced the crime using almost exactly the words that Talantire had come up with. For fifteen minutes, he fended off all questions about suspects, the crime commissioner's background, and speculation about whether this was an attempt to steal the Bychecombe Hoard.

It was at this point that Talantire, sitting next to Ross, interrupted.

'As it happened, I talked to the commissioner here in this house just a few days before this incident. He did disclose to me that the Bychecombe Brooch was in the safe, along with some other items from the hoard. We haven't been able to get into the safe as yet, but I have no reason to believe it has been taken.'

This prompted lots of further enquiries from the press, which Talantire fobbed off. However, there was one well-aimed question from a BBC Radio Devon reporter about whether there was a link between the theft of quad bikes from the farm and this crime.

'It is certainly something we are actively looking into,' Talantire said.

At that point Ross called the proceedings to an end, and Hallett said she would take down any further questions they had and would get back to them in due course.

–

News that Helena de Courchevel had been moved from intensive care at the Royal Devon Hospital in Exeter prompted Talantire to dispatch Maddy to go and interview her. As she was led by a nurse to the private room Helena had been allocated, she noticed that a female PC was outside on guard. Maddy asked them both whether Helena had spoken at all.

'She asked about her husband, ma'am,' the PC said. 'I wasn't briefed to confirm anything.'

The nurse said, 'I let her look at my phone, at the news, so she knows I think.' She led Maddy in and explained that she would be allowed just ten minutes to avoid tiring out the patient, who had been partially sedated. Helena was swathed in bandages on her head, neck, arms, and presumably elsewhere. Her face was bruised around the eyes, one of which was almost shut.

'He's dead, isn't he?' she whispered. 'My husband.'

'I'm afraid so,' Maddy said. 'I'm sorry for your loss.'

Her face began to dissolve. 'I saw from the news that there were two dead. Who is the other one?'

'He's not been formally identified yet, but he was in the control room in the barn.'

She lifted one hand to her face, the other being hooked up to an IV with a cannula. 'That must be Bassin. Almost everybody else was at the party. Poor Bassin.' The crying continued for several minutes.

'Where's Talantire?' Helena asked eventually.

'She's tied up at the crime scene. I'm afraid you'll have to make do with me.' Maddy suddenly flushed, realising she'd used insensitive language.

'She saved my life. I was dangling on a chain in the well.'

'I know. I'm here to try to find out who did it. Do you know who he was?'

She began to cry again, huge shuddering sobs. 'It's really hard for me to think about it,' she whispered.

'I know, take your time,' Maddy said, looking anxiously at the clock. Half of the allotted ten minutes had passed already.

'He was using a voice disguise device and had a microphone taped to his neck, so he sounded robotic.'

'Did you recognise his face?'

'I didn't see it,' she said between sobs. 'He was wearing a ski-mask and was dressed all in black. It was very frightening. He had a knife, and he kept cutting me with it…'

'I think this is too much for her,' the nurse said. 'She's had a traumatic experience.'

Maddy nodded, realising that no useful identification at this stage was going to be possible. 'I'll come back in an hour, if that's all right.'

'I don't think that's possible,' the nurse replied. 'The doctor said it might be better if we wait until tomorrow. We've got to change her dressings, and she should be going for another MRI scan.'

'Fine,' Maddy said, then turned to the PC at the door. 'Has she had any other visitors?'

'No.'

'She won't be allowed any until tomorrow,' the nurse said. 'We made an exception for you.'

Maddy realised she had gone about as far as she could.

–

Back at Bychecombe Manor, the mobile incident room had arrived on the back of a lorry. It was essentially a large Portakabin with two meeting rooms, secure storage areas and a refrigerator for perishable evidence. It was also cramped and quite noisy when the air-conditioning was running. Dave Nuttall and one of the CSI technicians got it all in order, while Talantire scanned through the CCTV from the Griffon again. She picked up a call from Maddy, who gave her the news that the assailant was using a voice changer.

'Right,' Talantire said. 'That pretty much confirms that we're talking about an insider. Someone who felt his voice might be recognised.'

'Exactly,' Maddy said. 'And he was dressed head to toe in black.'

'With size ten boots,' Talantire said. 'CSI has confirmed that. I'm going to have to wait until they're finished with the commissioner's office before I can access the computers and find out for certain who might have been fired or left his employment in the last few years.'

'I'm coming back now because I can't interview Helena again until tomorrow,' Maddy said.

'How badly injured is she?'

'The nurse said she had lots of superficial cuts designed to be painful rather than lethal, and she's very bruised and battered. She is distraught about the death of her husband.'

'Poor old Bagpuss,' Talantire said. 'At least somebody loved him.'

After terminating the call, Talantire wondered if the assailant had ever intended to kill Helena. Presumably he just wanted to terrify her into passing across the code to the safe. If she couldn't identify him then there was probably no danger of her being killed in hospital. Still, best to be on the safe side.

Dave Nuttall came back into the drawing room to announce that the mobile incident room was now fully commissioned.

'Good,' said Talantire. 'Let's start by interviewing Digby Robinson. He is the only person still alive who we think has permission to use the security system inside the main barn.'

'He's been waiting outside for hours, hoping to get into his cottage,' Nuttall said.

—

Digby Robinson was thirty-five, lean and dark-haired. He had already given a statement to a uniformed officer, in which he had described entering the manor house with John Rice after finding Soraya, the housekeeper, in hysterics by the front door.

'But what prompted you to leave the party?'

'John persuaded me that the second bangs were definitely gunshots and wanted to investigate. So I went with him. Then we saw Soraya.'

Talantire took him through the statement in detail, in which he described trying to move the commissioner's body to see whether he might still be alive. That was how he got blood on the cuff of his sleeve. It was he who had closed the door to the office, to hide the grisly sight of the body from any other members of staff who came in. His clothing had now been packed up for analysis.

'It says here you are the IT chief for Sleepy Monk Creameries.'

'That's right.'

'And were you responsible at all for the CCTV system in the barn?'

'I didn't install it, but yes, I have helped solve some of the teething problems and can certainly find my way around it.'

'Who else among the employees would you say had the skills to be able to use it?'

'I think quite a few of the duty staff could turn it on and off, position the cameras, that kind of thing. Bassin would always run the utilities and backup once a week. I'm not sure if any of the others knew how to do that, but I can soon look on the system and see how many identities there are. If you need to see any of the backups, I can certainly let you.'

'Thank you, I'll bear it in mind.' Talantire didn't disclose that the system had been tampered with and the cameras turned off at the time of the murders.

'Are you based here at the Manor?'

'No, I work from home and spend most of my time in the marketing office in Exeter. There's not enough office space for me here, and I can do most of what I need to do remotely. I don't deal with any of the milking machines because there is a specialist technical support who comes over from Switzerland.'

Talantire assessed this straightforward-seeming man. He didn't manifest any of the symptoms of shock that she had seen on John Rice's face, but then he may well not have worked so closely with the victims.

'Did you report directly to the Honourable Lionel?' she asked.

'Notionally, I suppose, but since he was elected crime commissioner I've reported to Bassin.'

'What was he like?'

'Smart, ambitious. He had worked his way up from being a farmhand, having got a summer job here a decade ago.'

'Were there any work rivalries, problems with ex-employees, anything like that you are aware of?'

Robinson shrugged. 'I know they fired Bassin's brother a couple of years ago, but for anything more up to date I suppose you should ask those who work here at the farm. I'm not really in the loop.'

She continued to look at him quizzically, letting the silence stretch out.

'Well, there was a general feeling that the big boss was a bit of an idiot. That he'd spread his limited talents a bit thin by taking on being crime commissioner. The creamery had been in difficulties since Brexit. It was no longer worth accessing the European market because of the new bureaucratic hurdles, and the British cheese market was oversupplied, so margins were poor. The general feeling was that he wasn't up to the scale of the challenge.'

'I see.'

Robinson leaned forward conspiratorially, his dark eyebrows arched. It was almost as if he imagined that there were just the two of them in a pub, which was exactly the kind of atmosphere Talantire had hoped to create.

'Look. It was well known that he drank too much and was a bit, let's say, old-fashioned when it came to dealing with women.'

'I had my own experience of that, in particular the way he treated a young Muslim colleague of mine.'

Robinson smiled and spread his hands. 'Of course, none of this justifies the appalling thing that happened to him.'

'Absolutely not,' Talantire said. 'Tell me about Bassin's brother.'

'I don't think I ever met Luka. I just know that he was sacked for gross misconduct and sent packing back to Slovenia. If you want to get chapter and verse, you should speak to Geoffrey Wheatcroft, Sleepy Monk's solicitor. He would have dealt with it.'

Talantire made a note of the contact details. Inspector Tony Thompson had been tasked with tracking down all the staff and hopefully had tried to make contact with Wheatcroft already. Now it was time to put Robinson on the spot.

'So who do you think perpetrated these terrible crimes?'

'I assume someone connected with the previous robberies of quad bikes.'

'Were you involved?'

He looked absolutely shocked. 'Of course not.'

'Do you know the combination to the safe?'

'I don't even know where it is.'

'Have you ever used a shotgun?'

He hesitated. 'Yes, I went on the pre-Christmas estate shoot. I had to be taught how to hold the thing.'

She smiled at him. 'Just had to ask, that's all.'

'Have you spoken to Lionel's adopted son?'

'Was Rustam here?' She had heard he was living in London, estranged from his adoptive father.

'Yes, he was pointed out to me in the pub this afternoon.'

Talantire opened her iPad and pulled up the video file of CCTV footage from the Griffon. 'Show me,' she said.

Robinson set the screen size to maximum and dragged the slider beneath the footage to advance the time. It was towards the end of the video, when there was already a disturbance in the bar with the news of the shootings, that Robinson pointed to a slightly built figure dressed in black jeans and a dark sweater. They seem to be drinking a Coke, from its colour. 'That's him.'

Talantire made a note of the time, 2:42 p.m. It was when the disturbance in the bar was at its most intense that Rustam finished his drink and, without talking to anybody else, made his way out of the pub via the terrace and disappeared up the track towards the manor house. In total, he was on camera for less than a minute. Talantire switched to the CCTV footage that showed the moped rider just a few minutes later. 'Is this him, do you think?'

'It looks like him,' Robinson said. 'I don't know whether he had a moped or not.'

The timings looked very tight indeed, but otherwise this was an extremely promising lead: motive, if the reports of a rift with his adoptive parents were correct, and opportunity, given that he was down from London for the party. It would also explain the voice changer. They now had the moped's registration number too. There was more to be done, but Talantire felt they had the makings of a plausible suspect.

—

Inspector Tony Thompson was having the devil's own job dealing with the farm employees. Many of them were drunk and demanding to return to their tied cottages on the estate. Others had more plausible and perhaps pressing reasons for being back in their homes by the early evening. The majority were still milling around the marquee that had been placed in the Griffon's garden, even though the free beer had stopped and much of the food had been scavenged. The search of the various homes was going slowly, even though Thompson now had more than a hundred uniformed officers working for him. Two teenage brothers had already been caught sneaking back through the woods to the terraced Victorian cottage where they lived with their parents. A young couple with a baby had been given permission to return to their own house under escort, and when the PC arrived with them, the front door was opened by their father, whose conversation made it clear that he had been in the Griffon earlier too.

Thompson had decided to allocate Creamery Nook, the largest of three Airbnbs on the estate, as accommodation for those not able to return to their homes. The Nook was hardly bijou, but in fact a four-bedroomed, beautifully restored gatehouse on the southern edge of the estate, vacant at the moment, and one of the first buildings to be thoroughly searched. A lot of the staff and their families, especially the older generation, were not happy with this either.

The press had made matters worse, of course, with the resources to interview a great many more bystanders than the police had yet managed. DCS Ross seemed to be out of his depth and was spending most of his time wrestling with the PR difficulties of the case. No one had ever murdered a police and crime commissioner before, and of course it made for a terrific headline.

The call from Talantire wasn't unexpected. Thompson had promised to attend her informal incident room meeting, but he hadn't been able to get away. All he had provided so far was the CCTV from the Griffon. It soon became clear that this was what she was calling about.

'Did any of your officers interview Rustam Hartington, the commissioner's adopted son?' Talantire asked him.

'The name's not familiar.' He looked up and saw an elderly couple sitting in their Range Rover on the drive just beyond the crime tape. 'However, I do have here Elizabeth and Ted Beauchamp, sister and brother-in-law of the commissioner's late wife Gillian. They're both directors of Sleepy Monk Creameries, and I suppose you could call them community leaders here at Little Bychecombe.'

'Can you get someone to escort them into the Manor for interview?'

'Certainly.'

Elizabeth and Ted Beauchamp looked to be in a state of shock as Talantire sat them down for interview. Talantire recognised them from the CCTV footage at the Griffon, where they had been holding fort at one of the larger tables in the corner of the lounge. Elizabeth was one of those ethereally fine-boned middle-class women, immaculately dressed, with her snowy white hair in a chignon, while her husband, in a saffron blazer and brick-red corduroy trousers, sat glassy-eyed beside her. He was clearly tipsy, to say the least.

'First of all, can I say how sorry I am that we are here under such tragic circumstances,' Talantire said.

'It's been the most ghastly shock,' Elizabeth said. 'Nothing like that *ever* happens around here.'

'The place has been going downhill for several years,' Ted said in a rumbling baritone. 'I wasn't Lionel's greatest fan, but this is absolutely terrible.'

'Can I ask you to confirm your movements this afternoon?'

'We were at the Griffon throughout,' said Ted. Talantire had no trouble believing it. The CCTV showed them only leaving when there was a mass exodus from the bar as the police arrived.

'Can you tell me about Rustam?'

Ted blew a huge sigh and rolled his eyes.

'I don't know who invited him,' Elizabeth said, 'but he was there in the lounge bar, sticking out like a sore thumb.'

'He was Lionel's adopted son, I believe?'

'Yes,' Elizabeth replied. 'A Bosnian orphan whose parents were killed when their car went over a landmine. My sister Gillian was barren and so desperately wanted a child—'

'Damn little tyke turned out to be a mistake,' Ted interjected. 'Not right in the head from the start.'

'When exactly was he adopted?' Talantire asked.

'About 2002, when he was seven,' Elizabeth said.

'Threw *awful* tantrums,' Ted said. 'He bit my sister-in-law many times.'

Elizabeth took over. 'Gillian showed boundless patience with him throughout, though Lionel was less forgiving. When my sister died in 2012 and Lionel shacked up with the harridan—'

'Are you referring to Helena?' Talantire asked.

'Bloody gold digger,' Ted said. 'Came down from London with her airs and graces, but not an ounce of breeding.'

Talantire made a note to check up on the commissioner's will, the beneficiaries of which might well explain the enmity she had just witnessed. 'So does Rustam live here at the Manor?' she asked.

Ted let out a huge sigh and folded his arms.

'Not any more I'm delighted to say,' Elizabeth said. 'He was a thief in his teens and at eighteen disappeared up to London, since when I understand he's been delivering takeaway meals,' she said with distaste. 'He's sneaked back from time to time, and Lionel was even considering giving him one of the cottages and creating a job at the creamery for him, but thankfully that came to nought.'

'Do you know where he is now?'

'Haven't a clue,' Ted said. 'But I wouldn't be surprised if he was the culprit.'

'Why do you say that?'

'He is a violent criminal. You should check your records. He has convictions.'

'We shall certainly be looking into it,' Talantire said. She thanked them and ended the interview. She then messaged Thompson with a picture of Rustam and asked him to keep an eye out for him. 'As of now, he's our number one suspect.'

Chapter Six

Rustam Hartington did indeed have a criminal record, though not one of notable violence. His contact with the police started with an unconditional discharge for shoplifting in the gift shop at Great Bychecombe in 2009, a conditional discharge for the theft of a bicycle in Little Bychecombe, and then, aged sixteen, another conditional discharge and a fine for affray in Barnstaple. At eighteen, while living at no fixed address in East London, he was arrested for stealing a mobile phone. There were numerous other arrests at which no charges were preferred. A mobile phone number was on file for him, but it was several months old and she had no confidence that it was any longer in his possession. She rang the phone and left a message for him to call her back. If he did, she would fall over in surprise.

Talantire contacted her opposite number at the Met Police's Barking division, which covered the area where Rustam had appeared to live, or at least where most of the arrests were made.

The last address for him was a shared rental property in Dagenham, but a phone call to the landlord revealed that he had moved out some months previously. She then put out an alert for his arrest.

Even as she did so, Talantire was dubious that Rustam could have prepared a plot of this complexity. Nothing he had done in the past showed much foresight or cunning. Some minor violence, yes, with the affray charge relating to fighting outside a pub, but not much ingenuity. Perhaps he had a partner in crime.

It was eight o'clock when Talantire looked up from her work in the cramped confines of the portable incident room. DC Dave Nuttall had been manning the phones to take the pressure off her, filtering through the most promising leads that had come through on the public information line and tips passed on through the press office. He had still found time to pursue his own pet theories, one of which he now presented to her.

'I've been looking on Companies House,' he said. 'The board of Sleepy Monk Creameries Ltd includes our good friends Detective Superintendent Timothy Weaver and Superintendent Paul Shortland as non-executive directors.'

'That's interesting,' Talantire said.

'Weaver is also finance director of HHW Properties Ltd – based in Devon – and is on the board of which Bagpuss served until just a year ago.'

'Serving officers are not barred from holding direct-orships of companies,' Talantire said. 'So long as they have been disclosed and vetted as not compromising their duties and rubberstamped by the chief constable.'

'Well, I'm certainly going to check that,' Nuttall said. 'And there's always scope for motive when there's money at stake, isn't there?'

'Agreed.'

'HHW properties, which I presume was formed from the initials of Hall-Hartington and Weaver, owns that great chunk of land between Great Bychecombe and the A361, with application in for 273 executive homes. The other director is Bill Hoskins, the former head of planning for Devon County Council.'

'The crucial word there is "former", Dave.'

'Well, yes, but he's bound to have lots of mates in the planning department.'

'You will be happy to know that I already have requests in for a financial order on all the Hall-Hartington businesses and bank accounts. The fraud specialist at Middlemoor will be combing through it.'

'I hope none of them work under Shortland or Weaver. By the way, were you aware that Shortland and Weaver, along with the commissioner himself, were all members of the local branch of the Freemasons?'

'No. It's not against the rules, Dave.'

'I know, but just saying.'

Talantire gave her subordinate a piercing look. 'Scepticism is okay, Dave, but let's not go for paranoia. Not at least until we have more to go on.'

Nuttall returned to his desk, where the phone lights were blinking on the handset. Talantire stood and stretched, taking in the dismal blank walls and the ceaseless drone of the air conditioning unit. She hadn't yet had a call back from the commissioner's personal lawyer, Geoffrey Wheatcroft, who was also the legal director of Sleepy Monk Creameries. Emails to his accounts bounced back with out-of-office notifications, and it being a Saturday night probably explained why they didn't forward to a receptionist.

She needed a break and to have a think, so she decided to take a short walk.

–

Emerging from the Portakabin and descending the stairs from the back of the lorry on which it sat, Talantire was suddenly aware of the beautiful spring evening. It was gone eight o'clock, and the birds were still singing. Bychecombe Manor was set in the most beautiful landscape, a broad valley of pastureland, with the main thoroughfare lined with horse chestnut trees. In one of the fields opposite, she spotted a green woodpecker with its red cap and characteristic swooping flight. It alighted briefly upon a section of blue-and-white crime tape, setting it swinging, before flying up into the tree above.

The search of the tied cottages was still ongoing, but more than a dozen had now been turned over to their residents. Most of the rest were waiting in the luxury of Creamery Nook, ordering takeaways from South Molton and further afield. She went on a brisk ten-minute walk, greeting uniformed PCs as she did so.

Something about this ghastly crime was bugging her. The meticulous planning, the inside knowledge not only of the CCTV system but of the ancient well, the safe's location, and presumably of what lay within. But if robbery was the motive, why the violence? A professional burglary might have accomplished as much, more elegantly and without the gunshot noise that attracted attention.

None of it sat right with her.

At the door of one cottage, still being searched by CSI, she got into conversation with the uniform guarding the door. PC Robert Howcombe actually lived in Little Bychecombe, though he was on the South Molton community team. He told her he had been off duty, in the pub at the engagement party, but had been called in for the emergency.

'Did you see anything suspicious amongst the party-goers? Anyone you didn't know?' she asked him.

'Well, I didn't know a lot of the older folks. There were quite a few from beyond the village, relatives of the betrothed.'

Talantire was amused to hear a young man use such an anachronistic term, especially conveyed in his strong Devon accent.

'However, there was this young fella standing by himself. He wasn't wearing party rags like the rest of us, and he had a London accent. I heard it when he was ordering a drink.'

Talantire got out her phone and accessed a still from the CCTV that showed Rustam.

'Is this him?'

'Yes, ma'am, it is.'

'Was he there the whole time?'

'I couldn't honestly say that, but I did notice him towards the end.'

'He's the adopted son of the commissioner and his first wife.'

His boyish brow furrowed. 'Then I'm surprised I ain't seen him before.'

'He doesn't live locally. But keep your eye out for him. I would like to talk to him.'

'Will do, ma'am.'

At that moment, the door to the cottage opened and one of the CSI team came out, dressed in a crackly Tyvek bodysuit.

'Nothing in that one either,' he said to PC Howcombe. 'Oh, sorry, ma'am, didn't see you there,' he said to Talantire.

'Any sign of bloodstains in any of the cottages?' she asked him. 'Bloodstained boots, anything like that?'

'Plenty of muddy ones, but not much else. I think they found an unregistered shotgun in one of the other cottages,' he said. 'Venka's got all the details. She's down at the evidence van.' He pointed back down the footpath towards the main house. In the yard at the back, there were now a dozen police patrol cars and half a dozen vans, including the gold command vehicle.

Talantire thanked them both and made her way back. The evidence van was a long wheelbase Mercedes, unmarked, that was meticulously fitted out inside with shelves and a small refrigerator. The doors were open, and Venka was inside with another CSI technician.

'How's it going?' Talantire asked her.

'Not too bad, Jan,' Venka replied. 'We've taken lots more DNA swabs right around the well chamber, so the labs are going to be busy tonight.'

'I heard you found an unregistered shotgun in one of the cottages?'

'That's right, but don't get your hopes up. It doesn't look like it's been fired recently. The owner is the father of one of the farm employees, and he must be in his seventies. I've already sent the firearm off with the courier for ballistics testing. All the blood samples have gone off too, along with the DNA, by motorcycle dispatch rider to Exeter. We've been promised answers on the first batch of samples by midnight.'

'That's good,' Talantire said. 'The post-mortems are set for Monday, but I don't expect to learn too much.'

'That's shotgun victims for you,' Venka said dismissively. 'Give me a good poisoning any day. Now, I'm very interested in your opinion of this.' Venka

73

turned away and lifted down a heavy object in a clear polythene evidence bag the size of a suit carrier. She held it up in front of Talantire. It was the doll that had been hanging on the back of the door into the well chamber. 'There was a knife at its feet, one that had clearly been used to attack the commissioner's wife.'

'Yes, I saw.' Talantire had photographed both the doll and the knife on her way into the well chamber. 'It's a weird thing, isn't it? It gave me the shivers when I first saw it.'

The doll's coarse gingery hair and wizened leathery face sat in contrast to the childlike way it was dressed. It looked like an elderly witch going to primary school.

'It's clearly some kind of collectable item,' Venka said. 'There's a unique number stencilled on its neck.'

'I'm hoping to interview Helena de Courchevel tomorrow, so maybe we can shed some light on it then,' Talantire said. 'I also want to know where the murder weapon is, and those bloodstained boots.'

Venka shrugged. 'They could be anywhere.'

'Not really. There wasn't that much time for the assailant to escape. They could well have been dumped somewhere in the house, or down the well.'

'Well, we haven't done all the upstairs yet. It'll be another day at least.'

Talantire was interrupted by a call. It was from a detective inspector at Barking Police who was trying to trace Rustam Hartington. 'We think we'll get him pretty soon. He's been working for Deliveroo, so through them we've got an up-to-date mobile phone number for him, and we have some location details. As you suggest, he has been down in Devon and seems now to be en route back to London.'

'On the train?'

'We don't think so, based on the cell site pattern. It could be a coach.'

'He left here on a moped,' Talantire said. 'But DVLA records show it's not his.'

'A moped would be an exhausting way to travel back to London. The triangulation and handoff speeds seem to indicate something faster.'

'Do you have an address for him yet?'

'No. We haven't had much success finding associates who could give us that information. But I'll be in touch when we have any more.'

Talantire thanked him and hung up.

–

Talantire went back into the mobile incident room, where Maddy and Dave were working away on their terminals. It was gone nine o'clock.

'The DCS phoned for you,' Maddy said, without looking up. 'He's back in Exeter.'

'I was wondering why I hadn't seen him. The gold command van is gone already.'

Maddy finally looked up. 'Ross was probably getting dizzy with all this country air, and felt the need to hide behind a desk and get the reassuring feel of chipboard against his thighs.'

Talantire smiled and rang the number, which was engaged. She left a brief message and had no sooner put the phone down when it rang.

'Drayton Ross here,' he said. 'Have you got any suspects for me, Jan, apart from the adopted son?'

'No, Rustam's the main line of enquiry. It's still pretty thin until we can speak to Helena properly and find out what the relationship was like between him and the commissioner.'

'As you can imagine, I'm getting a lot of pressure from upstairs for a quick win. There is international press interest, you know. *The New York Times*, French and German papers. The chief constable had a call from the Home Secretary too.'

That's your job, don't complain about it to me. Talantire didn't voice the thought but instead said, 'There's a lot of forensic work still to do, and we need a full financial over-view of all the commissioner's business interests. We don't want to be outflanked by any hard-working investigative reporters.'

'I don't think we have any suggestion of financial skul-duggery, do we?'

'We won't know until we look,' she replied. 'I just need to make sure that those resources are being deployed.'

'Absolutely. I promised you anything you needed, so long as we get results.'

She was just in the process of formulating some further reassurance when Ross killed the call. 'It sounds like Ross is feeling the stress,' she told Maddy.

'That's his job, and why he gets a fat salary,' Maddy replied.

Once Nuttall had finished on the phone, she called them into an impromptu meeting. Nuttall swung his chair around to face her and Maddy sat on the edge of her desk as Talantire turned the whiteboard to face them. Below the three words PLANNING, KNOWLEDGE and VIOLENCE, she added one more: SPEED.

'The whole speed of this crime is quite troubling to me. We know from the CCTV at the Griffon, which captured people looking up on the terrace, that the first pair of shotgun blasts took place at 14:21. The second pair were at 14:26.' She wrote the times on the whiteboard. 'Soraya raised the alarm at 14:36, having ventured out onto the landing to get her phone. She didn't report hearing an intruder at that time.'

'Maybe the assailant was still downstairs?' Nuttall asked.

'It's almost certain. In that ten-minute window from the second pair of blasts, the assailant could hardly have managed to throw Helena down the stairs, start cutting her with the knife, manoeuvre her to the safe, and then presumably getting no joy about the combination, drag her another fifteen yards down another set of steps, into the antechamber where the doll was found, open that door if it was locked, shackle her to the chains, and then lower her down the well.'

'That is a lot to do,' Maddy agreed.

'So assuming he was still inside the house when the 999 call was received, he may have slipped into one of the many rooms to change and emerged wearing clean clothes and footwear to mingle with the other guests. Neither Soraya Hinton, John Rice nor Digby Robinson saw anyone. Tony Thompson has collected the bedroom keys from the five sets of guests who were staying in the main house,' Talantire said. 'So we can take a look.'

'Are there other exits, apart from the kitchen and the main front door?' Maddy asked.

'Yes, two others. A basement exit at the side leading to the walled garden, which was locked when we found it, and a first-floor fire escape, also locked. But anyone leaving there would have been visible from the main drive.'

'Maybe if the perpetrator knows the place so well, he could still be there,' Nuttall said.

'Yeah, in a place that hasn't been searched like a loft or a cupboard,' Maddy added.

'All right, Dave, let's suit up and have a good look around,' Talantire said. 'I'll check with Venka to see what areas they still have to cover within the house.'

'I'll see if we can get a floor plan of the entire place,' Maddy said.

'I couldn't find one online. There is only a historical one that covers the medieval building,' Nuttall said.

'Elizabeth Hartington probably has one,' Talantire said. 'But I'm not sure if they have access to their own home yet to get it.'

–

It took half an hour's work with uniforms to locate Elizabeth and Ted, and to discover that, yes, there was a floor plan. The bad news was that it was in an office inside the very building that they intended to search. Talantire and Nuttall were working on very partial information as they entered the manor house through the front door – to avoid getting under the feet of the CSI team – and ascended the grand staircase to the first floor. They were accompanied by PC Adrian Close, who was armed with a Taser. Just in case. Talantire had the list of guests and their keys. Another dozen guests had been staying at the Griffon, and all attendees had now given statements to the uniforms, except for four individuals who had already left, including Rustam.

It was ten o'clock, and dark enough to need the lights on. There were grand chandeliers in the carpeted corridors, but the light they gave off was rather diffuse, so they used phone torches as well. They started in the western wing, where Soraya had been, the part of the house that was still in daily use, and which, according to Elizabeth, included all the guest rooms. They took photographs as they entered each room, and PC Close's bodycam captured further details. There was plenty of luggage, but the beds were mainly made. While PC Close stood by, the two detectives looked under beds, in cupboards, and inside cavernous dark wood wardrobes.

At the end of a corridor, they found the commissioner's bedroom. It was a magnificent light and airy room, with enormous lead-lighted windows that looked out over the courtyard and avenue of horse chestnuts along the drive to the north, giving a wonderful view of the rising slopes of the coombe and the woodland at the top. The room was tidy, evidence of the cleaner's attention, with the bed professionally made, neatly folded clothes on it, and dry cleaning hanging on the back of the wardrobe in its plastic bag. Elizabeth had explained that this was originally the room he shared with Helena until her mobility worsened four years ago and she couldn't manage the stairs. The commissioner had put a lift in at vast expense just over two years ago, but she had never returned to the marital bedroom.

Talantire routinely managed a professional detachment and was no particular fan of the commissioner, having crossed swords with him on numerous occasions, but seeing the unused clothing and the freshly pressed suit that he was presumably going to wear for the engagement party was poignant. All these everyday preparations so dramatically interrupted by his murder.

PC Close waited outside while Nuttall took photographs and Talantire took DNA samples from door handles and window catches. She went into the large, rather antiquated ensuite, which on its parquet tiled floor had a claw-footed bath big enough to drown a cow. The commissioner's toiletries were all neatly laid out, again evidence of the cleaner. There was a separate walk-in shower stall, still damp on the floor inside, with smear-free glass panels. Not used since the cleaner whizzed through. Talantire had a rising sense of respect for Soraya on seeing the enormous workload that had fallen on this woman's shoulders.

Making her way back into the bedroom, she went over to the mantelpiece, on which were large framed photographs of the commissioner and Helena on their wedding day. She looked absolutely beautiful, long-limbed, delicate features, with those amazing cheekbones, and of course fully ambulant before the onset of her MS. One heck of a catch for Brian Hall, as he had been, who even in those days was a paunchy and rather homely-looking individual. She couldn't help herself thinking about Helena's motivation for this match. Was it the money, the inheritance? Or did she see burning within him some passion, wit or allure that had escaped the notice of all his underlings in Devon and Cornwall Police?

There were other photographs too. The two of them skiing, sharing meals in foreign climes, and a whole series of skiing competition pictures of a teenage Helena clutching fistfuls of medals. What an incredible burden her multiple sclerosis must have been, a progressive loss of mobility, snatching away not only the adventure sports that must have meant so much to her in her early years, but even the ability to walk that we all take for granted. All these photographs showed something else too: this was his shrine to the woman, casting aside any doubt about the intensity of the love he had felt for her. And what man in his place wouldn't feel the same? She couldn't help wondering to what extent that love was requited.

Once they had finished all the bedrooms, which were all on the outside of the wing, they looked into a series of cramped offices and storerooms on the inside of the building. There were five of these, mostly with narrow and grimy barred windows looking out onto an interior light well, just twenty feet square and seventy feet high, going up to the complex roof. With drainpipes, wiring and window ledges, it was mainly a grubby roost for pigeons.

In the third of these inside rooms, Talantire found a sash window. Though it was painted in, it looked like it might open. With Nuttall's help, they managed to haul it up and peer out. The cavity was dismal and grubby, and it seemed to go down to at least the first basement level. It would have been a perfect place to dispose of a pair of bloodstained boots. But there was nothing there except half a dozen dead pigeons, a paint tin, and some paint-stained rags. From the amount of pigeon excrement on these items, it was clear everything had been there for many months if not years.

Returning to the corridor, they worked their way methodically around the first floor, finding nothing that would indicate the presence of the perpetrator. Talantire made a mental note to do a Bluestar treatment of all the staircases, which would at least indicate if somebody had walked up in bloodstained boots. Even the most microscopic deposit would then be picked up.

There were so many rooms to check, and each took at least ten minutes with all the DNA samples and documentation, so it was almost midnight when they got to the second floor. No guests were being accommodated here, according to the list they had. It wasn't a surprise. The carpet up here was thin and threadbare, the lights much more basic low wattage bulbs that seemed to have been there for decades. Period architectural features were few and far between, and there was clear evidence of the penetration of damp that stained the walls a nicotine brown in numerous places. There were more than a dozen bedrooms up here, many of them clearly unused for years. Talantire and Nuttall entered one room after another where the furniture was dust-sheeted and the curtains drawn. Many had individual fireplaces, the grates filled with pinecones to show they were no longer in use.

Finally, they found a narrow wooden staircase, ascending to yet another floor. Small side windows showed they were near the apex of the roof. At the top of the stairs was a room that had a name: Summerheath. It was not on Tony Thompson's list. They opened the door into a pitch-black chamber filled with the stench of stale cigarettes. Their phone lights revealed it was hexagonal, a little larger than the other bedrooms, with windows on all sides. The exquisite wood panelling, decorated with carvings of forest creatures, stood at odds with the clothing littering the floor and three empty bottles – one vodka, two wine. At its centre was a four-poster canopy bed.

Occupied.

For a heartbeat she thought it was a corpse, but a gentle susurrus of breathing was a relief. A third body would be too much. Talantire approached, her phone light showing the child-sized figure wreathed in covers. A large eye mask covered the face, and only one slender arm in what looked like a Victorian nightdress protruded from the sheets.

'Hello,' Talantire whispered.

The figure moved slightly, and a hand lifted one edge of the eye mask. The face beneath was like a porcelain doll, smooth and almost shiny.

'What time is it?' It was a woman's voice, thick and croaky.

'Quarter past one.'

'In the afternoon? Fuck! Why didn't you wake me?'

'No, in the morning. Early Sunday morning.'

The woman turned away, pulled out ear plugs and tore off the eye mask, releasing a cascade of dyed copper hair. She clicked on the light on the bedside cabinet, almost knocking off a largely drained bottle of vodka that stood there.

'I'm a police officer, DI Talantire. Can I ask who you are?'

'I'm a guest,' the woman rasped as the light came on. Now she could be seen more clearly. The hidden half of her face was old and heavily lined, but her cheek and forehead on the other side were preternaturally smooth. 'What the hell are the police doing in my bedroom?'

'We've not come to eat your porridge, that's for sure,' Nuttall muttered.

'Are you not aware that there's been a double murder here in the last twenty-four hours?' Talantire asked.

'What!' She slid out of bed on the far side and grabbed her phone from the bedside table. 'Who's been killed?' she asked as she began to scroll.

'The Honourable Lionel Hall-Hartington, and one of the farm employees.'

She looked astounded, her mouth hanging open on the one side where it had the freedom to do so.

'Didn't you hear the gunshots, the sirens, the banging down of doors?' Nuttall asked.

'I'd taken a couple of sleeping pills… but my God, old Bagpuss!' she exclaimed in a gravelly, smoky voice. 'Finally. So the party's been cancelled…'

'The party was *yesterday* afternoon,' Nuttall said.

'Yesterday? Christ, that's the last time I mix those two tablets… Is Helena safe?'

'She was injured, but yes, she is out of danger now,' Talantire said.

'Thank God.'

'So can you please identify yourself?' Talantire asked.

'You couldn't get me a coffee, could you?' She smiled ingratiatingly, but it only lifted one side of her face. Turning back to the nightstand, she poured a glug of vodka into a mug, popped a pill and swilled it back. She reached for a packet of cigarettes, lit one up and took a long drag.

'No, we're investigating a murder,' Talantire said, and gestured for Nuttall to look in the woman's suitcase, which was lying open at the foot of the bed.

As he crouched to start searching, she cried out, 'No need for that, I'm Paula Zucketort!'

'I need to see ID,' Talantire said, holding out her hand. The woman appeared alarmed that Nuttall was going through her things, which seemed a pretty good reason to carry on.

'What's this then?' Nuttall said, holding up a Ziploc bag of pink tablets.

'Medicines,' she said, holding a skinny arm out for them.

'Prescriptions normally come in blister packs,' Talantire said.

'Yes, but I get them pressed out for me because I have trouble with my arthritis,' she said. 'Then I keep them in a handy bag.'

'And this?' he said, pulling up a smaller bag containing the distinctively shaped leaves of the cannabis plant.

'Oh for goodness' sake, it's only weed. It's for Helena, for her MS.'

'I'm afraid we are going to have to look after these for you for now,' Talantire said. 'Charges may be preferred. You are not obliged to say anything, but it may harm your defence if you do not mention when questioned something which you later rely on in court.'

'Oh, so you've got two murders on your plate, but you'd rather spend your valuable time persecuting me over this chickenshit,' she said.

'No, I wouldn't "rather" but I can hardly overlook it,' Talantire responded.

Eventually, Ms Zucketort handed over her driving licence and begrudgingly agreed to a cheek swab. Talantire and Nuttall, with better things to do, left PC Close to carry on, aided by another couple of uniforms, who in booties and gloves came up in the lift to take Ms Zucketort down to a separate room for questioning.

It took the two detectives until two a.m. to finish all the rooms, and they still hadn't tackled the lofts. The discovery of the sleeping beauty, as they called her, didn't blind them to the fact that they were looking for a killer; one who was powerful enough to drag a woman along a corridor and throw her down a well. If he was up in the lofts, it would have to wait until morning.

The two detectives returned to the mobile incident room to make some checks on Ms Zucketort. Nuttall looked her up on the national crime database while

Talantire, intrigued by a familiar name, googled her. Inevitably, Talantire got her answers first.

'She's the fashion designer and avant-garde artist Venus Z, aged seventy-three. Uses her own body as a canvas. She made her name during the punk era, was best mates with Vivienne Westwood and Malcolm McLaren and the King's Road crowd. She was on *Top of the Pops* in 1979 with *Uproar!*, a one-hit wonder.'

'I don't remember that,' Nuttall said.

'Neither do I,' Talantire continued. 'Wikipedia says the 2021 film *Cruella* drew on her early life history.'

'I'm well impressed that she could sleep through a double murder and all those sirens,' Nuttall said. 'Ah, look, I've got her now. She's got plenty of form, but most is quite old. Assault on a police officer at Orgreave Colliery, June 18, 1984. That was the peak of the miners' strike. She was fined, got a suspended sentence, but refused to pay and got sent to jail for twenty-eight days. So she's a martyr.'

'Or principled,' Talantire said.

'There have been quite a few drug offences since, but no prison time. Cannabis, cocaine, ketamine – that was just a year ago. It's all possession but not dealing.'

'She might well be adding to that now,' Talantire said. 'She surely can't be the perpetrator, but she might know something.'

'Maybe she wasn't asleep the whole time,' Nuttall said. 'Perhaps she sleepwalks.'

Talantire guessed that Nuttall was joking, at least about the second part. But she certainly didn't intend to take the woman's account at face value. She requested a warrant to search the woman's home in London.

They had one final bedroom to do: Helena's. Elizabeth's map clearly showed it on the ground floor, above the laundry. They found it quickly enough, though it was locked. They didn't have the keys, and it was too late to disturb Ted and Elizabeth, or whoever else might hold them. Nuttall leaned on the door and from the free play reckoned the lock was fairly flimsy, and they could break it easily enough.

'It's a listed building,' Talantire said. 'We can't cause any damage.'

'Well, I'm too fat to squeeze under the door, but maybe you can manage it,' he said with a smile.

'Flattery will get you nowhere,' she said. She looked through her go-bag, came up with a small spray of WD-40, sprayed it into the lock, then brought out a hair grip and a tiny screwdriver of the type you would use to fix a pair of spectacles.

'I didn't have breaking and entering down as one of your skills, Jan.'

'I learned it in prison.'

Seeing Nuttall's raised eyebrows, she continued: 'From Mickey Harper, when he confessed to doing over the Grand Hotel. It's all right for old locks.'

It took five minutes of fiddling and prodding with a carefully bent hairpin, but the click of the lock was distinctive. Talantire opened the door and flicked on the light. It was a large modernised room with an adjustable bed and disability handrails in a couple of places. There was a folding wheelchair and some gym equipment, including a pull-up frame over the bed. The room was tidy but didn't look like Soraya had worked her magic on it, and that made sense because Helena's account was of just having left the room, further along the same corridor as her husband's office, when she heard the shots.

Talantire took a few photographs while Nuttall turned to her. 'Shall we search it then?'

'We don't have much excuse. She is a witness, not a suspect.' Talantire went through to the ensuite, which had been entirely modernised to deal with Helena's disability, with a wheelchair-accessible shower and a low wash basin.

When she came back in, Nuttall looked up guiltily from a laptop. 'I found this in a drawer,' he said. 'I'm just looking through the search history.'

'I suppose we can't rule out her complicity entirely,' Talantire said.

'Nah, there's nothing much here for the last couple of weeks,' he said, standing up. 'Still, she's got a sex toy.'

Talantire put her hands on her hips. 'A woman is allowed her privacy. Her sex life was probably a bit limited because of her MS, depending on how much nerve damage there was.'

Nuttall shrugged. 'I'm sure most women couldn't bear the idea of Bagpuss undulating about on top of them.'

'Thank you for that unnecessary image, Dave.'

Chapter Seven

It was half past two in the morning, while Talantire was reading the witness statements collected by the uniforms, when her phone buzzed. It was Venka, to let her know that the analysis of early DNA and blood samples from the basement and corridors were back. She was still reading through the email as she called Talantire.

'Okay, Jan, so it's quite predictable so far: lots of blood from the commissioner and his wife, in the places you'd expect to find it. The blood on the boot prints matches that of the shooting victim in the barn, so we can confirm that as the first death. There's also some of the wife's blood on some boot prints down in the basement, which makes sense. It's her blood on the knife... We've got quite a lot of unknown DNA, on light switches, on door handles, yada yada yada... Aha! We've got someone on the database. Criminal conviction flagged up!'

'Let me look them up,' Talantire said, putting her mobile on speakerphone and logging into the national criminal record database. She looked across at Dave Nuttall, who was in discussion with a group of three uniforms who had brought in the latest statements.

'Paula Venera Zucketort,' Venka said.

'Ah, yes, we found her upstairs asleep,' Talantire said. 'She's the fashion designer and avant-garde artist Venus Z.'

'Never heard of her,' Venka said.

'But where did you find her DNA?' Talantire asked.

'In one of the bedrooms on the first floor, door handle, ensuite, in the well chamber and on the doll.'

'So she was right down there, eh?' Talantire said. 'But as for the doll, I think it's one she made, in her own image.'

'What?'

'She's a blatant self-publicist. The pictures make her look a bit like the doll we found. Wikipedia says her most famous exploit was to get a half facelift, so that one half of her face looks smooth and unwrinkled, with the addition of Botox, while the other half has aged naturally.'

'That sounds grotesque.'

'Yes, you should see her!' Talantire said.

'I've got enough weird stuff on my plate as it is.' Venka continued to read out various results.

'She claimed to have slept through the gunshots.'

'Really? I'd be even more impressed if we had her DNA on the handle of the knife,' Venka said.

'Absolutely. The woman's five foot tall. She clearly doesn't wear size ten boots or have the ability to drag a disabled woman thirty yards down a corridor.'

'So a red herring then?' Venka asked.

'She might know plenty,' Talantire said. 'At a guess I would say that Helena invited her. We found suspicious pharmaceuticals in her possession, so we have an excuse to interview her.'

'Agreed,' Venka said.

'So what does that leave us with?'

'Well, plenty of unknown samples including some in the basement level.'

'Any others in the well chamber?'

'Apart from yours and Boxall's, we've got the commissioner's and two unknown others. Both these last samples were on the cords in addition to Helena's. We've sent a sample of the rope off for analysis, to see where it may have come from.'

'That's crucial, if we get whoever tied her up,' Talantire said.

'Of course, we don't yet have the results back from any of the samples that were taken later, or anything from the various tied cottages.'

They finished up the phone call. Venka said she was going home and leaving the CSI investigation in the hands of her deputy, Chris Boxall. She'd be back at seven in the morning.

Talantire knew that she wasn't going to get any sleep. She'd given Maddy Moran permission to go home, because she had young children, but needed her back in at dawn. She and Nuttall would hold the fort until then. Starting with an interview of Paula Zucketort.

–

Talantire found the woman making herself at home in one of the lounges, under the guard of a young PC. She was lying sideways on a leather settee, dressed in a child's tartan pinafore dress, with white ankle socks and black patent leather T-bar sandals. She was smoking a cigar and blowing smoke rings. Someone had brought her coffee in a china cup.

'Ah, our intrepid detective,' she said, looking Talantire up and down as she approached.

Talantire raised one eyebrow in response as she pulled up a hardback chair and sat down. She brought out her notebook and set a digital recorder on the coffee table between them. 'We'd like to ask you a few questions, Ms Zucketort.'

'Ask away, my dear,' she said with an airy gesture of the cigar.

'Who invited you to stay here?'

'My dear friend Helena. We've known each other for years.'

'And when exactly did you arrive?'

'What's today?'

'2:47 a.m. on Sunday.'

'So it must've been Friday afternoon. I distinctly recall having afternoon tea, just here.' She gestured at the sofa opposite. 'She and I had a couple of drinks over dinner at around seven, and then I said I was going up for a lie down, as I had a headache. And then you found me.'

'What about Saturday?' Talantire asked.

She shrugged and blew a smoke ring. 'You tell me.'

'So you claim you were asleep from Friday night right through until the early hours of Sunday morning?'

'I'm not claiming anything,' she said. 'I wasn't awake at the time.'

'Tell me about your relationship with Helena de Courchevel.'

'As I said, I met her years ago. She was a fashion student when I was getting going with Malcolm.'

'Malcolm?'

'Malcolm McLaren. I worked in his boutique for a while on the Kings Road. Helena was just a teenager, but she came to some of my parties and told me how she wanted to be an actress. Apparently she had grown up next to the Hammer Films studios at Bray and spent a lot of time hanging around there hoping to get a bit part.' She giggled, a peculiar girlish noise compared to her deep, smoky speaking voice, but much more in keeping with the schoolgirl attire. 'She had the looks, of course, and managed to get a bit part in one of the James Bond films, but never the Bond Girl part she wanted. I guess she was unlucky. The nearest she got was when she shacked up with that handsome cad Yves, who spent all his time on the ski slopes and chasing other women.'

'What about Lionel Hall-Hartington?'

'Ah, yes, good old Brian.' She exhaled a cloud of cigar smoke and gazed admiringly at it. 'Hard-working Brian Lionel Hall, son of a trade unionist, who married above himself and clambered up the greasy pole of life, the ultimate cheesy magnate.'

'So you weren't a fan?'

'Let's just say Helena could have done better.'

'When I told you he had died, I noticed that you said "finally", as if it was something you had been waiting for.'

One side of her face frowned at Talantire, which came off like a peculiar wink. 'One can always hope I suppose.' She leaned forward, grabbed her coffee and spoke to the PC. 'Would you mind getting me a fresh one? This has rather gone cold. Thank you so much.'

The PC looked at Talantire, who shook her head. 'Ms Zucketort, we are conducting a murder investigation, not running a tearoom.'

She folded her arms and rolled her eyes. 'Look, I slept through the whole damn thing and missed all the fun. I'm quite pissed off, actually.'

'We'll see what the forensic tests say. You really don't seem upset that Helena's husband has been murdered.'

'Well, I'm enormously sympathetic to her, for her loss. But I never had any time for him, and it would be hypocritical to say otherwise now just because he's dead.' She stubbed out the cigar and sat up on the settee.

'I see,' Talantire said.

'So where is Helena? Can I go and see her?'

'She is recovering in hospital in Exeter. But I'd prefer if you remained here for now.'

'Am I under arrest?'

'No. You have been cautioned and you should expect to be called back for further interview in the next couple of days.'

'For a couple of leaves of weed?'

'This isn't Amsterdam, it's not legal here.'

'More's the pity,' she murmured. 'A little bit more nuance and practicality would go a long way towards allowing people to have nature's safest and most effective painkiller.'

'Save it for the judge.'

She laughed. 'I've shared a joint with quite a few legal professionals over the years. And they are such buggers for cocaine. If you don't believe me, try taking swabs from the cisterns of the toilets in Britain's Crown Courts. Half of our barristers are as high as kites.'

Talantire knew that she was right. But this wasn't a forum for scoring points. She handed Ms Zucketort over to the uniforms, asking them to make sure she stayed locally and handed her passport in.

–

Talantire had been waiting for a quiet moment to return a call from Adam. His voice message said that he would happily talk to her any time, day or night. 'I'm thinking of you,' he said. 'You're my superstar.'

It was three in the morning, not a great time to wake anyone up. But she appreciated his message, and it was probably the only time she would get. So she rang, and after the fifth ring he picked up sleepily.

'Hiya,' he said. 'Christ, what time is it?'

She told him and said sorry and explained it was the only chance she would get.

'It's okay, I meant what I said.'

'It's so wonderful to hear your voice, Adam.'

'I've missed you. The nearest I can get to you is by keeping tabs on the local news.'

'I don't have a moment to do that,' she said.

'I'm glad I didn't go to that posh party. Apparently some important local bigwig has been murdered, along with some other bloke. A brutal and unprovoked crime, so they say.'

She chuckled. 'Brutal, certainly. It's far too early to say whether it was unprovoked.'

'Any suspects?'

'Yes, but I can't really tell you anything much.'

'I have the perfect alibi,' Adam said.

'Oh yes?' She laughed lightly, enjoying this moment of relief from the weight of her responsibilities.

'Yes. I was murdering somebody else at the time. That berk at Teatime Fancies Ltd, who's just decided he wants a complete redesign of his website, because his wife doesn't like the spec he gave me, and has some other idea involving an online shop. He wants it incorporated at the original price quote and doesn't want to pay me for the work I've already done.'

'Shall I go around and arrest him?'

'If you'd be so kind.'

She laughed again, enjoying the harmless fantasy. She wanted nothing more at this moment than to be in his arms in bed in Tiverton.

'Adam, can I ask you something?'

'Of course, as long as it doesn't involve me getting out of bed right now.'

'Can I move into yours, while we look for a place to share?'

He laughed, which she took as a good sign that this idea didn't seem entirely alien. 'I've got some room in the shed, if you don't mind sleeping with my windsurfer and wetsuit.'

'I really need to get out of Cornwallis Avenue as soon as possible,' she said. 'Bad associations.'

'I know. You can come and stay with me here, honestly.'

'Ultimately, I need to be close to Barnstaple, though, for work. There are some nice places for sale in the outlying villages, and I thought we could buy one soon if we put our resources together – probably a doer-upper.'

'Um, right. I thought we would wait six months.'

'Well, I think we can manage.'

'You certainly pick your times, don't you? I presume it's the same interrogation technique you use with prisoners,' he said with a sigh. 'Wake 'em up at three a.m. and ask shocking questions.'

She laughed but let him continue.

'You do know that I can't easily get a mortgage on my freelance earnings?'

'I know, you mentioned it before. But I can get a mortgage against my salary, just about, and you can contribute. I've been stashing away my overtime pay too.'

'And you know I have zero practical skills,' he said.

'Keeping me happy is a very practical skill.'

He laughed. 'You have an actual place in mind, don't you?'

'I do.'

'Oh my God, don't say "I do". That's a whole different kettle of fish. So what's this place like?'

'It's an extended two-bedroom Victorian cottage on the B road, in a village that's authentic but not touristy. It's got half an acre of land and some fruit trees, and the village has a pub that I've never arrested anyone in.'

'So nobody knows you there or what you do?'

'Yes, it's an important consideration,' she said.

'I'll happily take a look but not until the morning, proper morning, when it's light.'

'Okay. Good night, Adam.'

'Good night, Jan. Stay safe. I love you.' He hung up, leaving her with a warm glow inside.

'I love you too, Adam,' she said to the phone, before placing it gently in her pocket.

—

Talantire managed a nap in the cramped ladies' bathroom of the mobile incident room between half past three and quarter past four in the morning. She locked the door of a cubicle, sat on the closed loo seat, turned off her phones, and leaned an airline-style inflatable neck pillow against the wall as a pillow. That way, she managed enough of a doze to stop her feeling spaced out. She had honed this technique over many years of being able to grab a forty-five-minute power nap while working through the night.

She awoke when someone banged the door of the adjacent cubicle. She emerged gradually, stretched in front of the mirror, and opened one button in her blouse, enough room to reach in with a roll-on deodorant and freshen herself up. She took a toothbrush from her handbag, and with a small squirt of paste from an airline freebie mini tube, gave her teeth a quick going over. As she was doing so, the woman from the next cubicle flushed the toilet and emerged. She was a young uniformed officer who Talantire didn't recognise.

'I admire what you've done, ma'am,' the PC said. 'You are a great example to us younger officers in the force, especially in the way that you challenged the behaviour of senior male officers.'

'Thank you. Never take it lying down, that's my motto.' Talantire spat out her toothpaste and wiped her mouth with a paper towel from the dispenser. She asked the woman's name.

'I'm PC Sarah Rice.'

'Any relation to John?'

'He's my cousin. So who is the main suspect in this killing, ma'am?'

Talantire advanced cautiously, wary of the connection to a witness. 'We are keeping an open mind at the moment.'

'What about that foreign employee who was fired eighteen months ago?'

'Do you know anything about that?' Talantire was even more wary now.

'Not exactly, but some of the party guests were talking about it when I escorted them to the gatehouse. He's Luka, the brother of Bassin Horvat, the shift manager who was killed.'

'You think he killed his own brother?'

'They hated each other apparently,' the PC said.

'Okay, we don't want to get into rumour and speculation, but I'd certainly like to speak to someone who knows a little bit more about this.'

'It's one of the employees,' she said. 'I'll get Inspector Thompson to tell you which one.'

It was half an hour later and already getting light when Talantire and Nuttall made their way over to one of the tied cottages. No. 4 Creamery Row was a basic Victorian brick built two-up two-down, with a damaged trampoline in the front garden and half a dozen children's bikes spread along the path. They rang the doorbell and the door was opened by a woman wearing a bath towel, who ushered them in rapidly. She excused herself, saying she'd only just got in after waiting hours in the gatehouse. She asked them to keep quiet because the children, having been woken up by the police search, were only just now asleep. She led them through to a very untidy and cramped lounge where her father, Dale Stotfold, was sitting in a stained armchair. He was a rough sixtyish man of ample girth, husband of the Bychecombe Manor cook, and was clearly suffering the effects of a hangover. His eyes were glassy and bloodshot.

'Are you all right to talk?' Talantire said dubiously, as he gestured for her to sit down.

'Yeah, I guess so. I must've had fourteen pints and some chasers at the Griffon, but I had some coffee at the gatehouse. Trouble was they poured brandy in it, didn't they? While we sat and discussed the murders.'

'I hope you haven't driven anywhere,' she said.

'Nah, I staggered home on Shanks's pony,' he said, slapping his legs.

'I understand that you worked with Bassin Horvat and his brother.'

'Yep. Luka. He was a great laugh, and a bit of a joker. The ladies used to like him; I think that's what got him into trouble. He was sacked three years ago.'

'What was your job at the time?' Talantire asked.

'Chief creamery technician.'

'What does that involve?' Nuttall asked.

'I oversee the machines that add the enzymes and cultures to the curds. After that they go off for moulding and to the storage sheds for maturing. Luka worked in the sheds.'

'I understand that he and his brother didn't get on.'

'Yeah. Something to do with inheritance back home originally. Bassin went home for a while after their father died, and when he came back they were at daggers drawn. Then there was this argument in the sheds between them one day, about a woman. It was only a week later when he was sacked by the big boss. Something to do with his behaviour with the girls, they reckon. I wasn't there at the time, but I heard about it. Next day when I came into work he was gone. The caravan where he lived was empty.'

'Do you think Luka was the kind of person who could have done this?' she said, waving a hand back towards the farm.

'I don't know. I really don't know. Luka had a temper certainly, and he had good enough reason to want to get back at the boss as well as his brother. But murder, well. That's something else, innit?'

Talantire was intrigued by the tale, for all its circumstantial nature. 'Who was Luka's best friend at work? And do they still work here?'

'You might be best off speaking to Kelsey Thornwater, who works at the Griffon. She was his girlfriend for two years. No one would know him better than her. She reckons he was furious about being sacked.'

Stotfold's daughter had returned, fully dressed, with a glass of water and a handful of tablets. 'Get these down for your headache, Dad,' she said. 'Every time Gladys is away, you hit it hard, don't you?'

'I'll leave you to it for now,' Talantire said. 'Please let us know your whereabouts because we may need to speak to you again.'

As the two detectives were leaving the cottage, Talantire got a call from Barking Police in London. Rustam Hartington had been arrested at London Victoria Coach Station, where he was waiting to board a bus for Dover. He had a cross-channel ferry ticket on his phone. The young man was being taken by police van to Exeter police station and would be there by eight a.m.

After thanking the officer and ending the call, Talantire punched the air. 'Yes!' Fifteen hours since the murder and the prime suspect had been apprehended.

–

Talantire looked at her suspect on the CCTV screen. Rustam Hartington lay slouched across the interview table at Exeter's main police station at Middlemoor. He was a slight individual, ill-shaven, with dark hair and a crucifix earring. According to the custody officer, he had complained bitterly about being arrested throughout the long overnight journey down to Devon. After being cautioned, he had slept fitfully in a cell. It was now 8:15 a.m.

While she was looking at the screen, Maddy Moran arrived. The detective sergeant looked fresh as a daisy, the benefit of having been able to get some sleep. She was wearing what appeared to be a new dark trouser suit.

'You look shattered, boss,' she said cheerfully.

'Managed a forty-five-minute kip, leaning against the wall in the cubicle of the ladies' toilet,' she replied. 'But I'll be fine as long as I get some shut eye tonight.'

'So what do you reckon?' Maddy asked. 'Did he do it?'

'I'm really not sure. CCTV shows him in the Griffon at 2:42 p.m. for less than a minute. That is only twenty minutes after Bassin Horvat was shot. Okay, there's enough time to kill the commissioner, but not much left to try to break open the safe, drag Helena to the well chamber and winch her down. Unless he did it before coming for a drink.'

'That would be brazen,' Maddy said.

'Yes. I'm also really unclear how he would have got out.'

Maddy looked at the screen and saw that the lad was wearing cheap prison-issue plimsolls. 'I see we've taken his footwear. I wonder what size they are?'

'Seven,' Talantire said. 'He's got small feet, unfortunately.'

'A few extra pairs of socks would make it up to twelve, I'm sure.'

'Maybe, but we don't have the boots. He was arrested in trainers. Right, let's go in.'

The two detectives made their way inside the interview room, waking up the detainee. A male PC stood at the back of the room, and a female duty solicitor sat next to Rustam. Once the tape was primed, they began.

'Good morning, Rustam. I'm Detective Inspector Jan Talantire, and this is Detective Sergeant Maddy Moran. We're investigating the murder of your adoptive father,

Lionel Hall-Hartington, and one other man yesterday at Bychecombe Manor.'

'It wasn't me.' He had a surprisingly soft voice, quite at variance with his dark-eyebrowed scowl and affected a London accent.

'All right, perhaps you'd like to account for your time since midday yesterday.'

He yawned and stretched and glanced at the brief, who no doubt had earlier told him that he didn't need to answer any of the questions.

'I came down with Venus from London on Friday.'

'Venus? Do you mean the artist and fashion designer Paula Zucketort?' Talantire asked, thinking about the interview tape that might later be used in court.

'I don't know her by that name. She's kind of a godmother to me.'

'By what means of transport did you arrive?' Maddy asked.

'In her chauffeur-driven car. It was pretty cool.' He grinned.

'I have to say, you don't seem very upset that your adoptive father has been murdered.'

The brief interrupted: 'That's not a question and you don't have to answer it. People respond to bereavement in different ways.'

Talantire gave her a tight smile. 'Of course they do.'

Rustam put an elbow on the table and propped up his face with his hand, such that one half slid upwards. 'We didn't get on, him and me. He was always telling me how to behave.'

'And did you resent that?' Maddy asked.

'I left, that's what I did. I needed my freedom.'

'Tell me what you did when you arrived on Friday afternoon,' Talantire said.

'Me and Venus had a meal with Brian and Helena.'

'By Brian you mean your adoptive father, do you?'

'Brian Hall, that's his real name. I can't stand any of this "Honourable Lionel" double-barrelled shit. Lionel is his middle name. He was always trying to pretend to be something that he wasn't.'

Talantire could imagine how annoyed Hall-Hartington must have been to be called Brian.

'I only stayed for ten minutes, they were arguing as usual, and I couldn't stand hearing him spout off.' He scowled at the two detectives. 'Prawn sandwiches with the crusts cut off, eaten off fine china.' He rolled his eyes. 'Pretensions galore.'

'Where did this meal take place?'

'In the small dining room at the manor house.' Talantire thought she knew the room. It was on the ground floor, adjacent to the one in which she had interviewed Soraya.

'Did you go anywhere else in the house?' Talantire looked at her notes. Barking Police had already taken a cheek swab and fingerprints from Rustam, but the results weren't in yet. It would be interesting if his DNA turned up anywhere else inside the house.

'The toilet maybe, I don't remember.'

'When was the last time previous to that that you visited?'

He shrugged. 'Perhaps a year ago. I remember it was summer, but it could have been two years.'

Talantire made a note. There were relatively few places that DNA would survive that long. If Rustam had left traces in the office, or the basement, that would be strong evidence that he was involved in the crime.

Maddy took up the questioning. 'So when you left the meal, where did you go?'

'I stayed with a friend in the village.'

'Who?'

'I can't tell you.'

'It would be a lot better for you if you did,' Talantire said. 'As things stand, you are a potential suspect for the killings. So the more you tell us, the better.'

An expression of frustration crossed his face, and he shook his head angrily.

'What about your movements on Saturday? We need to know exactly where you were and when.'

'I went to the pub around one. Said hello to a few people I knew. It was getting a bit boring, so I left in the middle of the afternoon.'

'We have you on CCTV in the main lounge of the Griffon at 2:42 p.m.,' Maddy said, showing him a still on her iPad. 'But there's only a glimpse of you before that, near the pub kitchens.'

'I was upstairs talking to a friend.'

'The name of the friend?'

He hesitated. 'Chris Tolworth.'

Maddy flicked through the printouts of the names of people who'd given a statement. 'We don't have him here,' she said to Talantire.

'He is a chef, at the pub,' Rustam said.

'How long did you stay with him?' Talantire asked.

'Less than an hour. He had to work.'

'Did you go inside Bychecombe Manor at any time on Saturday?'

He thought for a moment before saying: 'No.'

'Did you hear the gunshots?'

'I heard something. I thought they were killing pigeons.'

'You were then caught on CCTV riding away from Bychecombe Manor at 2:46 p.m. Where were you heading?'

'Back to London. Didn't seem any reason to hang around.'

'Didn't you meet up with Ms Zucketort again?' Talantire said.

'Nah. I didn't know where she was.'

'Whose moped was it?'

'Chris's. He said I could borrow it.' That made sense. It corresponded to a local address that the DVLA had.

'Where is it now?'

'Tiverton town centre. I left it there when I caught the bus back to London.'

Talantire nodded and made a note. That seemed to fill in the blanks on his movements on Saturday. 'Where were you about to head off to when you were arrested at Victoria coach station?'

'You've got my phone,' Rustam said, rolling his eyes. 'The ticket was on there.'

'The coach ticket was to Berlin, but what was your ultimate destination?' Talantire asked.

'I hadn't decided.'

That was about as far as Talantire reckoned she could go on his intentions, but she was interested in his past history.

'Can you tell me about your relationship with Helena?' she asked.

He shrugged. 'She's all right. Quite cool, I suppose, for an old fogey. Is she okay?'

'Do you mean "is she injured"?' Maddy asked. 'Yes, she was badly hurt. She was stabbed several times and is lucky to be alive.'

'Wow,' he said. 'Amazing. And I thought nothing ever happened here.'

Talantire was struck by how estranged this young man seemed to be from the couple who had brought him up. There didn't seem to be any emotional connection whatsoever. But neither did there seem to be an enmity or hatred that would have fuelled the savage attacks meted out. Just a complete detachment.

'Isn't this the woman who looked after you after your first adoptive mother died?' Maddy continued, obviously picking up the same vibes that Talantire was.

'Calling it "looking after me" is a bit of a stretch. When my mum became ill in 2010, Brian moved me into a boarding school in bloody Dorset, claiming they couldn't cope. So I didn't even see her in the days before her death.' For the first time he genuinely looked upset.

'When you say "your mum", you're referring to Gillian Hall-Hartington who died in 2012?' Talantire asked.

'Obviously.' He rolled his eyes. 'I mean, I don't remember my birth mother. She and my dad died when I was five after our family car ran over a landmine near Sarajevo. That's how I got this.' He pointed to the back of his head, from which a faint white shiny scar extended down his neck on one side. 'That's what gives me all the trouble.' He tapped the side of his head.

'Once you were at boarding school, how often did you come back to Bychecombe Manor?'

'Not often. I was invited for quite a few weekends, by Helena who presumably thought she had to make an effort, but I preferred to go home with some of my friends from school, or to go up to London with them. I often used to stay with Venus. She had some great parties. Then, when I left school, I went to London for good.'

'Did you work?'

'Yeah, I did some delivery jobs and crashed at various friends' flats. Brian used to offer me some money, to bribe me to come down and stay. But Devon is so boring, unless you're a wrinkly.'

'So why did you come down for this party?' Maddy asked.

'Well, the booze was free, and I got a lift with Venus.'

None of this looked incriminating to Talantire, but there was still the question of the lad's criminal record. She quickly scanned the documents in front of her, and then said, 'You've been in quite a bit of trouble with the police over the years.'

'Yeah, but I'd been diagnosed with ADHD,' he said.

'That doesn't excuse shoplifting, setting fire to a parked car or graffiti.'

He shrugged. 'Tell that to the shrink; they have a different view. It came from the trauma of my early life.'

Talantire knew they were making no progress here. She was increasingly convinced that this young man had nothing to do with the killings, something reinforced by the very tight timings that would have been required. The DNA tests of Rustam and for the wider area of the manor house were due any time, and then they would know.

When he was returned to his cell, he complained bitterly, calling Talantire a bitch. Talantire had some sympathy. If they had any more promising suspects in the frame, Rustam might have been released from custody. The truth was, she would be under great pressure to provide evidence of a quick arrest in the case. DCS

Drayton Ross had already left a message for her this morning and was clearly looking for results.

As soon as the noise of Rustam's complaining departure had dwindled, Talantire called DCS Ross back. He picked up immediately, the first time she could recall getting straight through to him. She hadn't quite prepared what she was going to say.

'Hello, sir,' she began.

'Have you charged him? The commissioner's adopted son?'

'No. I think it's unlikely that he was the perpetrator. He wouldn't have had time—'

'For God's sake, Talantire, we need results!'

'No one is more aware of this than I am. I'll make a final decision when his DNA swab comes through, and we can see where it matches.'

'Those tests should be through by now, dammit.'

'Yes, I agree they are late. But the second batch was a huge number of samples, well over 1,500, so you've got to have some sympathy with the lab. We've got cheek swabs from every employee at the farm, and of most of the members of their families who lived on site, and we have samples from every light switch and door handle in the entire manor house and adjoining outbuildings. Venka and her team have done an absolutely fantastic job, and as we speak they are spraying Bluestar through much of the building to see where those elusive gory boots might have been.'

'Yes, I do appreciate the workload you've got.'

'CSI is also going to take a closer look at the well this morning. We are hoping to lower in some divers to search for anything that got chucked in there. It would seem an obvious place to dispose of incriminating items.'

'Like boots,' he said.

'Yes, sir, like bloody boots.'

Ross thanked her and hung up. Maddy, who had been standing nearby, said, 'You turned that around pretty well.'

'He's obviously stressed.'

'A typical middle moron. Can't handle the frontline,' Maddy said.

'Well, he's useful. Without people like him absorbing all the pressure from senior management, politicians and the press, my job would be a great deal more difficult.'

'That's very charitable,' Maddy said.

Talantire checked her watch. 'Come on, we've got a very important witness to interview now.'

—

Helena de Courchevel was looking a lot better when Talantire and Maddy Moran went to interview her on Sunday morning. Although it was only 9:40, she was sitting up in bed, her hair brushed, and the deathly pallor of the previous day had been replaced by a little more colour, though many of the bruises were worse. She was wearing a little lipstick and had applied some face make-up under one eye, the other being covered by a dressing. She had added just a touch of eyeliner. Nevertheless, she still looked gaunt, and the doctor who let them in said they couldn't stay more than fifteen minutes.

Maddy, who had interviewed her the day before, began by asking her to start at the beginning and tell them the first thing she'd noticed.

'I was in my own bedroom, which as you probably know is on the ground floor, and had put on my trouser suit for the party. I was planning to be there by three but was running late. I wanted to remind Bagpuss that he had to get ready and stop watching the rugby.'

'Bagpuss being the commissioner?'

'Yes, sorry, that's just my name for Lionel.' Her smile of endearment dissolved into tears, which ran freely down her face. 'And now he's gone.'

Maddy plucked some tissues from the box by the side of the bed and handed them to her.

'What happened then?' Talantire asked.

'I heard some noise in the corridor, just as I was coming out, then Lionel's shout, then these two massive bangs in quick succession.'

'Do you know exactly what time that was?'

'Not exactly. I was a bit caught up in events. But I wheeled myself along to within five yards of the office and saw this man, standing there with a gun. Then he spoke to me in this horrible robotic voice and pointed the gun at me.' She sobbed. 'I tried to grab for the gun, and did briefly get hold of the barrel, but then he bashed me with the butt of the weapon, which explains this,' she said, pointing to the dressing over her eye. 'He then threw me down the stairs in the chair.'

'That was very courageous of you,' Talantire observed.

'Not at all. I knew he had to reload after shooting my husband and wouldn't have had time, so I had to act quickly. I was furious!'

'Amazing,' Maddy said, shaking her head.

'You have used a shotgun, haven't you?' Talantire asked.

'Years ago, yes. Only pheasants, mind.'

Maddy then asked, 'You said yesterday he was all dressed in black with a ski-mask. Could you say anything about his height or build?'

'He was well-built, certainly. It was hard for me to guess his height because I was in the chair and later being dragged along the ground...' Her voice broke off into tears. 'This horrible voice, robotically altered, demanding that I give the code for the safe.'

'Why didn't you comply?' Maddy asked.

'I did! I'm not a hero. I gave him the code that I knew, which was our wedding anniversary, and it didn't work. Lionel must have changed it when we got the relic back from the Ashmolean.'

'What happened then?' Talantire asked.

'He punched the code in that I had given him, and then he swore horribly at me, using that disgusting C-word. He stamped on me, kicked me, and then he pulled out this knife and gave me five seconds to give him the correct...' She dissolved into tears, sobbing uncontrollably. Talantire rested a hand on her arm and said she should take her time.

A nurse came in, heard her crying and looked accusingly at the two detectives. 'Are you okay, Helena?' she asked.

She nodded, her hands over her face. After another minute, and once the nurse had left, she continued. 'He put his face close to mine, the knife against my throat, so the blade was really pressing in, and he said he would cut me slowly so that I bled to death if I didn't give him the correct code. He stank, BO, horrible, like the stench of death.'

Talantire and Maddy looked at each other, the digital recorder eating up all the details, every breath, every sob. The harrowing tale.

'He jabbed the knife into my scalp, which really hurt, and I could feel the blood, then he dragged me along the corridor and down the steps by my feet, so my head banged. I used my arms behind my head to shield it.' She wiped tears away from her eyes. 'I kept thinking, if he knows about what was down there then he must know the place really well.'

'That's certainly what we are thinking,' Talantire said.

'And the fact that he disguised his voice meant...'

'He expected his voice would be recognised,' Maddy finished for her. Talantire turned to her and waved a finger. *Don't put words into her mouth, even obvious ones.* She got the message immediately and mouthed, 'Sorry.'

Helena had her hands over her face and was shuddering.

'Was there anything he said to you that gave some indication of who he was?'

She shook her head and removed her hands from her face 'I've racked my brain, honestly, and I can't think of anyone who would do this to me, or to Lionel. We've always got on fine with everybody. There must be somebody we've really upset somehow.'

'The last thing you should feel is guilt,' Maddy said. 'You've had a terrible ordeal. Don't feel sorry for your attacker, in any way, shape or form.'

'He did say one thing, when I asked him why he shot my husband. He said, "You know exactly why. He had it coming."'

'Can you think of anything that would have prompted that remark?'

'No, not really. I thought of Luka, who Bagpuss had fired, but he's abroad now. Why would he come back?'

'Do you have an address for him?' Maddy asked.

'No, but there might be one on file. You should ask Geoffrey Wheatcroft.'

'He's the company solicitor, isn't he?' Maddy asked, looking down at her notes.

'He did the HR for us too,' Helena said.

'We've already got a call into him at work and at home,' Talantire said.

'Look, whoever it was, please catch him, because I don't feel safe. I've had horrible nightmares and woke up screaming.'

'I promise we will,' Talantire said.

'The hospital has been getting phone calls from the press. They want to speak to me,' Helena said. 'Can you stop them?'

'Sadly, elements of the press are a law unto themselves,' Talantire said.

'Don't take those calls,' Maddy said. 'We'll have a word with the hospital about it.'

'What about your own phone?' Talantire asked.

'I don't have it. I never saw it after he threw me down the first staircase. Have you not found it?'

'No, I'm sorry, we haven't,' Maddy said.

'Now, Helena,' Talantire said. 'It's probably a bit upsetting, and I want you to take your time doing it, but I'd really like to ask you about being winched down the well.'

This brought on a new bout of tears. When she was eventually able to speak, she said, 'I thought I was going to die, to drown in whatever filth is down there. I begged and pleaded. He said he was going to lower me into the water, headfirst, up and down until I told him the code. He said it was what the Mafia did.'

'Your legs were tied onto the chains with thin rope, like that used for washing line,' Talantire said. 'They were intricate knots. Did he take off his gloves at all?'

'I couldn't see,' she said. 'I had blood dripping in my eyes. But I don't recall seeing his hands at all.'

Talantire realised that she was asking for extraordinary levels of perception from a woman who must've been terrified. 'Of course, I realise it must've been very difficult for you. It's just that it's very hard to tie knots with gloves on, and we are hoping we might find some of his DNA when these tests come back.'

Before Helena could answer, the nurse came back in and terminated the interview. 'I think she's had enough for one morning.'

Chapter Eight

The Bychecombe Well in North Devon is, at 197 feet, the second deepest well in the UK. Although it is nowhere near the nineteenth-century Woodingdean Well, which is an incredible 4,560 feet, it is the deepest still usable well with a working windlass mechanism, and one of the oldest. The only medieval wells in Europe that are any deeper are in Germany, at Kyffhausen Castle (176 metres or 577 feet), Königstein Fortress (152 metres) and Hohenberg Castle (150 metres). The Bychecombe Well was first referred to in the late eleventh century as the Bychyecombe Crevice in writings by the monk Geoffrey de Anjou of Buckfast Abbey, who referred to its 'sweete waters, much used in the creation of ale.' Archaeological discoveries, including that of a sixth-century skull, and some associated pottery fragments, indicate the water source had been used back to Anglo-Saxon times. The water level seems to have dropped over the centuries, because when the fortifications and manor house above were possessed by Parliamentary forces during the English Civil War, the water was said to be inaccessible by 'a hundred feete of stronge rope'. Levels have dropped by roughly seventy feet since, though recent measurements show that an increase in seasonal rainfall is now increasing water levels again.

The Jacobean manor house which Oliver Cromwell's forces occupied had only been built thirty years previously, for Sir Robert Berkeley, Justice of the King's Bench, who was seen as a key supporter of King Charles I. This was a major prize for parliamentarians, who had already been impeached by the Long Parliament in 1641. There were rumours that the well had been used for witch ducking in Devon, but contemporary sources disagree about the location of the trial. What is clearer is that by 1902, the lower reaches of the well where it enters a limestone cave system had been catalogued by a local historian called Charles Cornford, who uncovered various relics going back as far as the Anglo-Saxon era. Water from the well still finds a modern use, being used in some of the unpasteurised cheese made by the Sleepy Monk Creamery, which now occupies much of the site, and has its own borehole.

Woodman Trust Guide to Exmoor National
Park, 1997

Talantire arrived back at Little Bychecombe just after eleven. She immediately headed to the medieval basement and then to the well chamber. It was crowded with a dozen men from the Devon and Cornwall Police Dive and Marine Unit. Despite the arc lights, the place was cold and damp, but peering over the edge she could for the first time see clearly just how immensely deep the well was. The first two divers were ready to be lowered down on harnesses from a cliff rescue frame in full potholing regalia, while the officer in charge, Sergeant Jim Blakemore, briefed them to look out for ledges and other irregularities on the lower reaches of the well.

The head torches of the two divers showed the full medieval character of the brick-lined well. There were rotted wooden pegs in the wall where presumably a ladder had once been anchored, and numerous corroded iron hooks too. As the lower reaches of the well came to view, it changed to a more rugged stone construction and became narrower, with one shallow ledge about eighteen inches wide, just a few feet above the water level.

Talantire introduced herself and asked how deep the well was.

'It's supposed to be 197 feet to the water, which is about sixty metres,' Blakemore said. 'That's according to the medieval record, but we've just measured it at 174 feet, so the water level has risen a lot. Of course there's a significant cave system beneath, this whole area being limestone, and the lowest point of that is 687 feet, but that is three miles further west. Since the passages are too narrow, no one's ever explored the whole thing.'

'I had no idea it was so extensive,' she said.

'Well, it all makes sense. I read up about it on the local historical society's website. Access to fresh water and the ridge at Great Bychecombe overlooking the valley explains this as a defensive position going back to Iron Age times. The original motte and bailey castle was near here, and the Norman keep and fortifications followed it. The Bychecombe Hoard was found here for a reason.' He grinned at her.

'I'm particularly interested in anything modern you find. We're looking for a pair of boots that may have been worn by the assailant, a shotgun, plus gloves, ropes, anything that might have been dropped down here in the last couple of days.'

'I know, I've been briefed by the CSI boss, what's-her-name.'

'Venka.'

The lights down the well dimmed as the two divers sank beneath the water. For a minute or so there was no conversation, just the echo of the splashing and disturbance from down below. Blakemore turned away to an associate, who held a tablet computer that showed murky images from beneath the water, relayed via wire to a floating transmitter on the surface. Talantire peered over his shoulder.

'That's what I suspected,' Blakemore said, turning back to her. 'There is a corkscrew-type chamber beneath, with no flat surfaces. Whatever was dropped may have slid and be much further down. It might turn out to be impossible to retrieve anything.'

'Just do what you can.'

'There was a good attempt back in 1902,' Blakemore said. 'The water level was lower then, by a good ten feet. A local historian called Charles Cornford went down with his son, presumably looking for coins or some Anglo-Saxon relics. They did find a skull, which is now in a museum in Barnstaple.'

Talantire was impressed. She hadn't expected this level of background knowledge. 'You've really done your research, Jim.'

'It's a hobby as well as a job. I like to know what I'm getting into. I do a lot of potholing, and a proper reconnaissance is absolutely crucial to safety... Jesus Christ, what is that?'

Images coming up on the TV camera to the tablet now showed two distinct stone steps, set into the curving edge of the well.

'Is that significant?' she asked.

'Yes, we're already three feet below the old waterline. These must be really old.'

'If someone went to the trouble of building steps they must have come down here regularly,' Talantire said.

'That's true. Maybe there was an escape route from the fortifications.'

'Underwater?'

'Well, it might not have been beneath the waterline whenever these were built.'

'Maybe that explains the corkscrew shape, the remains of an old spiral staircase along the inside of the well,' Talantire said.

Blakemore nodded and pursed his lips in appreciation of this idea, which he clearly hadn't considered. The image had moved down to a further and rougher step. And on it, lying sideways, was a boot of modern appearance. Even through the gloom and sediment-filled waters it was clear that this was a Caterpillar boot in yellow, the logo clearly visible underneath the dark ankle cuff. A large dark stain could be seen on the toe.

'That's it!' yelled Talantire excitedly. 'That's what we're looking for. Any sign of the shotgun?'

The divers descended another fifteen feet, but they didn't find the gun. It took half an hour for the boot to be carefully retrieved, brought up in a bucket, and placed in a plastic sheet under the arc lights. Talantire donned blue nitrile gloves before touching it. The first glance was inside, to find the size. Ten. A glimpse of the sole showed a still-thick caking of blood in the treads, which she expected would be Helena's. She scraped fragments into a sample tube. She then used tweezers to dig out bits from the bloodstain at the toe, and to extract scrapings from inside, where the innersole met the welt. There wasn't that much hope of DNA after thirty-six hours in water, except in the thicker bloodstains, but she might be lucky. She took samples from the laces and the cuff too, places that might have been grasped by the fingers of the wearer. She then labelled all the sample tubes, took some final photographs and parcelled the boot up in a large plastic evidence bag.

At this point she left the dive unit to it, took her treasure trove out of the room and up to the mobile incident unit. A whole blast of messages arrived on her phone as she emerged back into mobile phone coverage, including two from the press office. They could wait. They had a genuine piece of evidence to celebrate. Maddy Moran was there amongst a group of detectives working at their screens.

'Look what we've recovered,' Talantire announced to the group. 'I'm very confident this is one of the boots worn by the assailant and ditched down the well.'

'He must've had a spare pair to put on,' said DC Caroline Cheetham, one of six detectives who'd arrived that morning from Exeter to beef up the team. Caroline worked in the fraud team and was concentrating on the financial aspect of the investigation. 'That's a cold stone floor to pad about on in your socks.'

Talantire smiled. 'I wouldn't be at all surprised if this was planned right from the start, even down to the change of footwear. This is a perpetrator who knew where the safe was, who knew about the well, and may even have been able to gain access earlier.'

'Somebody must have seen him,' DC Cheetham continued. 'Either coming in or leaving.'

'That's not necessarily true,' said Dave Nuttall. 'There is a side entrance at basement level that exits to the walled garden. We've got some prints off the door handle that are currently being analysed.'

The discussion continued for several minutes until Talantire got an alert on her phone. 'The next raft of lab results are in.' Everyone turned back to their terminals to access the email.

'The adopted son?' Ross asked.

'No, one of the guests. She's been to the well chamber, as has the cleaner, Soraya.'

'But not the son?' Ross persisted.

'There is no forensic link with him in the lower part of the building, and having interviewed him I just don't get the vibe that he is involved. However, there was Soraya's DNA on the cord used to bind Helena, along with somebody else.'

'Why would Soraya's be on the cord?' Maddy asked.

'Think of what it is,' Talantire said. 'It is actually a cotton washing line, perhaps scavenged from the yard behind the kitchen. Soraya does much of the laundry, so it would make sense her dabs are on it.'

'Ah, that's an ingenious deduction,' Ross said.

'It's the unknown sample on it that I'm excited about,' Talantire said. 'This could well be the culprit.'

She turned her attention to Weaver. 'Sir, how are you getting on with the financial order investigation?'

'Should have something by lunchtime tomorrow,' he said.

'Banks are slow over the weekend,' said Maddy. 'Even when you've supposedly got privileged access.'

'That's true,' Weaver said.

'In the meantime, there's one thing I can do, and that's interview Ms Zucketort to see if she can explain why her dabs are all over the well chamber.'

'She's already arrived at Middlemoor apparently,' Ross said. 'Have you not seen the messages from the press office?'

Talantire looked at her phone to see three messages from press chief Moira Hallett. One was an email with a press release attached, headed *Venus Z to Ask Tough Questions of Police*.

Fashion icon Venus Z will this morning be making a statement outside Devon and Cornwall Police headquarters in Exeter. Following the tragic murder of Police Commissioner the Honourable Lionel Hall-Hartington, the killing of another man, and the savage attack on her friend Helena de Courchevel, the forces of law and order have major questions to answer.

How could an assailant simply get into the home of such an important policing official, and then vanish without being seen?

How was it that he and his wife did not have security present?

Last but not least, why has nobody yet been caught?

'Helena is a very close friend of mine,' Venus said. 'I am appalled and horrified that she is currently lying in hospital, having been stabbed and beaten, in what appears to have been a robbery attempt. I am here today to draw attention to the vulnerability of disabled women like my friend, to the wave of crime that is clearly sweeping even rural areas. I have a meeting with the police at noon and shall be putting some very sharp questions to them.'

Talantire was horrified that a witness had somehow managed to turn the tables on them. Moira's phone was constantly engaged, so she rang Inspector Tony Thompson, who was holding all the contact details of key witnesses. He said that Ms Zucketort, a.k.a. Venus Z, was staying in a hotel in Exeter and had contacted him first thing this morning, saying she planned to be at Middlemoor at noon. He had booked her in for interview, copied in the desk sergeant and arranged for a duty solicitor to be present.

'I've been waiting for you to return my call, Jan,' Thompson said. 'I assumed you would want to interview her.'

'I'm sorry, I've been in a no-reception zone for forty minutes. Can you get the desk sergeant to push the interview back until two p.m., which at least gives me time to get there?'

'I'll do what I can,' Thompson said grumpily. No sooner had Talantire hung up than Moira Hallett was on the line. She sounded harried and was clearly walking as she talked because the background noise changed.

'Jan, I strongly suggest you look at your TV screen,' she said. 'I'm going outside right now to give our point of view.'

Talantire flicked on the wall-mounted TV and saw the BBC local news feed. She immediately recognised the Middlemoor Police Station, and a crowd of reporters and TV crews. There, at the centre of them, standing on the steps just outside, was Ms Zucketort, wearing the most extraordinary get-up. It would have looked like a grandiose wedding dress, had it not been in stripes of black and red. There was a long train, which puddled on the lower steps of the police station. She was wearing a sombrero-style black mesh hat with a huge vertical streamer, and underneath it a partial Venetian mask that covered the right-hand side of her face.

'Good grief, will you look at that,' Talantire said to no one in particular.

Maddy, sitting nearby, glanced up. 'What's going on?'

'We are being upstaged,' Talantire said.

Ms Zucketort then went on to read a statement, very similar to the one on the press release, which ended with a declaration: 'We want answers.'

As she did so, Moira Hallett emerged from the police station behind her, flanked by two uniformed officers. Superintendent Paul Shortland appeared beside Moira, and she handed him a piece of paper.

'Devon and Cornwall Police would like to clarify what is happening here today. Ms Zucketort was actually asked to attend for questioning in connection with the murders at Bychecombe Manor, and as she was by her own admission in the building at the time of the killings, we can confirm that she is a person of interest in this enquiry. Yes, we all want answers, and on this occasion it is us who will be asking the questions.'

Just as he folded up the piece of paper, the camera turned once again to Ms Zucketort. The two uniformed officers had begun to shepherd her into the building. She walked in with her head held high, and one of the two officers with her even lifted the train and folded it over his sleeve so that it wouldn't snag in the doors. There were many shouted questions from the press, but Super-intendent Shortland ignored them.

Talantire now realised that the entire room was standing up and watching the show. 'Well, I suppose I'd better get down there and interview the woman,' she said. 'Maddy, would you accompany me?'

'You bet,' she said. 'I wouldn't miss this for the world.'

They didn't get to Middlemoor until half past one and had to run the gauntlet of the press to get in. Questions were thrown at her about the lack of progress in the case, but she ignored them all. Ms Zucketort had been installed in the rape suite, but in her finery still managed to make the soft furnishings and sofa look dowdy and stained. She was lying full length on the three-seater, while her lawyer, a very well-coiffed woman with eyes that matched her powder blue trouser suit, sat on the easy chair opposite.

When the two detectives walked in, Ms Zucketort exhaled from a vape the size of a clarinet, briefly filling the room with vapour.

'No smoking or vaping in here, I'm afraid,' Talantire said, a little annoyed that the desk sergeant hadn't made this clear already. She had already decided to come down on this woman like a ton of bricks. 'Please remove your hat and mask. We're not playing charades.'

The woman removed her hat carefully and slid off the mask, revealing the lined right-hand side of her face. 'I've come here voluntarily because there are questions that need answers,' Ms Zucketort said. 'This is Miranda Cummings, my lawyer.'

'No, you have come here to answer *our* ques-tions,' Talantire said, turning on the tape machine and identifying those present. 'Paula Zucketort, just to get things off on the correct foot, let me tell you that you are now being charged with possession of Class B drugs, in relation to the tablets and cannabis we found in your possession. You've already been cautioned.'

The woman grimaced and glanced at her brief.

Talantire continued: 'We've got back the forensic analysis from Bychecombe Manor, which reveals your DNA not only on the stairs and landing outside the room where we found you, but in the medieval sub-basement, in the well chamber and indeed – from our latest set of results – on the mechanism that controls the descent of the chains into the well. How do you explain that?'

Talantire had expected the woman to be completely floored by the question, but in fact she giggled gently and then replied, 'I was given a guided tour on Friday night by Lionel himself, after our evening meal with him and Helena. There's nothing remotely suspicious about it, surely?'

'Did Helena come with you?'

'No. She said she had dessert to make.'

'Was anybody else with you?'

'No. Rustam had been at the meal right at the start, but he left after arguing with Lionel.'

'Where did he go?'

'To see his boyfriend. Chris, I think it was. He works at the pub.'

'What did Rustam and his father argue about?' Maddy asked.

'Rustam was chewing with his mouth open, and his elbows were on the table. But really, underneath, it is always the same argument. Rustam feels estranged, particularly since the death of his adoptive mother. He feels he doesn't belong anywhere. He is Bosnian by birth but doesn't know the language, he's from Muslim roots but grafted onto an Anglican family. I feel for him, I really do. Our society is increasingly built to make most people feel like outsiders.'

'So Lionel showed you the mechanism in the well chamber?'

'Yes. He said that an earlier version of it had been used in a witchcraft trial, to dangle an accused woman in the water to get her to confess.'

Talantire hadn't heard of this and decided she would have to research more of it herself. Perhaps Sergeant Jim Blakemore knew about it.

'The other thing he showed me, in case you're interested, is the Bychecombe Brooch, part of the hoard.'

'That was in the safe, wasn't it?' Talantire asked.

'Yes, I believe so. I've very rarely seen a green garnet, which is such a gorgeous mineral.' She paused to get her phone from her handbag. 'Hold on just a moment,' she said, as she leafed through it. 'Here, look at this.' She passed the phone so that Talantire could see a photograph of the woman herself wearing the brooch.

'When was this picture taken?'

'On Friday afternoon.'

Talantire was nonplussed. This was a plausible argument for why the woman's DNA was found all over the well mechanism, along with the commissioner's. It put the police in a difficult position. If Helena confirmed Ms Zucketort's account, the woman would be in the clear. Her backing for Rustam's story further reinforced Talantire's suspicion that the adopted son had nothing to do with the deaths either.

The two detectives pressed the woman further on her movements during the afternoon when the killings took place, but she stuck to her story that she had slept through the whole thing. 'I'm afraid I can tell you absolutely nothing about it,' she said.

'What about these dolls you make?' Maddy asked. 'Did you hang the one that was found on the back of the door leading to the well chamber?'

'They are homunculi, not dolls; miniature people imbued with magic. That one was a gift to Helena from me. I noticed it on the door during my visit, but I don't know why it was down there.'

'But it's covered in your DNA,' Maddy persisted.

'Not surprisingly, as each of the homunculi has some unique part of me. At the very least, the hair is mine, and I use my saliva and urine in the glue. I can get you more details if you would like.'

Maddy exchanged a glance with Talantire, then said, 'No, that's fine, thank you.'

When they'd finished asking questions, Ms Zucketort said she had questions to ask, about why no one had been caught yet for the murders.

'I'm sorry,' Talantire said. 'We're not here to answer your questions, unless they are about the specifics of the charges against you.'

'Well, yes, I do have questions about that—'

'Then you can take it up with the desk sergeant.' Talantire tapped her papers on the desk, stuffed them in her briefcase and left the room. They headed outside, where the press throng had not diminished, and slipped away to the car park to return to the scene of the crime. Venka had messaged them about preparations for a full blood spatter test at the crime scene, and they both wanted to be there for it.

Chapter Nine

The two detectives got back to Bychecombe Manor at 3:45 p.m. There was still a significant uniformed presence, but most of the site, including the working farm, was now back in action. CSI had spent the last twelve hours going over the various cottages where items of interest had been discovered, and taking elimination DNA samples from many of the employees. A palpable sense of shock still lay across the whole site, with knots of subdued onlookers examining the wall of flowers outside the gates of the manor. Talantire and Maddy met Venka at the mobile incident room, and she told them that her team had been spraying Bluestar onto the carpets and walls throughout the manor.

'I think you might be surprised by the results,' she said.

The two detectives donned plastic booties and gloves and made their way back into the manor through the rear kitchen door, the same way that the assailant was presumed to have travelled. Both of them were aware of the powers of the chemical spray, which allowed minute traces of blood, even historical stains, to show up as bright blue pinpricks visible to the naked eye. It was a great improvement over Luminol, an earlier chemical that produced false positives from bleach and certain other compounds.

The corridor wasn't particularly dark, but the blue of the bloodstained footprints were almost luminous in their intensity. It was immediately obvious, too, that there were many other bloodstains: partial handprints on the wall, drops spilled on wainscoting and skirting boards. Venka, who was accompanying them, explained that what they were seeing was the building's full historical record of cuts, scrapes and other mishaps involving blood over many decades if not centuries.

'While the floors have probably been cleaned very regularly and retain only recent stains, walls, skirting boards, doors give us the history of every nosebleed, cut finger while opening tins, and all those agricultural workers over the years who trooped in here in order to get some wound or other dealt with.'

They moved forward past the boot room to the grand staircase ascending to other floors. Here there was a rapid diminution of the blood spattering on the carpeted stairs.

'I think it's clear that our assailant didn't go up the stairs, at least not wearing the same footwear. The stains here are only as old as the carpet, which we think might be from the 1980s, and because of that it is very useful for us to screen out older marks. However, if you look here on the banister, I think you can see a matching handprint to the one that we saw by the kitchen, which is in a child's size, and we are assuming to be historic.'

'Zucketort has child-sized hands,' Maddy said to Talantire.

'I think we can get the dabs matched on these, can't we?' Talantire said to Venka.

'When it's as big a print as this, yes.' Venka led them down the corridor to the office where the commissioner was shot and, unsurprisingly, that room was a blaze of blue. 'We looked for stains on the door handle and found several dots of blood that we think came from a hand. There was evidence of an elongated crease mark of blood too, which makes us think that whoever touched the handle was wearing nitrile or plastic gloves like our own.'

'Do you mean this is cross-contamination?' Talantire asked.

'It's certainly possible that of the half dozen of my colleagues here, at least one moved bloodstains from one part of the building to another. This isn't by any means the only crease mark we have seen, so I think it's going to be a problem for us. If the perpetrator was wearing nitrile gloves, he will blend in perfectly on the forensic record with those of us who came afterwards.'

'That's annoying,' Talantire said. 'We rely heavily on the bloodstained trail given the paucity of any DNA markers for unknown individuals. Okay, we know this killer was careful and highly forensically aware, but they must have left *some* trace.'

'It's exactly the same on the carpet in some places,' Venka said. 'We only have to have one clumsy tread by a single technician, and the others will walk the contamination all over the place, which shows up as a constellation of speckles.'

Maddy laughed. 'That's exactly like my kids when one has trod in dog mess. Once it's indoors on the carpet, it gets walked everywhere. You can follow it with your nose.'

Venka smiled at the analogy. 'That's exactly right. Let me show you.' She led them down the staircase, down which Helena's wheelchair had been thrown. It was lit up like a fairground, and the corridor beyond was a mess of colour.

'We think the commissioner's wife was stabbed here at the bottom of the stairs, because there was so much blood, as you can see, and here DNA tests show it is swamping that of her husband and the other victim.'

'What a vicious bastard,' Maddy said. 'Not content with tossing a woman in her wheelchair down the stairs, but to plunge a knife into her as well.'

'She describes grabbing hold of the gun here at the top of the stairs,' Talantire pointed out. 'That's probably enough to enrage the killer.'

Venka and Maddy both nodded.

'Now here,' Venka said, approaching the door to the walled garden, 'we have different footprints, probably from a training shoe, overlaid on the original bloody trail.'

Talantire could see the speckled outline of the outer edge of a series of right foot impressions on the carpet and the doormat.

'The interplay with the original footprints is quite confusing, though the blood was clearly wet enough to be transferred from the carpet to different footwear,' Venka said.

'The question is whether this is the assailant, having changed footwear exiting into the walled garden, or somebody else entirely having strayed into the crime scene,' Talantire said.

'These new prints look like they're exiting the building,' Maddy said. 'The originals, as far as I can see, do not approach this door.'

'Yes,' Venka said. 'But bear in mind you are only seeing in Bluestar the trail post-contamination. Whoever this is could easily have come in this way, or indeed another way, before exiting, but those initial prints are invisible to us because there is no blood on them.'

'Good point,' Maddy said.

Talantire crouched down to examine the new footprints, like a series of long, narrow question marks. 'I would say these are significantly smaller than the original footwear. Size seven or eight maybe.'

'That's my guess,' Venka said. 'I'm getting the prints pinged off on TreadMatch to the National Footwear Database, so we should get an answer within half an hour.'

'We also need to go into the walled garden,' Talantire said, 'to see where those prints lead. But first of all, I want to find the gun.'

'It must be in the well somewhere,' Maddy said.

'The divers couldn't find it, but then some of the lower passageways that lead to the cave system are too narrow for them,' Talantire said.

'Why not try lowering a big magnet on a rope?' Venka asked. 'If something so heavy as a shotgun fell, a heavy chunk of iron on a rope is likely to end up in the same place.'

'I'll speak to Jim, see what he thinks,' Talantire said.

Having completed their Bluestar tour, the trio carefully made their way back to the entrance.

Talantire stood with her hands on her hips and assessed what they had seen. 'I don't get this, Venka. Such gory crime scenes, in some ways so careless, yet no confirming forensic or observational data. We've accounted for most of the DNA here. Unless we believe that Paula Zucketort had the strength and the inclination to commit the murders, and to viciously assault her friend Helena, we are left with just one unknown DNA sample, found on both the rope and the metal grille.'

'What about Rustam?' Maddy asked. 'Let's say that after he went to see his friend on the Friday evening, he came back via the walled garden through the side entrance, then hid in the building until Saturday.'

'It's plausible, but there's no confirming forensics. The CPS would be the first to point out we didn't find any of his dabs or DNA on the lower two floors of the building. Even the boots are the wrong size.'

The Crown Prosecution Service had an inconvenient insistence on all the evidence being firmly in place before giving the go-ahead for a prosecution. While most detectives complained bitterly about the organisation making their job harder, Talantire found it a useful discipline to test her hunches against the unyielding assessment of CPS lawyers.

Venka left the two detectives, saying that she had to wrap up the investigation paperwork. 'We've done our bit so it's over to you now,' she said cheerily. 'I'll let you know if we have a tread match.'

Talantire and Maddy stood outside the rear kitchen door of the manor house, stripped off their Tyvek suits and stuffed them into the plastic bin bag for later analysis.

'If we don't get something soon, we are going to get it in the neck from the middle morons,' Maddy complained. 'I've got scapegoat written all over me.'

'We've still got leads to chase down,' Talantire said. 'We can get a PC to show Helena pics of the boot to see if she recognises it. We can also ask John Rice and the other employees to see if anyone knew who wore those type of boots.'

'Sounds a bit of a long shot,' Maddy said gloomily. 'We got DNA samples from both John Rice and Digby Robinson in the building, didn't we? What about them as suspects?'

'Yes, we can put them on the ground floor, but nowhere else. And they both have alibis at the time of the first shots, when CCTV at the Griffon clearly shows them there.'

'I'm stumped then,' Maddy said. 'But I don't trust the sleeping beauty, who claimed to have dozed her way through World War III.'

'Me neither, but she's clearly not capable of significant parts of the crime.'

The two detectives made their way back to the mobile incident room, each deep in their own thoughts. It was a lovely evening, the birds were singing, and the avenue of trees were decked in their finest foliage, fully unfurled, verdant and unblemished. They trudged up the steps into the Portakabin, and found it so crowded with detectives that there wasn't a place to sit.

Dave Nuttall looked up and greeted them, then said, 'I've just had a good look around the walled garden as you suggested. We got a beautiful set of dabs from the outside door handle, though the footprints you mentioned aren't visible.'

'We could try doing Bluestar at night on the exterior path,' Talantire said. 'We will have to wait until it's properly dark and make sure all the lights are turned off.'

'Isn't that CSI's job?' he asked.

'We've got more resources than them now. Besides, it's good practice to keep your hand in.'

'Right,' Nuttall said, seemingly unconvinced. 'Another thing. We just had a call from Geoffrey Wheatcroft. He had a weekend away in his boat, in the Solent, and has only just picked up our messages.'

'Finally,' said Maddy. 'A solicitor is always tardy, you can rely on it.'

'He's heading back straight away and will be available from first thing tomorrow morning.'

'First thing, i.e. half-ten,' she muttered.

'We need him in now,' Talantire said.

Nuttall continued: 'He was totally shocked by the killing, says he just can't believe it.'

'Well, join the club,' Talantire said. 'Were you able to ask him any questions?'

'A few. He's not aware of any threats or financial irregularities that might explain the killing. He has a copy of the commissioner's will at his office, along with the code for the safe here,' Nuttall said.

'That's a start, I suppose. Then we can find out if the Bychecombe Brooch is still in the safe. Right, let's get him in immediately. Dave, send a car for him. Take him to his office first so he can get all the relevant papers. We don't have time to waste.'

'Okay.'

'And, Dave, any luck tracing Luka Horvat?'

'We've got an address in Ljubljana for him, but the liaison officer from the Slovenian police who went round says the place is empty, though his car was parked outside. Neighbours apparently say he's abroad, but they don't know where.'

'Can the Slovenian cops get us an elimination DNA sample from the car? Ideally inside the vehicle, or even dabs from the boot? It might save us a lot of trouble to know whether or not his DNA is anywhere among the great mass of unknown samples we have here.'

'That's a good idea.'

'I assume he doesn't have a sample already on file with the local police?'

'No, he has no criminal record,' Nuttall said.

'Can we press them as hard as possible to get one? Tell them it's really urgent.'

He nodded and picked up the phone. Talantire finally felt that she had something to get her teeth into. Luka Horvat. A man with a grudge; could it be him?

–

Shortly after five on Sunday, Geoffrey Wheatcroft arrived at Great Bychecombe in a patrol car. It had stopped off at his legal office first so that he could pick up a stash of documents. Talantire met him in the same grand lounge that she had used for all the interviews, but he looked more at home in it than most. The man was informally dressed in what presumably was his yachting gear, polo shirt, white trousers and deck shoes, and with his patrician looks and thatch of white hair certainly looked the part. Once they had sat down and made their introductions, Wheatcroft confessed that he was still in shock at the murders and promised to do whatever he could to help them.

'As it seems to be an area of police interest, I've read through the commissioner's will on the journey here and am afraid there's nothing spectacular or unusual about it,' Wheatcroft said. 'Most of his money and assets would go to his wife Helena, with some five per cent in trust to his adopted son Rustam.'

'How much money are we talking about?' Talantire asked.

'Well, the entire estate would obviously be worth double-digit millions gross, though there is a considerable amount of debt from my understanding. None of the debt is of course documented in the will.'

'So Rustam's share would still exceed £1 million?' she asked.

'It's a reasonable guess,' Wheatcroft said, briefly removing his reading glasses and rubbing his face. 'But you have to bear in mind that the trustees would determine when the money would be released to him. There are two trustees apart from Lionel, those being Helena de Courchevel and Lionel's sister-in-law Elizabeth.'

'Would Rustam have known about his inheritance?'

'He was never present in any meetings in which I was involved, but there may be correspondence privately. I'm sure he would have guessed that he was in line for something. Is the young man your main suspect then?' Wheatcroft asked, looking over his spectacles.

'His involvement is only one line of enquiry we are pursuing,' Talantire said, with a sideways glance at Maddy. 'When was the last change made to the will?'

'There have been several changes to Rustam's trust over the last two years, but nothing to the main body of the will.'

'We you aware of any financial pressure or difficulties the commissioner faced in recent months?'

'I think you'd be better off speaking to the finance director of Sleepy Monk Creameries. All I'm aware of is that following Brexit, and the huge difficulties that cheese manufacturers faced in European export markets, the company took on some extra borrowing. However, my impression is that the company wasn't in overall financial difficulty.'

Talantire looked at her list of potential interviewees. The finance director of Sleepy Monk was Vernon Short-land, who she now confirmed with Wheatcroft was the brother of Paul, the uniformed superintendent from

Exeter who worked on rural policing. This was getting awkward. She had left the investigation of the financial connections to the fraud department in Exeter, which was headed by Detective Superintendent Timothy Weaver, who also happened to be on the board of Sleepy Monk Creameries as an independent director. As Nuttall had pointed out, he was a mason in the same lodge as both the commissioner and Shortland. This was all looking a bit too tangled with conflicts of interest. She hoped that Weaver had appointed somebody else to oversee the investigation, and believed might be better as a witness rather than an investigator. That would be the professional thing to do, but she couldn't force him to do it. DC Cheetham was too junior, surely, to be in charge, but there was no one else from his department present.

Wheatcroft passed across a thick briefcase full of documents and asked if he could be taken home. He promised to forward all relevant email exchanges regarding the finances of the company and of the commissioner himself.

'A couple of things we still have to ask you,' Talantire said, as the lawyer stood up. 'One is that you fired Luka Horvat, is that right?'

'Not exactly. I dealt with the paperwork for it, but the decision was Lionel's.'

'What were the allegations against him?'

Wheatcroft sat down. 'I wasn't told. The boss wanted him gone on the day, and I arranged it. He didn't share his reasons with me, but he did ask for an NDA.'

'A gagging clause?'

A smug grin spread across Wheatcroft's face. 'I wouldn't describe it like that. It's to protect both parties—'

'I know how they work,' Talantire said. 'And I see how it helps Sleepy Monk, but how does it protect him?'

'It keeps his behaviour secret.'

'What behaviour?'

'Exactly. Anyway, we paid him more than his contractually entitled severance for it.'

'So you really don't know why?'

'Well, I'm bound by client attorney privilege, as I'm sure I don't need to remind you. If you insist, I can show you the paperwork, but don't imagine it will give you any idea. It's very much legal boilerplate.'

Talantire was getting irked by this obfuscation. 'Why, exactly, Mr Wheatcroft, was Luka Horvat sacked?'

The solicitor sighed and checked his watch. 'From a subsequent email exchange with his brother, I understand that it was something to do with Luka's behaviour towards female staff.'

'If you didn't explain to him why he was being fired, might there have been grounds for unfair dismissal?' Talantire asked.

Wheatcroft smiled. 'Not on his contract, I can assure you. Besides, the NDA required him to give up his rights under employment law.'

Talantire could see she was getting nowhere on this point. 'All right, one final thing. You said you have the latest combination code for the safe,' Talantire said.

'Yes, of course,' Wheatcroft said. He accompanied them down into the basement. Although the police had finished working on the crime scene, they still had stepping plates in place. The lawyer, who was given booties to put over his shoes, knew exactly where the concealed safe was, pulling open the bookcase to reveal it, and from his phone tapped out the six digit code. It worked, and the foot-square steel door opened easily.

Inside, there was a stash of papers in manila envelopes, and resting on them a metal box about the size of a biscuit tin but much more substantial. 'I assume this contains the Bychecombe Brooch,' Wheatcroft said.

'Thank you, I'll look after things now,' Talantire said, easing out the box in her gloved hands and sliding it into a plastic evidence bag. 'I don't want to muddy the forensic waters. You seem quite familiar with the safe, Mr Wheatcroft. When was the last time you accessed it?' Talantire asked.

'I'm not familiar with it at all. The only time I've ever been down here was a few months ago, with Lionel. It was he who opened the safe.'

'We still need to take a DNA sample for elimination purposes.'

'If you must,' he said.

After Wheatcroft had been swab tested and escorted back to the patrol car that was to take him home, Talantire took the box into the incident room. Other officers, getting the idea that something important was to happen, gathered around as she slid the box from its evidence bag. She put it under an inspection light and checked it first for fingerprints, then DNA. There certainly appeared to be some partial prints that they could lift.

Talantire then slid along the clip and opened the lid. There, nestling in specially made packing material, was the famous garnet brooch, glittering green in the light. The gem itself was oval, about the size of a thumbnail and not much thicker, but its shifting pattern of light offered an apparent depth through some trickery in the mineral, as if the viewer was looking into hidden space beyond. It was mounted on a delicate silver setting, though whatever pin it had for attachment to a cloak seemed to have been broken off. It wasn't the only item in the box. There was a corroded iron belt buckle, which looked coarse by comparison with the brooch, and a tiny delicate golden clasp no bigger than a paperclip, which had been fashioned in the shape of a curvaceous woman.

'It's so pretty,' said Caroline Cheetham, peering at the brooch. 'So this is what the murderer was after?'

'Possibly, yes,' Talantire said. But even as she said it doubts were creeping into her mind. The gem thieves and art crooks she had read about rarely seem to operate with the kind of M.O. they had seen here. Subtlety, sophistication and stealth were the hallmark of professionals in this field, having a buyer lined up, and extracting their prize with the minimum of fuss. The blood and violence of this crime certainly marked a departure from the kind of thief who made a living from this speciality.

DC Kieran Meekings called Talantire over. 'I've got something very incriminating about Luka Horvat here,' he said. Meekings had been asked to monitor social media and had finally come up trumps. 'This was posted two hours ago, but the video call is over a year old,' he said. 'The woman who posted it has commented beneath: "Luka is probably the bastard responsible for the killings."'

Talantire peered at the post and saw it had attracted dozens of likes and some dozen follow-on comments agreeing. 'Ah, it's from Kelsey Thornwater; she was his girlfriend. We've been looking for her. Okay, hit play.'

The video showed a handsome bearded man, bustling about his caravan, cursing to himself. 'I hope for the love of God that you've not had anything to do with this, Kelsey,' he said, as he piled clothes into a kitbag. 'Because I've been fitted up.'

Kelsey's responses weren't recorded but could be inferred from Luka's replies.

'Yes, I *have* been bloody sacked. Gross misconduct. "Inappropriate behaviour while in employment". No, there are no fucking details. It's a stitch-up. Just an hour ago, my own damn brother led me into the office where that weasel lawyer Wheatcroft made me sign something. I get two grand if I keep my gob shut.' He paused for Kelsey's reply, then continued. 'Damn right it sounds dodgy. Yeah, I have my suspicions.' There was another pause as he looked into the screen. 'Okay, if it wasn't you, then who was it? Well, whatever… You think I can't do anything about it, do you?' His face turned angrily to the screen. 'I'm going to come back and fucking kill him, that's what.'

The video finished at that point.

'That's very interesting,' Talantire said.

'It sounds like he has it in for the commissioner,' Meekings said.

'Or the lawyer. Or his brother. Or whoever dropped him in it,' she said. 'But in each case, there's a clear motive for revenge.'

—

Kelsey Thornwater was quickly tracked down to a static caravan in the village of South Molton, then brought in by patrol car for interview. She was an attractive twenty-six-year-old, in tight-fitting denim cut-offs and a white low-cut shirt. She didn't seem at all surprised that the police wanted to talk to her. She breezed into the historic lounge in the manor house and sat down, making eye contact.

'I actually don't know anything about this. I was in the Griffon when it happened,' she said before any questions had been asked.

'It's all right, Kelsey, we know that. We want to ask you about Luka, and that Facebook post,' Talantire said.

'Ah, of course you do,' she said, with a resigned expression.

'We understand you were his girlfriend, part of the time when he was working here.'

'Yeah, me and loads of others, as it turned out.'

'When did you last see him?' Maddy asked.

She shrugged. 'The day he was fired,' she said. 'After he sent that video, he came into the pub with the lads. I'd just discovered that he was seeing someone else, about a month before that. We weren't together at that time, so I got somebody else to serve him.'

'He definitely wasn't here this weekend?' Talantire asked.

'Probably not. Well, I didn't see him. My friends would have let me know if they'd seen him.'

'But you still posted the accusation, that he did these murders?'

She rolled her eyes. 'I was having a laugh. I didn't *really* accuse him.'

'I think you did. It's a very serious act.'

She snorted and rolled her eyes again. 'C'mon, he was a bastard and deserves it.'

'Do you know where he is living now?' Maddy asked.

'Manchester, what I heard.'

This was new information for the detectives. 'How did you hear it was Manchester?'

'One of the lads who used to work here texted me. Luka was working as a doorman at a club.'

'And how long ago was that?' Talantire asked.

Kelsey shrugged and consulted her phone. It took a couple of minutes for her to find the message. 'Yeah, that was two weeks ago.'

Talantire excused herself and stepped out of the room. She messaged DC Caroline Cheetham and asked her to check out the report she had just heard. Doormen had to be registered with the Security Industry Authority, so they should be able to track him down fairly quickly.

Talantire noted the name of the friend who had relayed this information. From Kelsey's perspective, the lad was a friend of hers, not of Luka's. 'Luka was so competitive he didn't have many male friends.'

'How was he with you?'

'Well! At first, he was very charming and attentive.' She swiped through her phone and showed the two detectives a photograph of them together. Talantire had to agree that he was a ruggedly handsome fellow, the kind of man who women might imagine would rescue and protect them.

'Of course, that was just a front. He just wanted one thing: conquests.'

'Was he ever violent?' Maddy asked, finally getting onto the prepared questions that they needed.

'Not with me. He had a nasty temper, and he could be cruel as well as kind, but overall he was just slippery. You couldn't pin him down. In the end I realised he was just using me.'

'So he didn't hit you?' she persisted.

'No, I wasn't into it.'

'What?'

'S&M. He asked me once, I said no, and I thought that was an end to it.'

Talantire could see they were heading in a different direction, but if Luka had sadistic tendencies, then that could explain what he did to Helena. 'We just need to establish one thing: do you think he would have been capable of these murders?'

'Generally I wouldn't have said so—'

'Except you did,' Maddy interrupted.

'Well, I don't know. I realised before the end that there was a part of him I didn't know.'

'What d'you mean?'

Her eyes cut away. 'Just that sex thing, really.'

Talantire didn't want to go further down this path than she had to. 'What about the relationship between Luka and his brother?' she asked.

'Ah, well. There were tensions there all along. About the inheritance back in Slovenia, and the fact that Bassin as the oldest would get most of it. I was there with Luka when Bassin burst into his caravan and threatened to kill him. He was really angry about something.'

'When was that?' Talantire asked.

'A couple of years ago.'

'Did he say why?' Maddy asked.

'Not exactly, because they were shouting at each other in Slovenian. As he left, he turned to me and said: "Your boyfriend is a total…" Then he called him a C-word, and added: "He's a snake, don't trust him." That was when I first got the hint that Luka was playing around.'

'One final question, Kelsey. What size shoes does Luka wear?' Talantire asked.

She seemed surprised by the question. 'I don't know exactly, but big.'

Talantire allowed Kelsey to leave.

After the door was closed, Maddy grinned at her boss and said, 'So Luka was screwing around and he was kinky.'

Talantire looked levelly at Maddy while she rotated a biro between her fingertips. 'I'm happy to delve a bit further into the "he said, she said", but let's keep our eye on the big picture. Luka Horvat made a threat to kill, and that's enough for me.

'Maybe we can get Greater Manchester Police to interview him,' Maddy said. 'And there's always a chance we pick up a DNA match.'

'If we're lucky,' Talantire said. 'We've still got some unknown samples, including in the well chamber.'

'And there is a bit of a motive, isn't there, if he'd fallen out with his brother?'

'Yes, though we'd need more. A lot more. There's plenty of time to kiss and make up.'

Tanya Horvat closed the door on the police. It was their second visit, but she had barely started to process her grief about Bassin. She and their two children, Adam and Nikola, aged eight and nine, had maintained a continuous family hug since the news of her husband's murder. The boys had idolised their father and couldn't understand why anyone would want to hurt him. Tanya knew better, though never in her wildest nightmares had she thought it would come to this. For the first day she sat stunned, while the police family liaison officer spoke kindly, made tea, ruffled the boys' hair and dispensed advice. Not a word of it sank in. She might well have been listening to some boring play on the radio. She had robotically written a statement about her own movements on the day of the killings while the pair of uniformed male police officers sat with her.

She had been in the Griffon like everyone else, sitting with two of the newer Polish employees who worked in the cheese sheds, hearing news from home. Unlike them, she had only had soft drinks, with a baby on the way. She was one of the first to be allowed to return to her own cottage, but she hadn't seen the significance of that. It was only when the two boys, who had been playing football in the meadows, were brought in at eight o'clock by yet another officer, and the FLO arrived, that she realised all the care and attention she was getting was strictly personal. Up to this point, she hadn't yet begun to worry about Bassin because she knew he was still on shift, and he was always slow to return messages while he was working. Everyone had just been talking about the murder of the boss. Lionel Hall-Hartington was such a lofty figure in her life, and she could in a vague kind of way understand why somebody might want to kill him, or rob him, particularly with his job as police commissioner.

But when the liaison officer had sat her down in the kitchen and closed the door to keep the children out of earshot, she suddenly knew, and the floor of her life fell away from under her.

'Bassin!' She'd suddenly shouted his name, knowing everything from knowing nothing.

'Mrs Horvat, I'm really sorry to have to tell you—'

'Oh God.' *Bassin! No, no, no.*

'—that we have identified one of the bodies.'

Her scream sounded alien to her own ears. Who on earth was making that racket?

The kids weren't fooled for a moment. Nikola had burst in followed by Adam, and on seeing her their own tears began. 'What is it, Mummy?' Adam asked. 'Is it Daddy?'

She nodded her head and gathered them into her embrace. She remained in that stunned cocoon for hours, but the dark thoughts began to coalesce in her mind. Her own theories and suspicions. It was only an hour after she had been given the news that she asked the family liaison officer, 'Did you find his phone?'

The woman smiled and said, 'I don't have any information on that at this stage, but if we do find it, I think the investigative team will want to take a look at it before we can return it to you.'

She took out her own phone and looked at the pictures of their family together. Their happy life, two smiling children, good boys, born in Britain with a right to remain here. She had been here ten years and met Bassin that first summer when he was an apprentice in the cheese sheds. Her phone logged everything that was good and happy about their life, but his phone had contained other things: betrayals, hidden assignations, probably photographs of Luka's bitch he had screwed. She had only ever found the one thing, that text message.

> That first dance we had in the cottage yesterday, barefoot on your new floorboards, was wonderful to me. To be held, embraced, and to know that with him out of the way we will have a future together.

It was a year ago, and she had only glimpsed it for a few seconds when he was out of the room, but she had memorised every word. The sender's phone was identified only by a numeric code. 'Him out of the way' was obvious. Luka had just gone back to Ljubljana, so it could only be one person.

Kelsey.

She even guessed where they had danced together: Shepherdess Cottage. It was the one being renovated, and Bassin, originally a joiner, had replaced the woodwork, including reclaimed Victorian floorboards, which he had spent hours sanding. The next day after reading the message, she had walked the three quarters of a mile to the other end of the estate to see for herself. The secluded cottage, almost at the boundary of the estate where it joined National Trust land, had been derelict for years, but now it had been entirely rebuilt with a roof of reclaimed slates, and brand-new wooden sash windows. The door was locked, but she had taken Bassin's key. Inside there were no carpets or furniture yet, just the hardwood floorboards, carefully laid, sanded and varnished. Upstairs, just two tiny bedrooms, and in one of them was a new double mattress and a box of tissues.

The perfect love nest.

Tanya had even seen *her*. Kelsey came up here on horseback most Sunday mornings, exactly the same time that Bassin used to go and work on the cottage. Kelsey was an accomplished rider and used to borrow one of the livery horses kept at Bychecombe Stables, which had been owned by the boss's late wife, Gill Hartington.

Tanya had confronted him about it with the evidence on his own phone.

'Why are you having an affair with that bitch?'

'What?'

'Kelsey Thornwater. Don't you dare deny it.'

'It's not true,' he said. 'Who told you this?'

She showed him a photograph on her phone, of the message on his.

He looked at her. 'It's not what you think.' That's when she slapped him.

After days of arguments, Bassin had relented. He promised to break off the relationship, but in exchange begged her not to tell anyone else. Rumours spread fast in such a small community. 'You know what it's like to be foreign here; the locals gang up and I could lose my job.'

'Like Luka did?'

'Yes, just like Luka.'

'So stop behaving like him then!'

For proof, Tanya then took to visiting the Griffon. And yes, indeed, Kelsey avoided her. Bassin must have told her. For the next eighteen months, she and Bassin soldiered on, albeit now in separate beds, but in public they kept it together for the children. He worked long hours, while she worked longer and longer hours in the kitchen with the demanding and increasingly deaf Gladys Stotfold. But the joy was gone, because it couldn't survive in the absence of trust. One night three months ago, she'd discovered a packet of condoms in his trouser pocket when she was washing them. She confronted him about it and they had a huge argument, which ended with them sobbing in each other's arms. Then they made love for the first time that year.

A few weeks ago, she discovered she was pregnant. Their third child. Tearful and upset, she didn't at first dare tell Bassin that he was to be a father again. She arranged a family picnic in the meadows behind the house on a beautiful May afternoon. She had made traditional Polish peach cake and some Slovenian cottage cheese, *štruklji*, for Bassin. As she laid out the food on a blanket in the middle of the meadow, the boys came roaring in from playing football, hungry as usual. As the children gorged themselves, Bassin was looking wistfully away towards Shepherdess Cottage. She finally plucked up the courage, and announced to them all:

'Adam, Nikola, you are going to have a brother or sister.' She patted her tummy although there was nothing yet to see. She turned to Bassin, who looked paralysed with shock.

'Are you sure?' he asked.

'More than two months, yes.'

'Can I listen to your tummy?' Nikola asked.

'There's nothing to hear yet, *kochanie.*'

The boys grabbed some food and went off to explore. She turned back to Bassin, who was silently weeping.

'You're still seeing her, aren't you?' Tanya said.

He nodded and embraced himself, his shoulders shuddering.

'I knew it.' She pressed home her advantage. 'I knew you were seeing her again. I could tell. I need you to be only with me, Bassin. For the sake of our new little one.'

Bassin nodded and wiped his eyes. 'I'm sorry, I'm so sorry.'

'Put your hand on my tummy.' He did so. 'Swear on the life of our unborn child, you will tell this woman it is *over*, or I will march into the bar of the Griffon, when I'm heavy with child, and announce it to her and everyone else.'

'I swear,' Bassin said. 'From now on it is only you.'

And as far as she could tell, he was as good as his word.

Chapter Ten

DC Caroline Cheetham had been on the phone for some time. Whatever it was she was discussing, she sounded quite incredulous. When she eventually hung up, Talantire went over to her desk.

'What have you found out, Caroline?'

'Two of the commissioner's bank cards have been used.'

'When?'

'Yesterday evening, on contactless, all across Barnstaple. Eight transactions.'

'Good grief.' Talantire realised this pointed to a glaring omission in the case so far. She didn't recall seeing the commissioner's wallet on the evidence log. There had been so much else to look at, and she hadn't chased up Venka to see if all the basics had been catalogued. However, there was a sure-fire way to see what they were dealing with now: a quick look at the transactions.

'What was purchased?' she asked.

'Hold on, ma'am.' Cheetham logged into the system and pulled up the email from the bank that contained the details. 'Convenience store purchases, just under £100 each time.'

'Oh, what fantastic news!' Talantire shouted, punching the air. 'He finally did something really, really stupid.'

The other detectives gathered round, eager to hear about the breakthrough.

'Right, everybody, I want the CCTV from all these premises ASAP, and the receipts. Caroline has the details. We need to know who this is, and what was bought.'

'Hah, we'll get the little bastard now,' Maddy said.

'Yes, we're finally back in familiar investigative territory: a dim criminal trying to profit from his deeds.' She turned to DC Cheetham. 'Caroline, are you able to see whether this is part of any broader ransacking of the commissioner's accounts? I'm thinking cash withdrawals, anything like that.'

'There were two unsuccessful attempts to make a cash withdrawal, but nothing else,' Cheetham said.

'Good,' said Talantire. For all the jubilation, one nagging worry refused to go away. The wallet must have been somewhere that the killer could get hold of it, but she hadn't noticed it at the crime scene. She hadn't checked the commissioner's jacket, which would be the obvious place for him to keep it. It was even possible that the wallet or the cards had been somewhere else entirely: in his car, in his office at Middlemoor, in his bedroom at the manor.

It wasn't too late.

Talantire went to her iPad and flicked through the photographs that she had stored there from her own phone. There were a dozen taken of the blood-spattered office where the commissioner had been found. At the time, of course, she had focused entirely on the body and not the general surroundings. But as she looked again, she zoomed in on the desk he had been sitting at, the bookcase to one side, and the TV in the background. And yes, there had been what looked like a wallet on the second shelf of the bookcase on the right of the room. Then she accessed the images on the CSI database taken an hour later. None of the later images showed the presence of the wallet.

None.

The killer appeared to have taken the commissioner's wallet *after* Talantire had inspected the crime scene, while she was still in the building. She could so easily have run into him. She felt a cold shiver run down her spine. Running into the killer down there in the darkness would have been terrifying.

–

Talantire was just climbing the steps into the mobile incident room for the 6:30 p.m. incident room meeting, when Dave Nuttall burst out. 'Jan! We've just had a breakthrough. Ljubljana emailed through a DNA test from Luka's car. It matches two samples from the well chamber: one on the ropes, and one on the grille that covered the well.'

'Fantastic news,' Talantire said.

She called the meeting to order and shared the discovery of Luka's DNA with the rest of the team. 'This, I think, is more significant than any of the other DNA finds. I think it is fair to say we have been surprised by how many different people seem to have visited the well, and of course we can only make a case on samples that do not have an innocent explanation. It is, crucially, the suspect's contact with the bonds used to tie Helena to the chains that are the clincher.'

'Yes, but why aren't there any DNA traces from this person in the corridor, or on the safe?' asked one detective from the back of the room.

'It's a very good question and it troubles me, I have to say. We have a very slender evidential link to Luka Horvat, but that's a damn sight more evidence to a credible suspect than we had before.

'The discovery that the bank cards had been stolen gives us more time and eases one of the biggest areas that I've been worrying about. The perpetrator was, it seems, still in the building at the time of Soraya's 999 call, and for some time after my own entry at 15:10. I think we can now say that he was in the building for anything up to an hour longer than we had assumed.'

She turned the whiteboard, on which all the timings were written.

'CSI's photograph of the commissioner's office at 16:02 is the endpoint: it clearly shows no wallet present. So that window is over ninety minutes from the first shot at 14:21.'

'I bet some CSI operative nicked it,' muttered the same detective, which caused a ripple of laughter around the room. Talantire craned her neck to see who it was: DC Kieran Meekings.

'Well, we'll soon know, Kieran. There were eight purchases around Barnstaple last night. That's where you live, isn't it? What did you buy?'

He laughed as Talantire continued: 'But even on that schedule, our killer was busy: two murders, the assault on Helena, the attempt to open the safe, culminating in the complex operation of winching her down into the water on that antiquated contraption, ditching the soiled footwear, presumably donning some other shoes, hiding when I entered the building – and while Soraya was out in the corridor – returning to steal the commissioner's wallet, and then making his escape through the door to the walled garden.'

'I still think this woman in the attic has something to do with it,' DC Cheetham said.

'I agree that Ms Zucketort's presence in the house is suspicious, but I see no way she could have been the assailant,' Talantire said. 'She and Helena are friends, and there seems no motive. Now, to return to the issue of the killer's exit. We've found some footprints up to the door to the walled garden, and the database has given the match. An Adidas Galaxy tread style from 2022, which you can find on your iPads. We need to find those shoes.'

There were nods of agreement.

'Hopefully all these details will become clear, either when we get the CCTV or once we arrest Luka Horvat, but in any case, I'm going to propose a re-enactment of the crime on Tuesday morning. This is not for public consumption, because it would reveal too much that we'd like to keep confidential, but to double-check the timings.'

A number of officers nodded in agreement. 'That's a good idea,' Nuttall said.

'I'm glad you all seem to agree,' Talantire said, 'because we need a volunteer, roughly the same weight as Helena de Courchevel, so probably female, to be lowered, suspended by the ankles, upside down into the well.'

The room went absolutely silent. There was some chuckling amongst the male officers, no doubt of relief that it wasn't them required to volunteer.

'How far down is it, ma'am?' asked Caroline Cheetham in a small voice.

Talantire looked down at her notes. 'It's 174 feet to the water, and of course it's completely dark down there, so there will be lights provided.'

'It's about as deep as a twelve-storey building is high,' Nuttall said helpfully.

The silence was even more pervasive now. Talantire saw a couple of female DCs rolling their eyes at each other.

'They wouldn't have to go right down to the bottom, would they?' Caroline asked. 'You'd still get the idea.'

Talantire laughed. 'One of the crucial things for the reconstruction is how long it would have taken to lower the chains right down.'

'Isn't it dangerous? The chains are old and rusty. They might break,' one of the male DCs said.

'We'll make sure there are safety measures. Look, it's not compulsory. I'll see if we have a volunteer amongst the uniforms.'

'Good luck with that,' muttered one of the officers.

—

The big surprise was that they did have a volunteer. PCSO Amy Barrett, a slender recruit who looked even younger than her nineteen years, and as bubbly as a Welsh brook, had spent the last day putting up and taking down crime tape and directing traffic in the car park of the Griffon pub. She had asked to speak to Talantire because she'd heard about the reconstruction and wanted to be a part of it. Talantire went out to meet her on the steps of the mobile incident room. The young woman seemed almost to be hopping up and down with enthusiasm, her eyes bright.

'Did anyone explain to you what was involved?' Talantire asked.

'Yes, ma'am, it's being lowered down the well,' Amy said.

'It's dark, it's pretty cold, and you are a long, long way down. It would be the equivalent of being lowered off the roof of a big block of flats down to the ground.'

'That's all right, ma'am. I did lots of bungee jumping on my gap year in New Zealand. I threw myself off the Kawarau Gorge Suspension Bridge and absolutely loved it! That's forty-three metres, almost as much as the well, right?'

'Well, the extra eleven metres is twice the height of a house, so "almost" isn't quite right. But you won't have to jump off, you will be lowered on chains. We're going to use a dummy first, and when it's your turn later tomorrow morning, we'll give you some lights, attach you to a safety rope—'

'Great!'

'We'll have lots of experienced potholers and experts around, so there's nothing to worry about.'

'It sounds brilliant! If it helps to solve the crime, I'm up for it.'

—

First, there were other tests to make. It wasn't truly dark until a quarter to midnight, and though all the nearby lights had been turned off, the almost full moon was bright. The walled garden was a large square, fifty yards each side. Only in the shadows of the carefully clipped hedges and under the high exterior walls was the darkness complete. Talantire and Nuttall crouched by the steps leading down to the basement door, waiting for the Bluestar they'd sprayed to take effect. Beside them, a uniformed officer held up a large umbrella, creating a deeper shadow. The blue pinpricks of light emerged gradually, marking a print of the right training shoe. With the blood staining heaviest on the toe, this made a series of question marks ascending the stairs.

'He was in a hurry,' Talantire said. 'Climbing two at a time.' The clearest mark was on the top step and indicated the direction of travel. A little more Bluestar sprayed on the gravel path confirmed that the suspect had headed on the most central of the three radiating paths through the garden.

'It's a sprint,' Nuttall said, photographing the marks as he went, while Talantire placed yellow plastic evidence markers. There was about ten feet between observable treads, which, accounting the invisible left foot too, indicated a five-foot pace.

'We should be able to get his height based on this,' Talantire said.

'It looks like we're finally making some progress,' Nuttall said.

Talantire looked at the direction of travel and saw that the path skirted a rectangular ornate pond, then headed for a gate in the far wall about forty yards away. She made her way up to it and sprayed Bluestar at the base, where someone would have had to stand to open it. She also took a DNA swab from the latch. By the time she had done this, the Bluestar was working in the shade of the wall, and it was clear that the suspect had indeed come this way.

The gate had previously been padlocked with a police-issue lock, part of securing the crime scene. A uniformed officer proffered the key, and they went through. Beyond the wall, a tarmac drive ran left to a small car park for staff, and right towards the main road. On the other side of the drive was Bychecombe Manor Chapel.

Talantire knelt again to spray Bluestar around the base of the gate to get some idea of the direction the suspect had travelled. The image, when it arrived, was quite faint with just a few specks. The direction of movement was not clear. A beep on her phone distracted her for a moment. She directed Nuttall and the uniformed officer to check the chapel entrance for forensics and find out if there were any vehicle movements from the car park during the afternoon.

It was time to return to the incident room. The text she had received said they had an image of the card thief.

Chapter Eleven

Back at the incident room, Talantire peered over Nuttall's shoulder at the CCTV footage uploaded from one of the Barnstaple convenience stores. It showed a slim, apparently young man in a hoodie with a baseball cap and sunglasses, clearly intent on hiding his identity, making a purchase at the counter. There was some hint of a beard.

'Shit! It's not Luka,' Talantire said.

'Are you sure?' Maddy asked, peering at the screen from behind her.

'Yes, absolutely,' Talantire said.

'Luka Horvat is a bit bigger built than him,' Nuttall said, as they ran the footage backwards and forwards.

'We can't see his tattoos,' Maddy said. 'That would put it beyond doubt.'

Nuttall shook his head. 'Is this an accomplice rather than the killer?'

'If he is, Helena didn't see him,' Talantire said. 'And he didn't go downstairs through any of the heaviest blood-stains, because we'd have a second set of footprints down there.'

'Still, it would make sense if there were two of them,' Maddy said. 'They could get more done in the time available.'

Talantire shook her head: 'The time-consuming element is all in the well chamber, where we have very clear witness evidence there was only one person. Forensically, too, there's no suspect DNA apart from Luka's. Where is this guy's DNA?' she said, pointing at the screen. 'Absolutely nowhere.'

'Maybe he didn't do very much, just kept a lookout and nicked the odd wallet,' Maddy said.

'It's possible,' Talantire conceded. 'Maybe this guy was the stupid one, just along for the ride, which would allow us to crack the case. But I have a much bigger worry.'

Maddy and Nuttall turned to look at her.

'This guy is completely amateur, right?' Talantire asked. 'Using bank cards that any self-respecting criminal would know can be traced. What if he's nothing to do with the killing, just an opportunist, sneaking in to have a look around while everybody else was at the party at the Griffon?'

Talantire steepled her hands over her nose. 'Oh God! We were hoping that the exit footprints, the trainers leading into the walled garden, were evidence of a change of footwear by our killer. But if they belong to either an accomplice, or just an opportunist, then we would be back to square one tracing the exit path of the killer.'

'True,' Maddy conceded.

'But he's not just anyone, is he? The card thief got in and out through the door to the walled garden that we were told was locked,' Nuttall pointed out.

'An insider, then. But who?' Talantire stared at the pictures. Could this really be the man who killed Lionel Hall-Hartington, farm manager Bassin Horvat, and brutalised Helena de Courchevel? Or was he simply a chancer, a fellow employee who had sneaked into the manor and taken the opportunity to help himself to the commissioner's wallet while Luka Horvat was down in the well chamber? She didn't recognise what little they could see of the face, nor did any of the other officers nearby.

Maddy began a comparison with the CCTV from the Griffon, which didn't immediately yield any identical clothing. Talantire wanted to get in one of the well-placed locals like John Rice, who knew everybody, to see if he recognised him. A PC with an iPad was dispatched to his cottage. The poor bloke wouldn't thank them for disturbing his sleep, but sometimes there was no other way.

Rice turned out to be no help in getting an ID. It wasn't surprising. There wasn't much to see under the hooded top and sunglasses. The long-suffering Sleepy Monk employee was allowed to return to his interrupted slumber. Talantire wished she could do the same. The complexities of the case were doing her head in.

—

It was four a.m. when Talantire got the long-awaited call from Greater Manchester Police. Luka Horvat had been found working as a doorman at a club in Manchester. When approached by two uniformed officers, he agreed to voluntarily come in for interview at the end of his shift, just ten minutes off. They let him use the toilet first, but when he didn't emerge, went in after him. He had slipped out of an emergency exit. The detective constable who had been delegated to break the news to her was quite apologetic.

'We're really sorry, ma'am, but we'll track him down as soon as we can,' he said.

'We did warn you he was a slippery customer,' Talantire said. 'I want an all-points alert for him, railway stations, bus services, airports. This was a very high-profile crime, and we need to talk to him urgently.'

'I understand that, ma'am.'

After Talantire finished the call, she emailed the duty press officer and requested a press release saying that they were urgently seeking to interview Luka Horvat in connection with the murders. She realised she did have a photograph of him on file, one that had been taken on Kelsey Thornwater's phone, and forwarded it.

It was a better picture than the CCTV they had of the bank card thief. Still, when you appeal to the public, it's good to offer both your suspects. This was a very significant moment in the enquiry, with images of two men they wanted to interview, and they needed to be resourced to deal with the response. Perhaps reinforcements would be needed.

Talantire sat back and thought for a minute. 'I think it's time for us to wake DCS Ross up,' she said to Maddy. 'He'll get all the credit when we wrap this up, so perhaps he should earn it with a bit of lost sleep.'

'We can get the control room to do it, then they will get it in the neck, not us,' Maddy said.

Talantire laughed. The control room had personal mobile and landline numbers for all officers. All she had to do was tell them it was urgent. It took several minutes for Ross to call her back.

'A breakthrough, Jan?'

'Yes, sir. I thought you should know that we've now got images of two suspects, which I have forwarded to the overnight press officer for immediate distribution. Given that this will probably drop an avalanche of response from the general public, you might want to look at the resourcing for the public information line.'

'I take it the first is Luka Horvat,' Ross said. 'But who is the second one?'

'We don't have a name, but we believe he may be an accomplice. He's been caught in possession of the commissioner's bank cards, using them in Barnstaple on Saturday night.'

'That's a bit amateur, isn't it?'

'Absolutely, and thank God for that. We don't like too much professionalism amongst criminals, do we?'

'Okay, thank you. I'll take a look at getting you some more bodies first thing tomorrow.'

'Preferably more live ones,' she said. 'We've got enough of the other type.'

He sighed and hung up.

—

It took a long time for the next CCTV footage from another store to become available, but it was worth waiting for. Two detective constables had been working all night trying to get additional security camera pictures of the card thief. No less than three of the places where transactions took place had inadequate CCTV; either too grainy or not working at all. At the fourth, they struck lucky. The footage loaded up to GoodSAM was clear. The team gathered around Nuttall's terminal to take a look.

'This is SJK Stores, which has been done over numerous times,' Nuttall said.

'Is that the shop with the height markings on the entrance doorway?' Talantire asked.

'Let's see,' Nuttall said, fast forwarding to the time of the transaction. He then rewound one minute. The camera showed the doorway, which did indeed have a series of subtle line markings between roughly five and six feet from the floor. The same suspect came in, and a little bit more of his face was visible.

'Yes, that's definitely a ginger beard,' Talantire said.

'And five eight,' Nuttall said.

The man was conversing with an elderly Asian woman behind the counter, and as he reached for the vapes she passed across, a distinctive tattoo could be seen on the inside of his right wrist. They zoomed in on it as much as possible until the lettering became clearer. It was a name, in elaborate characters. Kev.

'Well, thank you, Kev,' Talantire said.

'Somebody must know this geezer,' Nuttall said. 'Should we try Rice again?'

'Have a ave heart, Dave,' Talantire said. 'The poor sod's only just got back to bed.' She asked the duty inspector to get a couple of uniforms to see who else was awake amongst the families on the estate.

It was fifteen minutes later when the PC radioed in that they had a name: Kevin Smith, a well-known local ne'er-do-well, not employed at Bychecombe Manor, who had been seen at the Griffon helping himself to free drinks even though he wasn't invited.

'There's more,' the PC explained, putting Rice on the line to her.

'I'm sorry, Mr Rice,' Talantire said. 'I hoped we weren't going to disturb you again.'

'It's all right. I couldn't sleep anyway. I think I guessed who it was even before I got to see the second picture. It's a bit awkward,' he told Talantire. 'He's my sister's new boyfriend.'

'What's your sister's name?'

'Daisy Rice. She's got a summer job working in the gardens here.'

To Talantire, it was all beginning to make a bit more sense. 'Where does she live?'

'Normally, in my spare room. But I think she is staying with him this weekend. I don't have an address for him but it's somewhere in Barnstaple.'

'Do you have her mobile number?'

'Yes.' He read out the number.

'Thank you, John, you've been very helpful as always.' Talantire hung up, then searched for a criminal record for a Kevin Smith from Barnstaple. It wasn't a precise enough search, and there were three possibles. She looked at the photographs attached to each record and discovered only one could have been the man on the convenience store CCTV. This was an individual with a long history of minor crime, but only a short period of imprisonment. There was an address for him in the town, so she dispatched a patrol car to make an arrest.

–

By six a.m. on Monday, Kevin Smith and Daisy Rice were in custody in Barnstaple. Talantire and Maddy Moran were there shortly afterwards to interview them. They started with Smith, in the grimmest of the interview rooms. He stared truculently at them, arms folded, next to a very sleepy-looking male duty solicitor. They had plenty on Smith. Not only was he wearing exactly the same clothes he was caught wearing on the CCTV, but he had the vapes, the cigarettes and what was left of the alcohol at his flat. There was no sign of the credit or cash cards or receipts, but he had already been cautioned by the desk sergeant and charged with theft, based on the store's transaction records and those on the commissioner's cards.

'How did you pay for this?' Maddy asked, holding up packet of cigarettes in an evidence bag.

'Pass,' he said.

'Is this you?' Talantire asked, showing him the iPad with a still from the CCTV of one of the convenience stores.

'Pass,' he said, without even looking at the image. They spent ten minutes asking him questions: whether he had been at Bychecombe Manor or the Griffon, whether he had seen the dead body of the commissioner, and so on. In each case, he responded in quiz show fashion with one word: 'Pass.'

Maddy leaned over the desk at him. 'You're no mastermind, Kevin, but crime is your specialist subject.' She read out to him his ten-year record of convictions ranging from antisocial behaviour, shoplifting and receiving stolen property right through to assault occasioning actual bodily harm. He smirked almost proudly as she listed his transgressions.

'Well, if you're not going to help us, I think we should charge you with the murder of the commissioner. What do you think?' she asked, turning to Talantire.

'You're our top suspect, Kevin,' Talantire said. 'We know you stole the wallet, which puts you at the crime scene.' They showed him an image on the iPad, of the commissioner dead in his chair, blood everywhere. 'Where did you leave the shotgun?'

'This is bollocks,' Smith said. 'I ain't got no shooter.'

Talantire was relieved they had rattled him enough to steer him away from the 'no comment' strategy. Smith may not have been the sharpest knife in the drawer, but his sense of self-preservation was kicking in when he smelled a fit-up.

'So tell me what happened when you went in there.'

'I never went in there.'

'Really? There's the commissioner's blood on your shoes.'

Talantire had in her possession a pair of size eight Adidas trainers that matched the second set of footprints at the crime scene, found under the bed that Smith was sharing with Daisy Rice. They hadn't yet tested the blood speckles that Bluestar had uncovered on the outer edge of the sole of the right foot, but she was confident whose blood it was.

'What shoes?'

'The white Adidas trainers, under your bed.'

'They ain't mine.' He rolled his eyes and looked at the brief, repeating for clarity. 'They ain't mine.' The brief simply smiled back at him.

'Kevin. They. Were. Found. Under. Your. Bed,' Maddy said, enunciating each word carefully.

'They. Ain't. Fucking. Mine. Okay?' he retorted.

Talantire saw that Smith was wearing knock-off Crocs, with no socks, presumably all he'd been given time to get at the point of arrest. She couldn't recall what Daisy had been wearing. Maybe they were her trainers? It was a possibility worth considering. Talantire was confident they could squeeze further details from this individual by actually charging him with murder. It would have the additional benefit of being a key development to offer to the PR team to keep the press off their backs. The trouble was, Kevin Smith almost certainly wasn't the murderer, and the CPS would be quick to see it. But threatening to book him for the crime was certainly a powerful lever.

Talantire stood up. 'Okay, DS Moran, would you be so good as to take this young man up to the desk and prepare the paperwork for the full charging?'

Maddy would know instantly that Talantire using her formal title was simply rehearsing a ploy, and she played along. 'Yes, ma'am. First-degree murder, yes?'

'Plus theft, handling stolen goods, possession of a firearm with intent to endanger life.'

Smith's pasty face turned a whiter shade of pale, enough to inspire a song written long before he was born.

'You can't do that!' he shouted. 'I was never fucking there!'

'Somebody was,' Talantire said, sitting down. 'Someone who gave you the cards. And who exactly was that?'

Kevin Smith glanced over his shoulder. There was nobody there, but she understood the gesture. He was incriminating his girlfriend, who was in a cell somewhere in the corridor behind him.

'Did Daisy give you the cards?' she asked softly.

'Pass,' he whispered almost inaudibly, his eyes cast down. The silent knife slipped between the ribs of their relationship.

–

Smith was taken back to his cell, somehow a slighter creature than he had been before. Talantire watched him go and heard Daisy banging on the cell door as he was taken past. 'Kev, Kev!' she shouted. 'I love you!'

Whether she would love him when she eventually found out he'd implicated her was another matter. Talantire kept the custody sergeant waiting until Smith was safely back in his cell at the far end of the corridor before bringing Daisy Rice out for interview. She was a hefty girl, seventeen and five eleven, with dip-dyed purple and silver hair, and a hooded sweatshirt labelled 'Harvard University'. As if. She was wearing flip-flops and beige skin-tight exercise pants that in the sallow light made her look pudgily naked below the waist.

Daisy plonked herself down on the chair with an exhausted sigh, while Maddy introduced her to the brief and made the preparations for the tape. Rice was chewing something, probably gum, so Talantire offered her a tissue and told her to take it out.

'Why?'

'You are under arrest, and you are not allowed to have anything that could be used to conceal or damage evidence,' she said.

Daisy rolled her eyes and spat the gum noisily into the tissue offered to her. Talantire dropped the gum and the tissue into a small evidence bag, which she sealed. That was the DNA elimination sample sorted.

'Are you a bit cold in the flip-flops?' Maddy asked. 'We've got your Adidas trainers here,' she said, offering the polythene evidence bag towards her.

'Thanks,' Daisy said, reaching for them just as Maddy pulled the bag away.

'They are not yours, are they?' Talantire asked. 'Size eight with a black stripe?'

'Yes they bloody are!' Daisy said, standing up from the table. 'I got them from Shoe Zone. They ain't nicked.' A uniformed PC at the back of the room stepped in to intervene and guided her back in her seat.

'Thank you for confirming that,' Talantire said. 'They're part of the evidence that we have to retain.'

'Why?' she said.

'Because they have the blood of a murdered man on the soles,' Maddy said. 'You have just proved that you were in Bychecombe Manor shortly after the killings.'

Daisy's hands flew to her face in horror. 'Oh no!'

Talantire couldn't help noticing that she had an engagement ring on. Like the gum, it was something she should have had removed from her on arrest and placed with other valuables. She'd have to have a word with the desk sergeant. If there was a diamond on it, it could be used to cut or at least deface the security glass in the cell. But on second thoughts, the gem looked so big it couldn't possibly be real, unless stolen. Almost certainly a gift from Kevin Smith. It reminded her of the old joke about a smash-and-grab merchant and his demanding girl-friend, which ended with the punchline: 'For God's sake, woman, do you think I'm made of bricks?'

Daisy was looking between her fingers at them, like a child.

'Did you steal the commissioner's wallet?' Maddy asked softly.

Daisy nodded gently behind her hands.

'Speak up, please, Daisy,' Talantire said. 'For the tape.'

'Did you give it to your boyfriend?' Maddy asked.

'Yeah, he was skint.'

'So it was a kind of present?' Maddy asked with a smile.

'Yeah.' She smiled back, dropping her hands.

Talantire approved how effortlessly her colleague had slipped into the role of 'good cop'. That left her with the other one.

'Daisy, have you ever used a gun?' Talantire asked.

Daisy turned away from her towards Maddy. 'Yeah, I have,' she whispered conspiratorially. 'Shotgun.' She mimed the aiming of the weapon, towards Talantire. 'Bang, bang, both barrels.'

The brief, suddenly alert, intervened at this point. 'I think we can all see that your interviewee is very vulnerable,' the man said. 'Should we not have someone here from social services?'

Talantire had been thinking very much the same thing. It hadn't immediately been apparent that Daisy Rice had learning difficulties, but it had become clearer over the course of the interview. The two detectives suspended the interview and stepped outside.

'I've no doubt that if we put it to her the right way, she would confess to the whole thing,' Maddy said.

'I agree. But is equally clear that she is not the murderer.' Talantire rang the out-of-hours helpline for Exeter social services and left a message. She also left one on the mobile number of the duty officer. 'I'd bet my pension that no one from social services could be here until lunchtime.'

'What about her brother?' Maddy suggested. 'If we could get John Rice to sit with her as the appropriate adult, we could carry on, at least get the theft element teased out from the main crime.'

'Good idea,' Talantire said. They went back in.

'Would you like your brother to be here, Daisy?' Talantire asked.

'Fuck off! John always takes over.'

'Is there someone else who you'd like to sit with you?'

'Kev.'

Talantire had anticipated this. 'I'm afraid Kevin is accused, along with you, of a serious crime. He can't be your appropriate adult.' She knew they needed to get on and make some progress.

She considered PC Sarah Rice, Daisy's cousin, but then realised that no police officer could take that role. 'Under the 1984 Police and Criminal Evidence Act, I am allowed to interview you in an emergency when no appropriate adult is available.'

'All right.' Daisy shrugged. Talantire was more concerned with the reaction of the solicitor, who seemed distinctly uneasy.

'Daisy, I'm going to ask you what happened from the moment that you came into Bychecombe Manor on Saturday afternoon.'

'All right.'

'What time did you enter the building?'

'No idea.'

'Did you hear any gunshots that afternoon?'

'Yeah. Kev and I'd been in the chapel, and we heard some bangs. Shooting rabbits, I thought, or maybe pigeons.'

'What were you doing in the chapel?' Maddy asked. Perhaps there was another theft that had taken place.

'Nothing.' Daisy's suddenly shy expression and downward glance betrayed exactly what they were doing.

'Did you have the key?' Maddy asked.

'Yeah. I got the keys to the garden and the chapel along with the workshop bunch, where the strimmer's kept.'

Talantire wanted to return to the main question, having established in Daisy's own account that she was a witness to the shotgun blast, not the perpetrator of it. 'Daisy, what did you do when you heard the bangs?'

'Well, we both got a bit scared about being caught, so we got off the altar and got dressed. The shots sounded nearby, so I said I'd go out and check what was happening.

I'm allowed to be in the garden, even when the house is closed, because I work there.'

'And you did this after the first bangs?'

'No. I reckon it was after the second lot, which sounded closer.'

'What did you do then?'

'Well, once we could hear sirens, we scarpered out of the chapel. I went into the gardens, while Kev hid in the woods.'

'And you went into the house through the side entrance.'

'Yeah.'

'Why did you do that?'

'I dunno. I was curious about what was happening.'

'Was the door locked?'

'Yeah, but I have the keys, like I said.'

This was the moment that Talantire really wanted to home in on.

'When you went in, did you hear anything?'

'Yeah. There was someone moving around downstairs, and I think there was someone in the kitchen from the noise.'

'What exactly did you hear?'

'Footsteps, mainly.'

Talantire was aware that it could well be her own movements that Daisy had heard, and possibly those of Venka starting the CSI process in the kitchen.

'Did you hear any male voices?' This was an absolutely crucial question, and Daisy considered it for a while, her eyes looking into the corner of the room.

'Yeah.'

'Definitely male?'

She squinted at them. 'Maybe not.'

'Could you make out what was being said?'

Again, she searched the room for inspiration. 'Can't remember.'

'Did you see anybody, at all?' Maddy asked.

'Not until after I'd picked up the wallet.'

'What did you hear then?'

'Talking from the kitchen area, so I scarpered downstairs, then back out through the door into the garden.'

'What did you see on the stairs?'

'A load of blood, and a wheelchair on its side. I didn't want to touch it.'

Talantire knew she'd done very well at that. CSI hadn't picked up any dabs from her at all; just her shoes. 'Then you went out the way you came in. Is that right, Daisy?'

'Yeah.'

'Did you lock the door to the walled garden behind you?'

'Yeah, it's a habit.'

That was highly significant. With Luka still in the house, he would've had to leave a different way. But which one? The only exits were the front door, where at that time John Rice and his mate were standing guard; the kitchen, which was full of CSI people just getting started; and the emergency exit on the first floor, which never seemed to have been opened.

Talantire wrapped up the interview and had Daisy escorted back to the cells.

Kevin Smith and Daisy Rice had upended the investigation. Yes, there were some small extra pieces of intelligence they had gleaned from interviewing them, but the bigger problem was the breach of such an important crime scene while officers like her were actually on site. It would be seen as an unforgivable lapse of security. And

179

undoubtedly it would be her fault. All she could pray for was a quick arrest and confession from their main suspect. Then maybe the security breach would all be forgotten about.

Fat chance.

—

Luka Horvat was arrested at 6:20 a.m. while waiting for a flight to Ljubljana from Manchester Airport, and by 10:30 on Monday he was in an interview room at Exeter Middlemoor Police Station. Talantire drove over from Barnstaple with Maddy Moran. They war-gamed their interview plan in the car, and then looked at him on the CCTV before going in. He was a tall, rangy individual, clearly gym fit, with the dark handsome looks she had seen in the photograph on Kelsey's phone. It was obvious why women were attracted to him. He looked nervous and fidgety, just what she had expected from a man who was guilty. Once a custody officer had arrived with the duty solicitor, they were ready to start.

The two detectives prepped the tape and introduced themselves. The brief was a young Asian woman wearing a hijab. She told Horvat that even though he had been cautioned, he shouldn't answer any questions that he didn't want to. 'No comment is just fine,' she said.

He took this a bit more literally than intended, refusing to even confirm who he was or where he lived. The brief corrected him, telling him that it would save a lot of time all round if he just confirmed the factual details. But he didn't change his policy.

Talantire decided to start with the biggest questions, to try to shock him into an answer.

'Where were you on Saturday afternoon?'

'No comment.'

'Let's be more direct,' Talantire said. 'I put it to you that on Saturday at Bychecombe Manor in Devon you murdered your own brother Bassin Horvat with a shotgun, then you killed the Honourable Lionel Hall-Hartington.'

'What evidence do you have for this assertion?' the brief asked.

'DNA at the scene, and motive,' Talantire said. 'He was fired a year ago by Mr Hall-Hartington. There is also evidence of a deep rift between your client and his brother, Bassin. We have threats recorded on camera.'

'Fucking Kelsey, what a backstabber,' Luka said.

'So you know what we're talking about?' Talantire asked.

'I was in Manchester on Saturday.'

'Oh yes?'

'Yeah, I was working at Wetherspoon's until eleven, and I'll be on the CCTV,' he said, folding his arms and looking directly at them.

Talantire and Maddy exchanged glances. This was a very forthright and confident assertion. Any verified CCTV alibi could kill the case against him stone dead. They asked for the details of the Wetherspoon's pub in question, then Talantire left the room to call Nuttall, who was at the mobile incident room. He answered immediately, sounding exhausted after working right through the night.

'Dave, I need an urgent CCTV check. See if it can be uploaded to GoodSAM straight away.' She gave the details of the time and the pub.

'Okay,' he said. She heard him typing away on a keyboard. 'If he's right, our only reasonable suspect disappears in a puff of smoke, right?'

'Unfortunately, yes. We've only got a couple of his DNA dabs in the well chamber. If he turns out to have an alibi on top of that, then we're stuffed,' Talantire said.

'I couldn't agree more,' Nuttall said. He yawned, and the noise easily carried down the phone. 'Maybe we all need more sleep because we're not thinking straight.'

'It's an occupational hazard,' she said. 'I'm leaning heavily on black coffee to keep me going.' Talantire looked at the interview room CCTV, where a smug-looking Horvat sat with his arms crossed while staring at the ceiling. And then she saw the time: 11:50.

'Dave, I'm going to have to go now. I've got a CPS meeting upstairs at noon. Maddy's going back to re-interview Soraya, and I'll be back with you later. Are you all right holding the fort?'

'Yep.'

Talantire hurried away, determined to get a coffee before facing the intimidating array of Crown Prosecution Service bigwigs.

Maddy went to see the desk sergeant, to get him to take Horvat back to his cell. Two minutes later, her phone rang. It was Nuttall.

'Got the CCTV already?'

'No. It's something else. Two squad cars from rural policing have just arrived and arrested one of the farm employees, and they're taking him back to Exeter. I wondered if you knew anything about it?'

'No. Did you try Jan?'

'Her phone's busy,' Nuttall said. 'Inspector Thompson was in the dark, and he's supposed to be kept in the loop about anything concerning the estate employees.'

'Talantire didn't say anything to me. Have you spoken to DCS Ross? He's the SIO.'

'No, but I think Inspector Thompson is trying to reach him now.'

'Who did they arrest?' Maddy asked.

'John Rice.'

'Do we know why?'

'It's at the behest of the National Crime Agency apparently,' Nuttall said.

'Well, Jan's in with them now. I didn't think Rice was a suspect.'

'Neither did I. But he did see the commissioner's body, so he has been inside the crime scene. Maybe they know something we don't.'

Chapter Twelve

Talantire hurried along the top floor corridor at Middlemoor with a takeaway coffee in one hand and her briefcase on its long strap over her shoulder. She had her phone pressed to her ear, finishing up a call with Primrose. It was 12:02, and the meeting was meant to start at noon. 'You've found *what!*' Talantire exclaimed, then looked in shocked amazement at the image the digital evidence officer had just sent her. 'Wow, amazing.' She thanked Primrose and ended the call.

She barged open the conference room door with her bottom to find most of the bigwigs already there: Chief Constable Hamid Sharif, DCS Ross, superintendents Paul Shortland and Timothy Weaver, Moira Hallett from the press office and no less than three lawyers from the CPS, distinguished by their Home Office lanyards. She recognised one of them because she'd seen him on the telly: CPS chief Kelvin Brunswick.

All eyes were on her as she ended the call and took her seat immediately to the right of Sharif, the side that didn't show the acid scars. Growing up gay in Pakistan had exacted its price, but it had also forged a man dedicated to justice. She placed her documents on the table, realising she was almost dizzy with fatigue.

'When did you last get any sleep, Jan?' Sharif asked her softly.

'Half an hour on Saturday night,' she replied.

'Thirty-odd hours ago. We'll try to keep this short and focused then.'

She didn't tell him that she had fallen asleep on the loo in the portable incident room. She was gratified that he had asked her. It was just the kind of thing that marked Sharif out as a good manager of people as well as a first-class organiser.

Sharif called the meeting to order and then asked DCS Ross to outline what had occurred at the crime scene. The detective chief superintendent read out from a typed sheet in front of him, managing to conjure something wooden and dull from one of the most shocking and unprecedented crimes in British history. Ross was clearly not comfortable; a slight tremor in his hands transmitted to the paper he was holding.

'So as of first thing this morning, we have three potential suspects in custody,' Ross concluded. 'I remain confident of a successful conclusion to this enquiry.' He looked across at Talantire, as did everybody else.

Unlike Ross, she'd had no opportunity to prepare a speech, but she knew the main points and launched in immediately. 'We do indeed have three male suspects, one of whose DNA traces are on the ropes used to tie the commissioner's wife to the chains from which she was suspended in the well.'

'Excellent, that sounds conclusive,' Brunswick said.

'Yes, that individual was also caught trying to fly out of the country first thing this morning.'

'A guilty conscience too,' Brunswick continued.

'It's not clear-cut yet, however,' Talantire said. 'He emphatically claims he was working as a security guard at a pub in Manchester on the day that the commissioner and the other man were shot dead. We're awaiting CCTV footage to back up the alibi.'

'He must be guilty,' Shortland said. 'How else did his DNA get on the ropes?'

'It's a secondary question for now,' Sharif said. 'What about the other two suspects, Jan?'

'Kevin Ronald Smith, a man known to us, was identified as using the commissioner's bank cards on Saturday night to make purchases in Barnstaple, and he has been charged with the relevant fraud offences. His girlfriend, one Daisy Columbine Rice, admitted entering the crime scene and stealing the commissioner's wallet. She is employed as a part-time gardener at the manor and had keys to the side entrance of the manor. She has been charged with theft.'

'No murder charges?' Weaver asked.

'No. Although there is forensic evidence that Ms Rice was in the house, from bloodstains on her footwear, and – as I've just been shown – a selfie she took with the dead body of the commissioner, there is nothing to tie her with the actual killings. She is a vulnerable individual, and I don't believe she had either the capability to plan, sufficient forensic awareness to prepare or the determination to execute such a violent attack.' She turned to the CPS chief. 'I simply don't believe a case against her would stand a chance in court.'

Brunswick nodded.

'What about Mr Smith?' Sharif asked.

'I don't think he even went into the house,' Talantire said. 'We certainly have no evidence for it.'

'You don't yet seem to have assembled evidence for very much, do you?' asked Hermione Scott, a barrister with iron grey hair and severe spectacles on a chain.

Talantire had prepared for this accusation with her call to Venka. 'My team and CSI between us have taken 8,917 DNA samples at the scene, 163 elimination swabs from those who were or might have been suspected to have been present at the crime scene, lifted 1,131 fingerprint samples, and taken 26,513 photographs in and around Bychecombe Manor crime scene. Let me tell you, categorically, that we are not short of evidence. What we're short of – and I'm sure you understand this – is the kind of evidence that will stand up in court when *you* have to do your job.'

The retort raised eyebrows right around the room.

'Point taken, Detective Inspector,' Brunswick said in an emollient tone.

Sharif turned to her and said, 'We do have a very big problem though, don't we? There is enormous pressure on us to get results.'

Moira Hallett was nodding emphatically and the chief constable gestured for her to speak.

'Yes, you're right, we do have huge pressure, from the newspapers, TV and radio, and of course the Great British public, who are as we speak are busily trading conspiracy theories on social media. I've been doing this job for over ten years, and I can tell you that the simple fact that two people have been charged with related offences relieves much of the pressure. The public will for good or ill focus on those in custody and assume that it's only a matter of time before they are charged with the more serious offences. It would be far worse if we simply didn't have *anybody* to put forward as a suspect.'

There was much nodding of heads around the table.

Ms Scott had something to add: 'I do accept that, and I'm hopeful we'll soon get what we need. However, I am a *little* concerned that the crime scene wasn't sufficiently secure to prevent the theft of the commissioner's wallet, and with that the consequent muddying of the forensic trail.'

Talantire had anticipated this too, which was just as well because Ross as SIO didn't look ready to volunteer an answer.

'I accept what you say,' Talantire said. 'But we do have to bear in mind that this was an exceptionally large crime scene and the lapse in security came very early in the investigation, just as we were getting control of it. The individual who got in was legitimately in possession of keys. My abiding worry is that Daisy Rice didn't in fact – despite her assurances – lock the door as she left, which may have given our perpetrator the opportunity to escape.'

'So what's next, Jan?' Sharif asked.

'We have a lot of re-interviewing to do today, of witnesses, also of Ms Rice to see if she can tell us anything about what she saw inside the house. I'm also looking forward to speaking again to the commissioner's wife who is due to be released from hospital this afternoon. Tomorrow morning, we have a reconstruction of the crime, which I'm hoping she will be well enough to attend.'

'Are there any other suspects that we haven't looked at?' Sharif asked.

'At the moment, no.'

'Actually, there might be.' This was from Shortland.

Talantire looked up. She hadn't heard anything from him relevant to the case.

'The National Crime Agency in Hull just tipped me off about the discovery of a shipping container full of quad bike parts being shipped to Rotterdam, and there is a connection to thefts at Bychecombe Manor.' He looked around the table, enjoying drawing out the suspense. 'They made an arrest at the scene, but following forensic tests have got a link via the national DNA database to somebody else, an employee at Bychecombe Manor. This individual was also, by his own admission, in the commissioner's office shortly after the murder, and I fear has rather been overlooked by DI Talantire.'

'Who exactly are you talking about?' she asked him.

'John Rice. An arrest by rural policing officers has recently taken place on the Bychecombe Estate.'

Talantire's jaw dropped open. 'Did you know about this, sir?' she asked DCS Ross.

'I was informed just a few minutes before the meeting and gave my permission.'

Ms Scott was on her like a hungry wolverine. 'I'm glad somebody is being proactive here. I have to say this investigation looks like it's a few sandwiches short of a picnic.' She looked at the faces around the room collecting various nods of agreement, including one – incredibly – from Shortland himself.

'Let me get this right, sir,' Talantire said to Shortland. 'You've gone behind my back with your own investigation—'

'Over your head, not behind your back,' Ross corrected her. 'I'm the SIO, and I was informed. I would have told you before the meeting, had you been punctual. As it was, I didn't get the chance.'

'DI Talantire, this was a tip-off that came to me as the head of rural policing from the NCA,' Shortland said. 'I wasn't trying to second guess you, but this is a big investigation, and everybody needs a bit of help.'

Trying to contain her fury, Talantire asked: 'Can I ask what exactly linked John Rice to this NCA investigation?'

'Well, the enquiry is only at its initial stages,' Shortland said, leaning back on his chair, cupping his hands behind his head. 'But we believe that John Rice may well have been complicit in the theft of quad bikes from Bychecombe Manor, which were then disassembled prior to being shipped abroad from Immingham on the Humber, with the ultimate destination of Turkey, where they would be reassembled and sold to middlemen. The NCA and Humberside Police have been working on this particular route for the export of stolen agricultural equipment for some years, and they regard this as something of a breakthrough.'

'Well done,' Sharif said. 'And I think some of this equipment has been traced back to the commissioner's farm?'

'Yes. A couple of matching chassis numbers.'

Sharif turned to Talantire. 'Were there any DNA markers from Mr Rice anywhere in the crime scene?'

'A few, which correspond to his presence near the body of the commissioner—'

'Or maybe he committed it?' Ms Scott muttered to her boss, Brunswick.

'—but nothing whatsoever in the crucial basement and sub-basement areas, where the commissioner's wife was assaulted and dragged along to the well chamber,' Talantire continued.

'But from my reading of this, you don't have anyone's DNA in this area that you haven't already eliminated,' Ms Scott continued. 'So isn't Mr Rice as good a candidate as any?'

'We do have one, if you count the ropes,' Talantire said. 'But as for Rice, he has a CCTV alibi for the time of the killing and no apparent motive. Indeed, he was visibly upset when breaking the news of the discovery of the body to me.'

Shortland chuckled. 'Well, given that his DNA was discovered 300 miles north in a shipping container on the Humber, I think we can be sure that he is not the tearful innocent he appears to be,' he said.

'Where exactly did you find his samples. Just on the components, or more generally inside the shipping container crime scene?' Talantire asked.

'I don't have the details with me,' Shortland said.

'Well, that's a shame,' Talantire replied. 'Because Mr Rice is the main mechanic who works on the Bychecombe estate's farm machinery. So it would be no surprise that residual traces of his DNA would be found on stolen equipment that he had at some previous time been working on. But that does not mean to say that he was involved in stealing them, does it? It would depend if his dabs turned up anywhere else where he wouldn't have a legitimate reason to be.'

'That's an extremely pertinent point,' Sharif said, looking at Shortland.

'We'll have to see,' Shortland said.

'If I were to hazard a guess,' Talantire added, 'I would say the excitement of finding John Rice listed on the national DNA database rather pre-empted rational enquiry. To be clear, he is only on it because I requested an elimination sample from him as part of the investigation. I would be very surprised if he doesn't turn out to be an innocent man.'

After the meeting, Talantire had a discussion with DCS Ross in the corridor.

'Can we have a look at the latest on the arrests at Immingham?' she asked.

'Of course, I have about fifteen minutes before my next meeting. Let's take a look.' They made their way to his office, then sat down together side by side at his PC and called up everything they had on from the NCA on the Immingham raid. She quickly established from the evidence file that John Rice's DNA was only found on some quad bike engine parts and handlebar controls.

'It's as I suggested,' Talantire said. 'I don't think Rice was anything to do with it.'

'Hmm, perhaps that is the case,' he conceded.

'I felt you could have been a bit more supportive, sir. The CPS don't need much excuse to start picking holes in an inquiry, especially as they were led to believe there was a firm suspect.'

'As I said, I wasn't given much notice myself.'

She turned to look at him. 'If you don't have full confidence in my ability to solve this crime, I'm happy to pass it over to somebody you do trust,' she said. This was a gambit she had thought about carefully on the way to the meeting. She was ninety per cent convinced he wouldn't take it.

'I have total confidence in you, Jan. You're one of the best officers in the force. But we do need results and I just can't see any right now.'

However, as they turned back to the on-screen files, they soon discovered that there was something of substance to one of the Immingham arrests. Gavin Stone, who had been at the party on the day of the killings, was detained by the NCA at the site of the raid, in possession of the keys to the shipping container in which the stolen parts were found. He was a twenty-six-year-old sometime welder, born and brought up in Newton Abbot, and had a minor criminal record. He had previously served a suspended three-month stretch for handling stolen property, a ride-on mower. He had claimed he didn't know it was stolen when he sold it. Looking through the evidence files that the NCA had forwarded to DCS Ross and Superintendent Shortland, she realised that they might be halfway to solving the mystery that had plagued the commissioner himself so much over the last few years: the theft of quad bikes and other gear belonging to Sleepy Monk Creamery. Perhaps it had been Stone who worked with Derek Cloddy, who had stolen the unattended quad bike.

Stone was being held at Grimsby Police Station, and CID there had plenty of questions for him. After Ross headed off to his next meeting, Talantire messaged them a few of her own, principally trying to establish where he was at the time of the Bychecombe Manor murders. His DNA was already on the national database and hadn't turned up at her crime scene, but that didn't mean to say he wasn't involved in some way. She would have to wait and see.

Right now, she had to go to Royal Devon and Exeter Hospital. It was just a couple of miles away from Middlemoor. That was where her only real witness was. Helena de Courchevel. Right from the start, everything revolved around her account. Was there anything else she could tell them?

Nuttall kept an eye on GoodSAM, but the promised CCTV did not arrive. He called Talantire's contact in Greater Manchester Police and was told that the alibi didn't hold. Wetherspoon's had CCTV of Luka Horvat there on Saturday evening from eight p.m., when the security detail began work, until eleven thirty. 'We got a confirmation email from the security firm that employed him that gave his hours,' the PC said.

'But was he in the pub before that, just as a punter?' Nuttall asked.

'No, not that we could see.'

Nuttall was checking Google while he was on the phone. 'It takes four to five hours to get to Manchester from Bychecombe Manor, the best part of 250 miles away by train or car. The murders were committed at roughly half past two, so he could have got to work at eight, just about, that same evening.'

'It would be a rush, wouldn't it?' the PC asked.

'Yes, but it's possible if he was determined to build an alibi. We need to find out how he could have travelled.'

'I'll get the details of any vehicles he owns.'

'And CCTV from trains arriving from six until seven-thirty,' Nuttall added. There was still a chance that Horvat was the culprit. A narrow chance, but worth pursuing.

–

While Talantire was at her meeting, Maddy Moran headed back to Little Bychecombe to re-interview Soraya Hinton. The housekeeper looked tired, her handsome features lined, and there were some grey streaks in her dark hair. Maddy wasn't there to give her a hard time, but Soraya was one of the few people who by her own admission had been moving around in the manor before Helena was rescued. It was she who made the emergency services call, after retrieving her phone from the laundry trolley on the landing on the first floor. What had she seen?

Maddy had the woman's statement in front of her and checked every detail of her account. She wanted to find out if Soraya could have seen or heard Daisy Rice on the floor below. The detective sergeant took her time, especially as Soraya was clearly struggling to remember exactly when everything happened. Some inconsistencies began to emerge about exactly when she had gone down to the ground floor and discovered the body of the commissioner. It was while going over these points that Soraya began to cry. 'I don't know, I just don't know. I started dreaming about it, men in black in the corridors with knives.'

'Okay, I'm sorry. Let's leave it there,' Maddy said, passing across a box of tissues. She looked down at the notes she'd made and realised that, rather than adding any extra information, they had simply undermined the confidence with which the first statement had been made. Then, as Soraya began to stand, she realised there was something else she needed to ask her.

'Just a final thing. Do you do laundry for the household? Hanging out clothing on the washing line, that kind of thing?'

Soraya's brow furrowed. 'There's a commercial laundry service. A few things get done on site from time to time, but we use the tumble dryers, which can handle anything.'

Maddy smiled. 'But there is a washing line in the back-yard of the kitchen.'

'Yes. I don't really get what you are driving at.'

'It's just that your DNA was recovered from the cords that were used to bind Helena's ankles to the chains, and we couldn't really figure out why that might be, until we realised that the cord was a commercial washing line.'

Soraya's neck flushed, and her eyes imperceptibly widened. 'Oh, I see. Well, I imagine there might be dish-cloths or something that I hung out when I was helping in the kitchen.'

Maddy continued to stare at the woman. 'So was some of the clothesline taken from the courtyard in recent days or weeks?'

'I don't know.'

'Well, the assailant must have had it with him to tie Helena up, and he must have got it from somewhere. As your DNA was on it, we assume he must have got it from the courtyard.' She was careful not to mention that there was somebody else's DNA on the rope too.

'I suppose you must be right, but I didn't notice. I haven't been back to the courtyard since the murders to check.'

Maddy leaned forward. 'I have, and there's no sign of any missing. Soraya, can you think of any other reason why your DNA might be on those cords?'

She shook her head and whispered, 'No.'

'Are you absolutely sure?'

She nodded and looked down. The woman was clearly lying, something she wasn't very good at. The flush on her neck was very telling. Maddy had a hunch about what the truth was, but she didn't want to press any harder. If she was right, it would explain something that had baffled her and Talantire since last night. There might be a chance to prove it if Primrose Chen was able to examine Luka Horvat's phone.

After letting Soraya go home, Maddy Moran returned to the mobile incident room. The place was a hive of activity. She picked up the evidence bag containing Luka Horvat's mobile phone, which was sitting untouched on top of the in-tray of a digital evidence officer, one of the many staff who had been drafted in from Exeter to help them. 'Mind if I borrow this?' she asked the man, who was fast-forwarding through some CCTV footage.

He glanced briefly over his shoulder at her and nodded. 'I won't get to that today, I'm afraid. It dropped down the priority list since we heard Horvat had an alibi.'

'He's still relevant to the crime,' she said. 'Where's the kiosk?'

'Behind here,' he said, pointing to one of the whiteboards. The Aceso Kiosk was a portable device that allowed untrained officers to be able to download the contents of mobile phones. It saved a great deal of time for investigations, which had previously required a lengthy consultation with phone service providers.

Maddy had only used the kiosk a handful of times, and it took twenty minutes to set it up on one of the few remaining tables in the crowded Portakabin. She took Luka's SIM card out of his phone and inserted it into the machine. She immediately searched for images and videos and found plenty. There were hundreds of pictures of naked and semi-naked women, in what appeared to be sadomasochistic settings. And dozens of videos. She kept the sound very low and the pictures small, in case her viewing habits were misunderstood. The majority appeared to be commercial porn, presumably that he had downloaded, but there were others that looked like they might be his own handiwork; not so professionally shot and no American accents.

Rope, chains, gags, whips, flails.

It would take hours to look through all of them. On a hunch, she searched for deleted files. Luka had been on the run for most of a day and would perhaps have got rid of incriminating files. Considering what he hadn't felt the need to erase, she had high hopes of incrimination for those that he did.

But there was a caveat. The kiosk could only retrieve binned data until it had been overwritten, which meant only recently removed content could be restored. She still found plenty. What she had been hoping to find was a picture or video of him with Soraya Hinton. If so, it would explain both their DNA traces on cords that were later used to bind Helena de Courchevel's ankles to the chains in the well. Ironically, such a discovery would actually exonerate him of suspicion of the murders, by providing a plausible and – in its narrowest sense – innocent explanation of the hitherto incriminating forensic trail.

But what she actually discovered was a little different.

The first deleted video was of a naked, gagged and blindfolded woman chained to a rusty piece of medieval ironwork in some authentic-looking dungeon, lit only by dozens of candles. And as the camera panned around, she recognised it. It was the Bychecombe Manor well chamber, and the ironwork the woman was fastened to was the grille on top of the well. A glimpse of the windlass, with its wooden barrel and loops of chains, confirmed it. Very little was shown of the man making the video, which seemed to be filmed on a headcam, but enough to be sure what was going on: a glimpse of a hairy male arm holding a leather flail, with which he was gently flogging the red-headed victim. His voice, threatening and dominating, did indeed sound like Luka's.

'Are you looking at porn, Maddy?'

She turned around to see Inspector Tony Thompson standing behind her.

Maddy paused the video. 'Yes and no.'

'It sounded like yes, yes, yes from what I heard,' he said, chuckling.

'Some of this was filmed just in there,' she said, indicating the manor. 'Using the well chamber as a dungeon.'

'Sounds thoroughly illegal to me.'

'Well... I'm not so sure.' She tried to think it through from a police perspective. The scenes were arguably consensual, and there were certainly no shrieks of pain. None of the participants seemed to be obviously underage, and setting aside the requirement to get permission to use Bychecombe's well chamber as a dungeon – which was surely a civil matter – there was nothing obviously illegal.

'So does this help us close in on the killer, then?' he asked.

'Not necessarily, no.'

'Then perhaps you shouldn't be watching it?' Thompson said, turning away.

Having heard the exchange, several officers in the incident room were now staring at her. Slightly embarrassed, she turned back to the screen. Thinking about it, she had been dead right: it didn't get them anywhere close to the killer. Quite the reverse. What these videos did, without doubt, was to remove yet another piece of forensic evidence. They offered a reasonable alternative explanation for how Luka's DNA got into the well chamber, without being involved in the killings. He was making porn.

Luka Horvat wasn't yet in the clear; after all he'd been caught trying to flee the country from Manchester Airport. But who else did they have left? Not Rustam, not Kevin Smith.

It was as if a ghost had committed the crimes. But ghosts don't fire shotguns, and ghosts don't leave bloody footprints.

–

Feeling gloomy, Maddy took a walk, admiring the warm evening and the birdsong. She passed the evidence van, in which lay many hundreds of so far unexamined evidence bags. A young Black uniformed officer was sitting on the steps at the open back of the van. Spotting Maddy, she stood up and pocketed the vape that she had clearly been using.

'Don't worry, I'm not going to dob you in,' Maddy said. 'I just want to take a look at some of the unopened bags.'

'There's enough in there to keep you going for weeks, sarge,' the PC said.

'Too right.' Maddy made her way inside, leaving the officer outside. There were ten racks of evidence lining the long wheelbase Transit, shelves laid out from ankle height up to the ceiling, carefully labelled with the location they were found and a number. She started first with the bags found at Paula Zucketort's room, but most of these had been examined and were cross-referenced to case files. Charges for possession of drugs were already in the works. On the shelf immediately above that was one labelled 'commissioner's office', and next to it 'commissioner's bedroom'. Maddy knew the former had been thoroughly searched, being part of the murder scene. She also knew that Talantire and Nuttall had looked into the commissioner's bedroom. However, it was clear most of the packets here had not been examined, something that she cross-checked with the evidence officer's clipboard. The labels gave some basic description. She found a bulky one labelled 'documents, right bedside cabinet, bottom drawer, locked.'

She opened the envelope and slid out a thick pile of papers. Most of them were typewritten legal documents, but under them was a tatty envelope containing a large greetings card, seemingly hand-painted, of a bird with a rose in its beak. She slid it out and saw a handwritten piece of poetry in a language she didn't recognise. But it included the name 'Helena'.

Moj golobček, Helena.

Ljubezen se ne spreminja s svojimi kratkimi urami in tedni, ampak jo prenaša celo do roba pogube.

Maddy immediately realised the significance. She didn't for a moment imagine that the commissioner would have written this himself. It wasn't a language that old Bagpuss might have been expected to speak. She got out her phone and went to Google Translate. The first two words, as she suspected, were Slovenian, making: 'My little dove, Helena.' It went on:

Love alters not with his brief hours and weeks, but bears it out even to the edge of doom.

Maddy had heard this famous line somewhere before. Suddenly it all made sense. Luka wasn't fired for groping a colleague. He was sacked because he was having an affair with the commissioner's wife, or had at least made a pass at her through the Valentine's card. She looked again at the envelope, addressed to Helena at the manor, postmarked February 12, 2022. Posted, perhaps recklessly, to arrive on Valentine's Day and presumably intercepted by the commissioner. It had been found in his bedroom, not hers, after all. She shuffled through the other papers and found a letter from Geoffrey Wheatcroft, dated March 3 the same year, giving a legal opinion about sacking without cause.

She bundled up the evidence bag, signed it out and took it with her back to the incident room. She then logged into the system and looked for the emails that Geoffrey Wheatcroft promised had been exchanged between him and the commissioner over the sacking.

None had yet been supplied. *Typical solicitor.*

She sat back in her chair and steepled her fingers over her nose. Helena was a rather beautiful woman, with fine and delicate features. Classy. For sure. But at sixty-one, she was twenty-five years older than Luka, and with her MS by then already using a wheelchair. This made her, to put it charitably, a very unusual choice for him to fall in love with. From everything they had heard, the photos and the videos and the testimony from Kelsey Thornewater, Luka concentrated on younger women. The only possible exception was Soraya Hinton, who was in her late forties, if they had indeed had an affair. Luka didn't seem a poetry kind of guy either. More a dick pic type.

Then it hit her like a bolt from the blue.

She'd got it all wrong. And so had the commissioner. She picked up the phone to Talantire.

that it did not feel a bolt from the blue. She'd got it all wrong. And so had the ... someone imposed on the phone to tell the ...

Chapter Thirteen

Royal Devon and Exeter Hospital was the usual warren that so many NHS facilities are, and Talantire took a while to find the doctor who had been treating Helena de Courchevel. Dr Luqman Hassan worked out of an incredibly tiny office, which seemed almost equatorial in its heat. He offered her iced lemonade, which she was happy to accept as she took a seat.

'How is our victim?' she asked.

'She's made a pretty solid recovery,' he replied. 'I've got the full report you asked for here, and I can confirm that she is well enough to be discharged first thing tomorrow.'

'That's excellent news because I need her to assist us in a reconstruction of the crime.'

'Yes, you mentioned that. She has been given a psychological assessment, and I have to say she seems remarkably tough. It is quite likely that PTSD will emerge at some stage, and I'll of course caution you that if she becomes upset, she should be excused from attendance.'

'Of course. I will have a dedicated family liaison officer whose responsibility will be for her well-being. Now, about her injuries.'

'Yes,' he said. 'I will spare you the technical jargon. She has suffered at least two dozen generally shallow cuts to her legs, arms and particularly her scalp, which resulted in fairly extensive bleeding.'

'This is one of the few cases where I have asked for a report on knife injuries to somebody who is still alive,' Talantire said. 'And I need the full medical background on her, as I mentioned.'

'Yes.'

'Were any of these knife wounds life-threatening, or intended to be?'

'Well, I can't talk about intentions, but I would hazard a guess that the assailant was intending to cause pain rather than death.'

Talantire nodded. That fitted with the narrative of the assailant trying to extract the combination for the safe from her.

'We did find traces of ketamine in the blood samples we took from her.'

'Was it something she had been prescribed?'

'No. It's really only used as a last resort analgesic in surgery, but it is sometimes used for depression.'

'I see,' Talantire said. She knew ketamine was in vogue as a recreational drug and could guess who might have illegally supplied her.

'I'll email you the whole thing by the end of my shift,' he said. 'Now, I'll take you to our patient.'

The consultant led Talantire along a labyrinthine corridor, down to the room where Helena was staying, now out of intensive care and in a general ward. The consultant left her there. An extremely pretty uniformed PC was at the door. She told Talantire that the patient already had a guest and showed her the clipboard.

Paula Zucketort, best friend and drug dealer. What a surprise.

Paula Zucketort had been staying at the exclusive Westcombe Fields private hotel, just a few miles from Little Bychecombe. She'd vacated her room at the manor, given that it was crawling with cops, but kept a promise to Talantire to be within easy reach in case they needed to re-interview her. Westcombe Fields had an expensive spa and numerous treatment rooms along with a heated indoor pool. By arrangement, she reserved the pool for her sole personal use every day from four p.m. until five so that she could swim naked. She had been waiting for a call from her personal spy, and at ten to two it came, largely confirming what she'd suspected, but adding a few surprising elements she'd never have guessed.

Shortly after visiting hours began at three, Zucketort arrived at the Royal Devon Hospital to see her friend Helena. Her chauffeur, Oliver, dropped her off at the main entrance in the vintage Rolls-Royce. As she'd been warned, there was still a uniformed cop on the door of the private room where Helena was staying, her final day in hospital. The female officer, young and rather pretty, recoiled a little at her appearance. But she checked her in on the clipboard then escorted her inside.

'Oh, Paula, so good to see you,' Helena said, holding out her arms to embrace her. The two women held each other closely.

'I've been so worried about you,' Zucketort said, sitting down on the edge of the bed. 'Those knife wounds appear to be healing well.'

Helena glanced up at the PC before answering. 'Yes, I might have a few scars under my hairline,' she said, showing her friend the criss-crossed linear scabs on her scalp. 'They did bleed so terribly.'

Zucketort opened a carrier bag that she had with her and said, 'I brought the dress you asked for, and added a few items I thought you'd like.'

'Oh, wonderful,' Helena said, sliding out a dress and hat.

Zucketort turned to the policewoman and asked, 'Darling, would you mind awfully getting us a coffee each? I'm absolutely parched, and there is a decent coffee shop on the ground floor. Helena says the stuff they serve on the ward is dreadful muck.'

'I'm here to do a job, madam,' the PC said. 'I can't do it if I'm running errands for visitors, or patients for that matter.'

'All right, never mind, I'll get Oliver to do it,' Zucketort said, rolling her eyes at Helena. 'But in the meantime, may we have a little privacy while she changes?'

The officer glanced at Helena, who nodded in affirmation. She then shrugged and made her way out into the corridor, closing the door behind her.

'What on earth is she doing here?' Paula hissed, eyeing the door, and then pulled the blue plastic curtain around the bed.

'She's supposed to be protecting me.'

'What, in case Luka comes back to "have another go"?' she said, rabbit-earing the final phrase.

Helena put a warning finger to her lips.

'They suspect me, did you know that?' Zucketort asked.

'Well, you *do* radiate suspicion,' Helena said, giggling, then put her hand on her guest's arm. 'So what have you found out?'

'Get this. Not long after Bagpuss was shot, a sneak thief crept in and stole his wallet while he was lying dead.'

Helena's hands flew to her face. 'No! How did you find out?'

'One of the detectives, DC Caroline Cheetham, used to work in my design studio before going over to the other side. She volunteered to keep me in the loop, though I expect she's going to want some designer clothing out of it.'

'A useful contact,' Helena said. 'So do we know who the thief was?'

'Someone called Daisy Rice. Gave the cards to her boyfriend, who went on a shopping spree.'

'Oh, gosh. I know the girl. I gave her a job in the gardens. Rather a sweet creature, she's got learning difficulties. I'm shocked she did such a thing.'

'She apparently took a selfie with Bagpuss's body too.'

Helena looked angry. 'I misjudged the girl. She's got no shame.'

'Well, you can talk, dear.'

Helena wagged her finger, and indicated the door with her eyes, where conversation could be heard from outside. There was a sharp rap on it.

—

Talantire stepped into the room, which seemed to echo with a conversation she had just missed.

Helena wasn't in bed but sitting in a chair next to it. She was wearing a green dress, a matching broad-brimmed hat and slingback sandals. Her bare legs exhibited purple and yellow bruises on her ankles, knees and thighs, and some scabbed cuts. However, several dressings looked to have been removed from her head, and the remainder were barely visible under the hat.

'My goodness, Helena, you look ready for a garden party!' Talantire exclaimed.

'It's important to keep up appearances,' she said with a smile. She was fully made up. The glamour was returning.

'How are you feeling?'

'She's recovering well,' Zucketort said. She looked like a doll, leaning back against the pillow, wearing a blue-striped pinafore dress and T-bar sandals: the wizened schoolgirl look.

'I'm tired and bruised but resolute,' Helena said. 'I still get nightmares, which I'm told is to be expected for some months. Of course, if you manage to catch him, that would make a huge difference.'

'We're doing our best,' Talantire said.

'Of course you are, darling,' Zucketort said. 'Hey, we've got enough for a party. Get the delicious kissogram girl in from outside and we can call it fancy dress,' she said with a laugh.

'Well, I can see that you're always ready for a party, except when you sleep right through,' Talantire said.

Zucketort turned to Helena, hands on hips, radiating mock offence.

Talantire continued: 'But I have work to do, and I'm going to have to ask you to wait outside while I do it.' She smiled tightly.

'Well, aren't you quite the spoilsport?' Zucketort said, sliding off the bed and stalking out of the room with a final wave to Helena.

Once she'd gone, and the door was closed, Talantire said, 'I just want to make sure you are all right to attend the crime reconstruction tomorrow morning.'

'I wouldn't miss it for the world,' Helena replied.

Talantire then explained how it would work, but before she had finished, her phone rang. It was Maddy, who said she had something important to tell her. Talantire stepped out into the corridor and saw Zucketort there, leaning against the external window, so felt compelled to walk further away to take the call.

–

After listening to everything that Maddy had told her, Talantire swallowed her amazement and made her way back to Helena's room, where she once again felt the need to remove Paula Zucketort, who was lying on the bed as if she owned the place.

Talantire followed her out and had a word with the PC to make sure no one was close enough to listen in. Then she came back into the room, closed the door and sat on the bed.

'Were you having an affair with Bassin Horvat?'

Helena looked stunned, then said, 'No, of course not. What on earth gives you that idea?'

'A homemade Valentine's card, dedicated to you, in Slovenian, which we found in your husband's bedroom.'

Helena stared levelly back. 'That was from Luka, not Bassin. It was why he was fired.'

'Luka doesn't seem to me the kind of man who would write poetry.'

She laughed. 'Quite right. But he was the type to copy it. It's one of Shakespeare's sonnets, and I think it was a joke. But as I say, it rather backfired. Bagpuss took it rather more seriously than Luka might have guessed, and he gave me a very hard time about it.'

Talantire eyed the woman intensely. Helena knew that with Bassin and her husband dead, it would be hard to disprove the story. But it somehow didn't ring true. Talantire stared at this glamorous and poised woman, who had undergone what was surely one of the most terrifying ordeals a human could experience, suspended by the ankles and winched hundreds of feet down into the abyss by a masked attacker. This truly was the stuff of nightmares. Yet here she was, cool as a cucumber, ready to be discharged from hospital. She wasn't telling the truth, Talantire was certain about that, but to what extent? An affair, whether brief or extended, with either of the Horvat brothers didn't necessarily bear on the crime at all. But secret connections tying victims together in unguessed ways were more than just gossip; Maddy was right about that. Motives were often held together by gossamer connections, unseen in physical evidence. Getting to that kind of information wasn't police work; it was spycraft.

Bassin Horvat was killed first, that much in the evidence was incontrovertible. If he was indeed Helena's lover, his death should surely have added to her grief. Certainly she hadn't seemed overwhelmed by loss so far. Yes, there had been tears at the start, some hysterics. The mysteries of psychological coping mechanisms were beyond the expertise and training of a detective. But Talantire was a woman, a human; she had a gut feeling. Helena seemed either of superhuman resilience, given what she had been through, or perhaps she was still in shock. But something just didn't feel right. And at the epicentre of that maelstrom of misgiving sat Paula Zucketort.

She and Helena were as thick as thieves. It wasn't just the things that they seemed to be talking about – the clothes, the jokes about having a party – it was what they weren't talking about, and the absence of any gravity in what she had witnessed of their discussions. Helena hadn't asked about the release of her husband's body, usually one of the first things that the bereaved sought information on. There was no discussion, that she'd been aware of, about the arrangements for a funeral. No conversation about grief or loss. So far, this was all just speculative. Certainly not the kind of thing to discuss with the CPS or even DCS Ross at this stage; not unless they got their teeth into something juicier.

Still, there was something they could do. Luka Horvat was still in custody at Middlemoor and would be for another few hours. That was just two miles away. They didn't have to release him until ten a.m. on Tuesday morning and could hold him for longer if there was a charge. He might be able to shed some light on the rumours of an affair. It was thin stuff, that was for sure. The whole case now seemed to come down to grasping at straws. None was thinner than focusing on a suspect who had an alibi.

She returned to her car and set off back to Middlemoor.

—

Talantire had rung ahead to make sure there was a duty solicitor available, and sure enough the same hijabed young woman, who had taken such an aggressive stance before, was already in place in the interview room with her client. Talantire prepped the tape, but before she could begin, the lawyer asked, 'Can I ask if my client is still a suspect in this case, given his cast-iron alibi?'

'It's not actually very strong. The murders took place at around 2:30 p.m. on Saturday. He could have travelled from Devon in time for the start of his shift at eight o'clock, which is when we first see him on the CCTV.'

Horvat rolled his eyes. 'This is unbelievable, I was in Manchester all day.'

'Where, exactly?'

'In my flat, with my girlfriend.' Credit to him, he managed to say this without smirking. Then he added, 'Also, I went to the Sainsbury's Local on the way into town to get a vape. I should be on the cameras there.'

'What's the address?' Talantire asked with a sinking heart.

He named the street.

'Any idea what time?'

'I heard the one o'clock news headlines on the PA while I was in the queue.'

Talantire made a note of this and stepped outside to ring Nuttall and tell him to chase Greater Manchester Police for CCTV from the Sainsbury's shop. For the next half hour, she paced around, standing on the second-floor balcony at Middlemoor, overlooking Exeter, fidgeting with her phone. When Nuttall rang her back, she could tell immediately from the tone of his voice that they had lost their best suspect. 'It's him at the Sainsbury's, Jan. Definitely. Got the same neck tattoos, everything.' The CCTV supported the alibi.

Horvat was off the hook.

Talantire felt her investigative world imploding around her. Horvat was her last best suspect, but she'd had this horrible feeling for some time, given the strength of his denials, that the alibi would stand up in the end. So it had proved.

There was no longer any unidentified DNA anywhere in the main areas of the crime scene. Fingerprints, perhaps, in a few places. But almost forty-eight hours after the unprecedented murder of an elected crime commissioner, they had precisely zero tenable suspects. Devon and Cornwall Police were going to be the laughing stock of the entire country. No murder weapon. No fingerprints. No DNA.

No clue.

One thing was certain: the middle morons were going to come looking for her with a vengeance.

Talantire returned to the interview room and confirmed to her detainee that the alibi looked solid. 'We've seen the CCTV from the Sainsbury's Local, and you are on it.'

Horvat closed his eyes and steepled his hands over his nose. 'Thank God,' he said.

'So is my client now free to go?' the brief asked.

'I still have a few questions to ask him. It shouldn't take long.'

Horvat swore and rolled his eyes.

Talantire continued: 'Your involvement is not our main line of inquiry any more, but you could still give us valuable insight as a witness. Remember, too, that the caution we gave you previously is still in force.'

The brief looked very dubious at this. 'Detective, you seem to want to have it both ways.'

'When you hear the questions you might modify your opinion,' Talantire responded. She showed him two of the bondage videos on her iPad and a number of the pictures that had also been taken in the well chamber.

He rolled his eyes. 'I thought you'd get to those at some point,' he said.

'Bit of personal porn, is it?' she asked him.

'It's all consensual, I promise you.'

The lawyer intervened: 'Can you explain what laws he is breaking?'

'None, that I'm aware of,' Talantire said. 'But I think it explains why his DNA is on some of the ropes that were used to tie the commissioner's wife.'

'Ahh. So *that's* why you suspected me,' he said. 'It makes sense now.'

Talantire could almost see the penny dropping in his mind.

'What we need from you now, though, is a list of the participants and any other people you ever went to your impromptu dungeon with. Give us that and we'll happily let you go.'

He blew a sigh and held his head. 'I can't do that.'

'And you don't have to,' the lawyer said.

'What is this, some kind of last-minute defence of confidentiality?' Talantire asked. 'The moment you took and shared videos and photographs, you violated their privacy. Agreed?'

'Not really.' He looked very uncomfortable.

'Seriously?' Talantire asked. 'My colleague, having found this lot in a deleted folder on your phone, then discovered that much of it had already been uploaded to three pornography websites. Did you ask the participants' permission before doing that?'

'What?'

'We found the evidence of upload on the phone, and your unique handle Dungeonmaster77, which also appeared on the sites.'

'All right, all right,' Luka said, holding up his hands. The brief now looked more unhappy with her client than with the police. Talantire swiped through the photographs, and Luka mentioned names. Soraya's never came up, but one that did was Sally Cropper, who was Helena's god-daughter and the bride-to-be from the engagement party. Most of the rest seemed to be outsiders rather than employees of Sleepy Monk or their families.

'How did you get the key to the well chamber?'

'From the cleaner. We had an arrangement.'

'Do you mean Soraya Hinton?'

'Yes. She let us in the side entrance on some evenings, which is when we did the filming. We picked times when nobody was around, but maybe I was wrong. Maybe that's why I got fired.'

The whole thing made a lot more sense now.

'Did Kelsey find out about these little nocturnal missions of yours?'

He shrugged. 'Why do you even care? It's nothing to do with the killings, is it?'

'It certainly could be, Luka. Perhaps you'd like to list the sexual partners you had while you worked at Sleepy Monk Creameries.'

'Why do you even want this? It's ancient history.'

Talantire passed him a pad and a pen, but he made no move to begin writing.

'I can't even remember them all,' he said.

'Did you ever send any of them Valentine's cards?'

He actually laughed at that. He shook his head. 'I'm not good with words.'

'I've got a couple of lines of text here, and I would be grateful if you could write them down.' She passed across a printout in English of the text from the Valentine's card and asked him to write it in Slovenian.

'What is this, a translation class?' he asked, but took the paper and pen Talantire offered him and wrote carefully. He didn't actually stick out his tongue with concentration, but from the effort seemingly required, he clearly wasn't used to writing by hand, and what he produced was in untidy block capitals. The translation was basically correct, but compared to what Talantire could see in a photograph of the card on her iPad screen, which was neat cursive writing, he couldn't have written it. It was completely different.

Talantire, working on the principle to never ask a question to which she didn't know the answer, then asked, 'Did you send this card to Helena de Courchevel?' She showed him a photograph of the original text on the iPad.

He laughed. 'You got the wrong man there.'

'So who is the right man?'

He shrugged and then laughed. 'I don't think it matters any more.' She knew exactly who he was referring to.

'Was it your brother, Luka? Was it Bassin?'

Luka shook his head. 'Don't stir it up. Tanya has been through enough. Why not leave her memories of her husband intact?'

He wouldn't say any more, though they rephrased the question several times. It was clear enough. Luka knew that his brother had been having an affair with Helena.

Talantire got back to the incident room at Bychecombe manor on Monday afternoon to discover that the Metropolitan Police had that morning actioned the search warrant for Pauline Zucketort's home. She lived in a two-storey apartment just off London's Carnaby Street in Piccadilly, above her ground-floor design studio. They had indeed found drugs, cocaine and ketamine, but only in small quantities, and not much else to get excited about. Talantire leafed through the details of what had been seized, which included a desktop computer, a laptop and so forth. There were hundreds of photographs of her home, taken before anything was touched. This included pictures of dress designs, of mock-ups, of the small ground-floor studio and the tools within it. This was all as a precaution. Zucketort was a famous fashion designer, and any damage would inevitably have to be paid for.

One curious discovery was a large and battered suitcase under the woman's round designer bed. Some cannabis had been found inside it, amongst dozens of DVDs and ancient VHS tapes. In its methodical way, the Met had laid out the entire contents of this retro treasure trove on the bedspread and photographed them. There seemed to be quite a lot of 1960s Hammer Films productions on VHS, including *The Devil Rides Out*, *Quatermass and the Pit*, and the Amicus film *The Skull*. That horror film, starring Peter Cushing and Christopher Lee, Talantire herself remembered seeing when she was a small child. It had terrified her. Amongst the DVDs was one called *The Well*. Talantire googled the film, which was an Italian horror production that came out in 2021. The trailer she saw on IMDb clearly showed victims of some infernal monster being thrown down a well.

To Talantire, that seemed like a bit of a coincidence: did Zucketort already have an interest in wells before the Bychecombe Manor murders? There could be a logical explanation, as Helena might well have told her about the medieval chamber.

She rang up the Met's drug squad, which had raided Zucketort's home for her. The officer she spoke to was quite downbeat, considering the raid a failure because of the small quantity of illicit pharmaceuticals seized.

'I'm afraid it's on the backburner for now,' he said. 'But we're happy to add extra evidence for your own prosecution.'

'And the computers?' she asked.

'Again, we are not likely to get round to looking at them. If you believe they will be useful in your own inquiry, we're happy to courier them down to you.'

Talantire could detect the sound of buck-passing. 'Yes, if you'd be so kind, that would be helpful.'

'Just the computers?' he asked.

'No, send me the suitcase and its contents too.'

'Right you are. Bit of a film buff, are you?' he asked with a chuckle.

'Yes, we've really been getting into the horror genre at this end.'

'So I heard. A damsel in distress, dangled down a well. Sounds like a real Hammer Films special.'

'You could put it that way.' Talantire thanked him and hung up. She really wanted to dig into the computers. If Zucketort had been involved in the crime, her computers and web search history might give some indication of how it was planned.

–

Paula Zucketort was arrested at Westcombe Fields hotel on Monday evening, just as she was getting ready to leave to go back to London. A member of her staff in London had notified her of the police raid on her home, and she had spent most of the rest of the day on the phone to solicitors. Although she had promised to stay close to

Bychecombe Manor while the investigation continued, the fact that they had seen fit to go tramping through her Piccadilly home without telling her in advance was an outrage.

However, she was not surprised to find two uniformed officers knocking on her bedroom door as she was getting ready to go down for a G&T before dinner. The two constables, one male and one female, were extremely polite but firm, and would not allow her to take more than a few personal items.

'Darling, I haven't even had my evening drinkypoo,' she said, as they escorted her downstairs, past the bar and out to a waiting patrol car.

'I haven't had mine either,' said the male officer. They told her she was being taken to Exeter, where she would be charged.

'What, for that tiny little bit of cannabis while I was here?' she asked.

'Not just that, from what I've heard,' said the female officer.

'Oh bugger,' she said.

—

Primrose Chen sat at her desk in Barnstaple CID and looked at the stack of evidence bags still on her in-tray. While she hadn't been rostered for the weekend, she had been called in for overtime. Exeter's digital evidence officer was swamped with CCTV and hadn't even begun on the phones. So she'd started yesterday afternoon and was still hard at it.

Talantire's message to her had been to look into the work and personal mobile phones of the police and crime commissioner, that of the other murder victim – farm manager Bassin Horvat – as well as that of the commissioner's wife, Helena de Courchevel. The slight snag, as Talantire admitted in the email, was that they only possessed three of the devices, and one of them looked damaged beyond salvation.

Primrose picked up the top evidence bag from the pile, which was labelled 'Bassin Horvat'. Inside the plastic bag, the device was a clump of plastic splinters held together with thick, dried blood. The SIM card, the beating heart of every mobile phone, was visible but peppered with shot. She knew immediately that there was almost nothing she could do with this device. If the SIM card had still worked, she could simply pop it into the kiosk.

Instead, she would now have to contact the service provider and get a full download of everything that had been held on that account for the last six months. That was the usual limit for retention of backed-up data. Helpfully, whoever had bagged up the evidence had supplied the number of the phone. She used an online portal to retrieve the service provider's details based on the number and then filled out the privileged access request. Answers would normally take a few hours.

The next envelope contained the commissioner's phones, both retrieved at the scene of the crime. There were indeed a couple spots of blood on them. Talantire's note asked her to look for anything that might be evidence of the threat against him. That was also why she wanted her to look into Helena's phone, the device that wasn't in their possession and hadn't been tracked down, but whose number she had given them. She again used the online portal to the relevant service provider.

Having got the form-filling out of the way, she donned a pair of blue nitrile gloves, slipped the commissioner's work phone out of the evidence bag, and with practised hands removed the SIM card, which was then inserted into the Aceso Kiosk on an adjacent desk.

She flicked through rapidly. Page after page of police bureaucracy, pleas for resources. Absolutely nothing of interest. She also realised with a sinking heart that she still had to go through the Sleepy Monk Creamery social media pages. She expected the personal phone might be more of interest, so she decided to concentrate her efforts there.

Having switched the SIM cards, she flicked quickly through the pages of texts and messages, most of which in the last week or so seemed to be arrangements for the engagement party, for which the commissioner was apparently footing the bill. There were plenty, many of them bad-tempered, between him and his wife. Her last message to him, less than an hour before he was killed, was:

> All right, I don't mind if you must watch the rugby, but I'm planning to be at the Griffon by three at the latest, as I have to bring the cake. Do make sure you change your trousers, because it looks like you've sat in some gunge.

To which the reply was:

> I'll only watch until half-time. Looking forward to cake!

And her final reminder:

The poignancy of such everyday conversation was not lost on Primrose. You never know which is going to be your last moment. Helena was still trying to chivvy her husband to improve his attire less than an hour before he was blasted to death with a shotgun, soon after which she would herself be dangled down a well by some sadistic bastard.

The videos and pictures on the phone revealed nothing untoward either. There were several pictures of an awards ceremony in the cheese shed, and a video taken outside of a blue tit entering a nesting box. Most of the exchanges with others were work-related matters concerning board meetings, accounts and so forth. She didn't dare imagine what must be going through Helena's mind now.

She worked away for the next two hours cataloguing everything.

Her eyes were tired, and after yawning she got up from the desk and helped herself to a yoghurt from the fridge. She sat back down and spooned the strawberry goop into her mouth as she continued to scroll through. She was now four months back into the commissioner's personal text message cache, and there was one that made her sit up straight and blink.

It was from Timothy Weaver, who she recalled was the head of fraud.

> Planning permission is in the bag. I've had a word with Bill, and the committee are fully on board now (finally!).

The commissioner's reply was short and to the point:

> Greedy buggers.

Weaver responded:

> The planning officers still recommend rejection, but can be overridden. Steve reckons we can get rid of the stipulation for affordable housing too, once we've got the main approval.

The reply was:

> Glad to hear it. See you at the Lodge on Friday!

Primrose re-read the messages, particularly the stark reply from the commissioner. *Greedy buggers.* It certainly didn't appear to be anything to do with the case, but it still looked dodgy. She picked up the phone to the incident room and got through to Nuttall. She described what she'd read.

'There is certainly a hint of corruption, isn't there?' Nuttall said.

'That's what it looks like to me,' Primrose said.

'I was already aware that the commissioner was a director with Timothy Weaver of HHW Properties, which has got a planning application in for hundreds of homes. He seems to be hinting that they greased the palms of the planning committee.'

'But Weaver's the head of Devon and Cornwall Police's fraud department! So we can't send it to them, can we?' Primrose asked.

'We might possibly send it directly to Sharif and copy in the professional standards people,' Nuttall said. 'The normal way of these things is that they get passed to another force to investigate. The most important thing is to make sure that something as serious as this doesn't get buried just because the commissioner is dead.'

'Are you prepared to be a whistleblower, Dave?'

There was a long silence. 'I'm not sure. We have to be clear-eyed about this. The police have an appalling record of harassing officers who speak up.'

'If it was possible to send this stuff to the chief constable anonymously, I'd be up for it,' she said. 'But my initials are indelibly on the case record examining this phone, so it would come back to me. And if Weaver is implicated, he might well turn on me.'

'I see what you're saying,' Nuttall said.

'I can't afford to lose this job, Dave. I can't afford to be harassed any more than I already am because of my race. My mom needs me.'

'Then don't tell Talantire,' Nuttall said. 'Because if you do, she is so bloody principled, she'll go for it guns blazing. We'll all have to duck for cover.'

'You're right. But I'd feel guilty if we don't do some-thing,' Primrose said. 'I just wonder if there's a way we can get the evidence "accidentally discovered".'

'You mean the press, don't you?'

'No, that way it might still come back to me.'

'I finish my shift at seven tonight, and I'm heading back to Barnstaple,' Nuttall said. 'Will you still be there?'

'Yes, probably. I've got heaps to do.'

'Let's go out and grab a bite to eat,' Nuttall said. 'I reckon we can find a way through this.'

'Sounds great!' Primrose replied.

–

Primrose had booked a table at a newly opened Japanese place, which surprised Nuttall because it was quite pricy. Was she expecting him to pay? He drove them both from Barnstaple police station over the bridge into town, and he was a little surprised to see in his peripheral vision Primrose removing her hijab and fluffing out her luxuriant long dark hair.

'I didn't check whether you liked Japanese food,' she said. 'But seeing as they do teppanyaki, which everybody loves, I thought it'd be okay.'

'It's all fine with me,' he said, screeching around a bend, and then turning at unnecessary speed into a car park. Nuttall didn't know what teppanyaki was, but he didn't want to appear an idiot by asking. However, he had already noticed that she was wearing more eye make-up than usual and had freshly applied lipstick. He immedi-ately tried to shut down his male brain. *This is not a date. She doesn't fancy you. You're a balding, middle-aged Teddy Boy.*

'What's your favourite?' he asked.

'The tuna sashimi here is unbelievable. It's so fresh, pink and just melts in your mouth. The wakame salad is fabulous too. I tried to recreate it at home, but the dried seaweed at most retailers just isn't as good as whatever version they have here.'

The place was quite swish. With few other guests on a Monday evening, the low lights created a romantic atmosphere. Nuttall was smart enough to take a back seat at the ordering, and did indeed opt for the teppanyaki grilled seafood after seeing it being delivered to the only other occupied table. She ordered fizzy water for them both, and a Hawaiian poke bowl for herself.

'So how are we going to place this evidence of corruption in front of the powers that be?' she asked him.

'I've been giving this some thought,' he said. 'Either we print it out and sneak it in the chief constable's in-tray, or we ring Crimestoppers, which as you know is anonymous, and make the allegations there.'

Primrose made a moue of doubt, just a subtle twist of the lips. 'I'm not sure. How much of his in-tray does he even read personally? And a lot of the stuff on Crimestoppers is discounted without firm evidence.'

'That's certainly true.'

'I've got an idea,' she said, leaning forward conspiratorially. 'I can copy the text files easily enough and plant them on a new burner phone, with the original time and date stamps. Now, if that is deposited in the chief constable's in-tray, I think there is a better chance he will look at it. All we need to do is label an envelope "confidential evidence of police corruption", and then sign it off from an anonymous Sleepy Monk employee.'

'That's a *very* cunning idea,' Nuttall said. 'It will completely break the link with the phone we have in our possession.'

'Yes, for all anyone will know, it could have come from Weaver's phone.'

Seated opposite his colleague, it was almost as if she was a completely different person from the Primrose he knew. She had big soft brown eyes, a beautiful smile and perfect teeth, and she radiated a great deal more confidence in this setting than she seemed to in the office.

'All right, if you can create phone records, I'll make sure it gets onto the chief constable's desk,' he said.

'It's a deal,' she said, offering him a high five. When their hands met, their fingers briefly entwined. It was almost electric. His male brain could no longer be suppressed. He hadn't had a date of any kind for several years. *She is not even thirty – fifteen years younger. Yet she fancies me.* Nuttall was old enough to know that romances at the office were usually disastrous, even when neither person reported to the other. They were detectives, after all: colleagues figured out in a nanosecond who was dating who. It might not be problematic for him, not at all, but it certainly would be for her. She was the supposedly virginal one, unusual and the butt of more than a few racist jokes. His rational brain urged caution.

'Well, I best be going,' Primrose said. 'It's a long drive back to Plymouth.'

He was aware that she had been doing this killer commute, sometimes two hours each way, since she started the job a couple of years ago. Before he could stop himself, he had said: 'You could stay at mine, if you like.'

Her eyes searched his, a smile playing across her lips – one not entirely of surprise.

'I've got a spare room,' he added hurriedly.

'Okay,' she said. 'My car is back at the office. I've got my overnight bag in the boot, and I need to ring my mom to let her know that I won't be coming home tonight.'

Nuttall couldn't help himself. He felt like a fourteen-year-old. He had to fight to keep his smirk under control. 'You can leave your car there, and I'll give you a lift.'

'That's not going to work, Dave. If they see us coming in the same car tomorrow morning, they'll put two and two together and make ten.'

'Good point.' He had been hoping for the full ten, but that was the first hint it wasn't to be.

–

Monday night gave Talantire the first good night's sleep she'd had for three days. She'd arrived at Adam's place in Tiverton little more than a zombie at nine p.m. Monosyllabic with tiredness, she had eaten the seafood risotto without fully recognising the enormous trouble Adam had gone to in making it. She had mumbled apologies for being such poor company, and after two glasses of sauvignon blanc, sank into his arms on the sofa. She had vaguely remembered him carrying her upstairs, already asleep, and being put into cool, crisp sheets. Once he joined her, she had snuggled into his embrace and disappeared into oblivion, falling down, down, down into the abyss of slumber.

She was woken at six by a call from the National Crime Agency, notifying her that Bychecombe's mechanic John Rice had been released without charge. She grunted, turned over, and drifted off to sleep again for another hour. When she next awoke, she realised she had to leave almost immediately to be on time. It was a good half hour's travel to Bychecombe Manor, and she needed to be there before eight to oversee the first practice run for the crime reconstruction.

She made herself a quick cup of coffee, gave the sleeping Adam a peck on the cheek and headed off into the bright summer morning.

—

Detective Constable Dave Nuttall pulled into the car park at Barnstaple CID at nine a.m., just about on time. The smirk on his face said it all, as did the unusually relaxed pace at which he had driven, listening to music. He'd overslept a little, and when he'd woken discovered that Primrose had already gone, leaving only a faint impression of feminine perfume on the pillow next to his. She'd left a little cryptic note on the kitchen table, signed off with a heart and a kiss. In the middle of the night, when she'd awoken him for the second time, she'd whispered that seeing as this was never going to happen again, they might as well give it a really good go. And, my God, they did.

The stairs up to CID seems steeper than usual, and as he pushed open the double doors, he sensed that everybody was looking at him. Primrose was at her desk, on the phone, and didn't glance in his direction. He turned left to go to Dr Crippen. The poisonous coffee machine's Americano would twist his giveaway grin into a grimace better than anything else he knew. After dispensing a toxic brew, he made his way across to his workstation and eased himself gingerly onto the typist's chair. It was only when he logged on and re-read the case notes that he was able to remind himself where all this had come from: the whiff of corruption around the commissioner and his two senior police colleagues. Once Primrose transferred the incriminating text messages onto a new burner phone, he had promised to somehow get it to the chief constable's in-tray. Just thinking about it gave him butterflies. Or was that from something else?

Chapter Fourteen

Helena de Courchevel was judged fit to be discharged from hospital on Tuesday morning. Talantire had arranged for a wheelchair-accessible taxi to bring her back to Bychecombe Manor, where she arrived at 11:30, accompanied by Soraya Hinton and Paula Zucketort. Talantire was a bit annoyed that DCS Drayton Ross and his sidekick Paul Shortland had turned up too, wriggling their way into what was a technical operation.

It was a gloriously warm morning with not a cloud in the sky, and Helena was dressed for the occasion in a floaty summer dress. A matching broad-brimmed hat was pulled down over the one still-bruised eye. A small knot of employees had gathered outside the manor to welcome her, and Helena waved to them as Soraya manoeuvred her in her wheelchair across the gravel. There was a round of applause and some cheers. Even the top brass joined in the clapping, and so in the end did Talantire. After all, here was a woman who had triumphed over the most terrible adversity, a veritable heroine.

When Talantire had rung her up yesterday evening and invited her to attend the reconstruction, she had asked: 'Are you going to drop me down the well again?'

'Good grief, we would never ask you to do that. You must be traumatised. We have a police volunteer who has agreed to do it.'

'Well, that's a bit of a relief.'

Helena had made a remarkable recovery, though she was clearly still in a fair amount of pain, which showed in her expression as she was being carefully wheeled into the house. Half an hour later, in the parking area between the back of the house and the main barn, Talantire addressed everyone involved. There were half a dozen cave specialists and police divers, plus Dr Tom Carnegie, a historian and archaeologist from Exeter University who was an expert on medieval machinery. There was a police film unit but no press. Talantire had made it clear to press chief Moira Hallett this was going to be different from most crime reconstructions. In a typical case, reconstruction would replay the movement and activities of a murder victim, in the hope of jogging the memories of potential witnesses. In this case, getting witnesses wasn't the objective. It was simply to try to shed more light on the tight timescales of the crime, to show whether it was possible for the murderer to have committed both killings, and lowered Helena all the way down into the well single-handedly.

While the professionals were getting themselves arranged in the well chamber, and Carnegie was studying the windlass mechanism, Talantire managed a quick five-minute debrief with Helena in her bedroom on the ground floor of the manor. After asking how she felt and how she was recovering, Talantire said, 'Are you sure that there was just one person involved? Did you hear or see anyone else?'

'No, just the one man in black.'

'And you confronted this person just outside your husband's office?'

'At the top of the stairs to the basement, yes.'

'You say that you were tied to the chains on the floor of the well chamber before being lowered down.'

'Yes.'

'The chains were definitely not already fully unwound?'

'No. How would he have got me down?'

'It's just that we had a dry run this morning, with no one on the end of the chains, and it took eight minutes to fully extend them.'

She blinked and looked away. 'I'm sorry, but my memory of the day's events isn't a hundred per cent.'

'I fully understand, it's just that I wanted to try and fill in some of the blanks.'

'I'm feeling really nervous about this morning, because it will bring back some of the bad memories.'

'I know, and if at any time you want to leave, don't feel you have to carry on.' There was a knock on the door, and Talantire opened it. PCSO Amy Barrett was there, in a similar blouse and trousers to those Helena wore on the day of the attack. Talantire had been told that the original ensemble was Karen Millen. This was M&S, and she was sure it would be ruined too.

'Hello, my dear,' Helena said, grasping both hands of the young recruit. 'You are a brave young thing, and you remind me of my former self.'

Talantire noticed Amy's tiny but definite curtsy, an understandable genuflection to the charisma of this woman. Helena said, 'When you are down there, Amy, it will be very dark. The light of the well chamber above you will be like a distant beam of moonlight—'

'Actually, there will be several lights attached to you, plus a bodycam and a head torch,' Talantire said hurriedly.

'We're not trying to create a psychological reconstruction. We don't want to terrify you!'

'Well, that's all to the good then,' said Helena brightly, clasping her hands together. 'So let's get on then.' Talantire looked at this woman who'd been through so much, and yet showed such a steely resilience.

–

The reconstruction began with the first pair of blasts, firearms officer Sergeant Ian Stonehouse discharging shotgun blanks inside the control room of the barn. The noise level was recorded inside the manor. He discharged the second set of blanks inside the commissioner's office, with Talantire and a number of uniforms watching. Then Amy wheeled herself out from Helena's bedroom in her still-bloodstained chair. She confronted Stonehouse, a black-clad assailant brandishing a shotgun, who was backing out of the office. Amy shouted at the man and propelled herself forward, managing to grab the barrel of the gun.

During the rehearsal, Talantire had been impressed that Stonehouse had managed to get hold of a robotic voice changer, which had apparently been last year's Christmas present for his son. Down here, the metallic threat sounded ominous, but Talantire noticed that Helena was shaking her head, indicating that the voice wasn't right. It didn't matter.

The next part was the one Talantire had been worried about: Amy being thrown down the stairs in her wheelchair. They had originally considered giving Amy a cycling helmet to protect her but then decided it would be easier to cushion the stairs with gym mats. The firearms officer didn't pull his punches, hurling the young woman head over heels down the stairs. Amy let out a squeal of agony as she landed, and then didn't move. Talantire put a hand over her mouth in alarm, unsure where the acting ended and the genuine pain began. Stonehouse ran down the stairs, pretended to punch and stab Amy, and with plenty of robotic shouting then began to drag her along the corridor, out of the view of the audience. Talantire glanced at Helena and saw that she was crying, her mouth distorted and tears running freely down her face.

'You don't have to watch any more, Helena,' she said.

'I do, and I want to, but it's very upsetting.' She wheeled herself off to the lift, while Talantire made her way downstairs accompanied by DCS Ross and Shortland to meet her at the bottom. The corridor was crowded with the official spectators and the film unit people getting under each other's feet. She couldn't even see the scene around the safe properly, and Helena, stuck trying to exit the lift, couldn't see it at all. It was only when they moved into the well chamber that there was enough space for everybody.

Sergeant Jim Blakemore, the potholing and rescue specialist, was in charge here. Climbing ropes had been attached to a clifftop rescue frame, Amy was inserted into a safety harness, cameras were attached, and the microphone was tested while Stonehouse, wearing blue nitrile gloves, struggled to tie the knots in the nylon rope. With Amy wriggling, as she was supposed to, a few robotic swear words could be heard. By Talantire's own reckoning, this was taking quite a bit longer than the actual crime. The practice at the dress rehearsal hadn't speeded his knot-tying. Attaching the ropes to the chains had been relatively easy, but Dr Carnegie cautioned that the ancient windlass mechanism could not be relied upon.

Finally, everyone was ready, and the plucky volunteer was lowered headfirst down the well. The chains clanked and grinded alarmingly, swinging Amy back and forth across the ten-foot width of the well, but her upturned thumb indicated she was fine. Talantire's eyes were on the ropes, which ran smoothly from the cliff rescue frame. It was clear within a couple of minutes that they were moving more slowly still than the implied timetable from the original crime. Helena confirmed it by saying that she had dropped much more rapidly than this.

Ross and Shortland were both leaning over the edge of the parapet into a seemingly bottomless void. 'My God, it's like the descent to hell,' Ross said.

'I don't know how she can do it,' Shortland replied.

Talantire was looking at the display screen mounted on the cliff harness support frame, which showed from the bodycam Amy's face, upside down, with her short dark plait dangling beneath. With Amy lit up like a Christmas tree and her own head torch, there was a much clearer view of the lower reaches of the well, the various cavities in the brickwork, the signs of repairs that had been made over the years, and the slimy mineral deposits that had built up over the centuries.

'Are you okay, Amy?' Talantire asked, leaning into the mic.

'I'm fine,' Amy said. 'But you do seem a long way up.'

Grinding sounds from the windlass distracted her. 'Stop! We've got a broken link!' yelled one of the technicians. He and two others crowded around the windlass, applying the brake, trying to make adjustments. The cliff rescue team put the brakes on their ropes, and far, far down, Talantire could spot Amy spinning round and round. Then there was a shout from the windlass team.

In trying to stabilise the mechanism, one of them had dropped a screwdriver over the edge.

It fell like a missile.

'Amy, watch out!' Talantire shouted. The tool shot out of view, flashed across the display screen, and exploded into the water, far, far below. The echo of that impact roared up to them, like the voice of Satan himself.

'It's okay, it missed!' Amy shouted.

'How much further do we need to lower her?' Talantire asked Blakemore.

'Twenty feet, but I don't think we can reliably use the windlass any more.'

'All right, let's leave it at that!' Talantire yelled across to the windlass team. 'Let's get her out.'

The broken chain was fixed with a climber's carabiner, which allowed the chain to be carefully wound in again. They took three times as long to get her out as they had to lower her down. Extricating her safely certainly seemed to take forever. There was a great cheer when Amy crested the parapet, and Talantire was there to congratulate her as she was gently lifted over the edge of the well and lowered onto the floor of the chamber.

'Wow, that was a blast!' she said.

'Well done, Amy,' Helena said. 'You were very brave.'

'Not as brave as you.'

'It's not brave if you don't have a choice,' Helena said, resting a hand on Amy's arm. 'It's really not.'

Talantire guided Helena and Amy out of the well chamber and arranged for a full debrief to take place at midday. The dive team still had experiments they wanted to do, including lowering a magnet into the water to see what else they could come up with. The hope of finding the shotgun had never quite disappeared. It would be great if it could happen, but Talantire wasn't going to hold her breath.

–

After thanking the various specialists who had helped, Talantire made her way to the mobile incident room and held an impromptu meeting with the other detectives, many of whom hadn't witnessed the reconstruction. She pulled across a whiteboard, and then said: 'We've got a problem, and I'm not sure how to resolve it. The reconstruction was designed to replicate the process by which the assailant shot dead two men, assaulted and threatened Helena de Courchevel, then lowered her down the well.' She paused to summarise the situation on the board with a marker pen. She had written in block capitals: TIMELINE.

'The reconstruction and rehearsal showed that just preparing the victim, tying her to the chain and then lowering it, takes at least ten minutes. That's all of the available time between the second set of shots, which killed the commissioner, at 14:26, and Soraya's entry into the corridor, as marked by the 999 call at 14:36. We have to allow time for the assault on the stairs, the stab attack on Helena, and an attempt to open the safe, plus time to escape. That means the assailant must still have been in the well chamber for some considerable time after the 999 call.'

Maddy put up her hand. 'There was the bloodstained boots to get rid of too, one of which we found down the well, and presumably some other footwear he then put on. That all takes time.'

'So I think we have to assume that the assailant was still busy in the well chamber for another ten minutes at least after Soraya's call,' Talantire said.

One of the DCs from Exeter put up his hand. 'What if there were two assailants?' he asked.

'Well, it's always good that someone is thinking outside of the box, but it doesn't work, does it? Helena was quite clear that the person who killed her husband was standing there right outside his office when she confronted him. And it's this particular part of the timeline that is the problem, from 14:26 onwards. It wouldn't matter if somebody else had killed Bassin Horvat, with a separate shotgun, and ignoring the clear trail of blood on the boot prints from one crime scene to the next. We still don't have enough time from the second shot. Unless, that is, our killer was still in the house when Soraya was moving about.'

Right at the back, PCSO Amy Barrett put up her hand. 'Ma'am, what if the assailant didn't lower Helena down the well but just released the brake? I don't know how long it would take, but it would almost be as fast as a bungee jump.'

Talantire was taken aback. 'I suppose we hadn't thought about that because it would be so dangerous. But if that took just half a minute instead of eight that would be where the lost time was. I'll ask Helena.'

'Could Soraya Hinton be the killer?' Nuttall asked. 'If it's her, she didn't even have to leave the house. She could have used a robotic device to disguise her voice.' A couple of the other detectives nodded in agreement.

'It's always worth considering, I agree,' Talantire said. 'Helena was quite clear that the assailant was male, and clearly violent, capable of throwing her down the stairs and stabbing her. I've interviewed Soraya and I would be astounded if she was capable of any of these things.'

'Everything hinges on the account of the witness, doesn't it?' Cheetham said. 'What if she's lying?'

'Yeah, maybe she blew her old man's brains out,' said the Exeter detective. 'She inherits, after all.'

'Don't think I haven't considered it,' Talantire said. 'But, quite apart from the fact that she uses a wheelchair, she would have needed an accomplice, someone who was capable of winching her down the well. It's absolutely impossible to do it without help.'

'There's the doll lady,' Nuttall said. 'We got some of her DNA in the well chamber. She could have winched her down.'

'If so, how did she get back up to her bedroom past me without leaving a trail of blood for the Bluestar to pick up, and without running into Soraya or Daisy Rice who we also know were in the building?' Talantire asked. 'The only way would be using the lift. Fortunately, it's a "smart lift", only installed three years ago. Kieran Meekings over here,' she gestured to one of the Exeter detectives, 'has downloaded the lift's history file, which shows that it wasn't used at all during the relevant period.'

'So what else do we have, ma'am?' asked DC Cheetham.

'Unless you think Helena is lying, we're still looking for a strong, violent man running amok and then apparently vanishing into thin air after committing the crime.'

'What about Luka Horvat?' yelled one of the detectives from the back.

'He's got a rather good alibi, thanks to CCTV in Manchester,' Talantire said.

'So what about his DNA found in the well chamber, ma'am?' the officer persisted.

Talantire wasn't quite ready to explain what she knew about this. 'Let's just say it must, by definition, have preceded the crime.' There was a certain restive muttering at the back of the room, so Talantire added: 'Wanting a particular person to be guilty doesn't make it so.'

–

The Bychecombe Manor drawing room was the perfect place for the debrief. Helena eased herself out of the wheelchair and, with a slight grimace of discomfort, slid onto the greater comfort of the leather cushions of the sofa. Amy Barrett, back in uniform, sat on the chair opposite, next to Talantire. Soraya had arranged for cakes and biscuits to be served along with a good fresh pot of coffee.

'Helena, do you recall how fast your descent actually was?' Talantire asked. 'Did the assailant just let the mechanism run freely?'

'It certainly felt like I was plunging, but I didn't actually see what he did. I had blood in my eyes from the cuts.'

'If that is what happened, it certainly makes the timings work better.'

Helena nodded, and Talantire turned her attention to Amy.

'So what did you see down there, at the lowest point?' she asked Amy.

'Well, it's really horrid and slimy, and there are vertical crevices in the stonework with things living in them. I definitely saw eyes reflected in the light.'

'All I can say is I'm glad that I was in the dark,' Helena said. 'I can't abide rats.'

'There is supposedly a stone shelf, just above the water level,' Talantire said. 'The potholers mentioned it.'

'Yes, there was, near the water. I think that's where the rats congregated. I saw their droppings,' Amy said, sipping her coffee. 'I wasn't going to put my hand down there, I can tell you!'

There was a knock at the door, and a PC put his head round. 'Sorry to interrupt, ma'am, but the magnet has come up trumps, if you'd like to come and take a look.'

She made her excuses, leaving the other two women to continue making friends. The PC led her down the two flights of stairs into the sub-basement and along to the well chamber. There were half a dozen people in the room, two of them in full potholing regalia. They were all standing around a sheet of plastic. On it were numerous clearly ancient rusty objects, including nails, a hammer, a belt with a buckle. There was also, right at the bottom, a rope.

'Is this what you brought me out of my meeting for?' Talantire asked.

'No, it was for this,' said Sergeant Jim Blakemore. He turned away and lifted an object that had been resting behind him on the parapet of the well. In his blue-gloved hands, he held a shotgun.

'Is this the murder weapon?' she asked.

'Well, we'll have to send it off the ballistics to be sure, but it's of the type and manufacturer that was used on the farm,' Blakemore said.

'It's another missing piece of the jigsaw,' Talantire said. 'I guess we've no chance of getting any DNA off it after the time it spent underwater.'

There was a general murmur of agreement amongst the assembled officers. She crouched down to look at the other detritus. 'How come a magnet picked up the rope?' she said, crouching down and putting on a pair of blue nitrile gloves.

'It was attached to something,' one of the technicians said. Talantire picked up the damp rope and sure enough saw that there was a rock climbers' belay device.

'What does this do?' Talantire asked, turning over the palm-sized metal object.

'It's a brake,' Blakemore said. 'If you're abseiling, it slows you down.'

'Did any of you drop this during the reconstruction, or the prior dry run?' she asked.

'No, I don't think so. This is a Petzl device, we use Black Diamond, so I think it means the rope isn't ours either,' Blakemore said.

Talantire stood up and looked more closely at the belay. 'It's not old, is it?'

'It's a modern device, ma'am, and so is the rope. I don't think it's been down there very long. I think we might have found carabiners too, except they're often made of aluminium.'

'Which isn't magnetic. Yes, good point,' Talantire said. 'Somebody's been down here, dropped the rope and other bits and bobs. It all hinges on *when* this happened.' She had to admit her technical opinion of the murderer was going up all the time. All these skills.

'We also found a nitrile glove, scrunched up, inside out, caught in one of the old bits of metal,' one of the technicians said. 'Obviously someone had taken it off, but it's probably one of ours.'

'Let's get it checked anyway,' Talantire said. 'I think we can probably check that from the growth of algae, compared to the boot that was found down here and the various other items. Let's get it parcelled up for analysis.' Looking again at the belay, she spotted something and pulled out the magnifying glass she normally kept in her jacket pocket. What she saw was very interesting, but she was going to keep it to herself for now.

—

It was one p.m. when Talantire returned to the mobile incident room. Finding DC Caroline Cheetham idling on her personal phone, she asked her to look after the newly discovered evidence. She passed across a very small evidence bag. 'Get this tested for DNA, and see if we can recover any fingerprints from the belay in here.' She passed across a larger plastic evidence bag, which contained the rope, the abseiling brake, and a fair bit of water that was dripping from a hole in the corner.

'After it's been underwater? Will we get anything?' Cheetham asked.

'It's unlikely we will get anything from the rope, as it's porous. But sebaceous deposits from fingertips easily survive a few days in freshwater on a non-porous surface like the belay. Still, our very clever perpetrator might have been wearing gloves. When you finish that, would you dispatch the shotgun to ballistics in Birmingham? It's down in the well chamber. Make sure you take DNA swabs from the trigger area first and have them sent off to the lab, express service.'

Cheetham blinked and started to fill out the details on the forms that needed to accompany the evidence. As she did so, Talantire noticed a police courier arrive, laden with evidence bags, delivered as promised by the Met. She directed him to the evidence van parked outside and followed. She watched as the evidence officer signed for the numerous large paper bags, including one enormous one carried on a sack truck.

'Actually, I'm eager to take a look at some of these,' she said. There was a large examination table at the front of the van beyond the shelves and some powerful lighting. Talantire donned plastic gloves, lugged the heaviest bag onto the table and broke open the seal. Paula Zucketort's suitcase was old and battered, emblazoned with vintage stickers. She unzipped it and was able to examine more closely the various DVDs and VHS tapes inside. Underneath the videos, she found a battered manila envelope stuffed full of photographs, including several of a youthful Helena arm in arm with a handsome man. He had a rugged upright body and quiff of blonde hair. She presumed him to be her first husband, Yves Montagne. She looked absolutely beautiful, with her bewitching pale green eyes. Real film star looks. Finally, there was a dizzying picture, taken from above, of the pair of them on some precipitous vertical rockface, high above an Alpine valley, all roped up with helmets and pitons.

One VHS case was blank. When she opened it, she found a diary from the 1980s, closely written in a tiny hand, with little illustrations and lots of scraps of paper added to it. She flicked through quickly then set it aside. There was even a Betamax tape in a hand-labelled case. It said 'Yves: most daring exploits'.

Talantire was intrigued but had no idea where to get a Betamax tape player. Even VHS players were rare enough now. Rumour had it that Helena's first husband was a ski fanatic and playboy. She googled him under the de Courchevel surname but discovered that Yves had never formally married her, even though they considered themselves man and wife. She had heard he was a professional stuntman in the 1970s and 80s who specialised in anything to do with snow and ice. YouTube had a whole series of his exploits, including an epic 800-metre jump on skis in 1973, which prefigured the famous James Bond *The Spy Who Loved Me* stunt by the American Rick Sylvester three years later. Yves's Wikipedia page mentioned Helena only in passing, despite the ten years they apparently spent together. He was a dozen years her senior, but from the other girlfriends and wives listed, it was clear he had a very broad interest in starlets and models. Life clearly lived *à la carte*. Talantire watched a few of his heli-skiing exploits on YouTube, filmed from a helmet cam to terrify the watcher. He died aged forty in an off-piste skiing accident in the Alps in 1992. It was Helena who raised the alarm.

This was entertaining enough, filling in several blanks on Helena's own biography, but it hardly got her closer to why Paula Zucketort had such a fascination with all this stuff. Then she realised. It almost certainly wasn't Zucketort's at all; it was Helena's. A collection of personal memorabilia from the time before she met the commissioner. Maybe old Bagpuss had been the jealous type and couldn't bear to be reminded of Helena's glamorous previous life. Maybe she was worried that he would destroy the stuff, particularly after what had happened when he intercepted a Valentine's card to her from Bassin Horvat.

The suitcase was a treasure trove of Helena's past life, but she didn't have the time to go through all of it. DCS Ross was on her back. He had left her a somewhat ill-tempered phone message an hour ago, demanding that she find a suspect, someone – anyone – they could throw to the wolves of the press to show that they were on top of this appalling crime. She had ignored it but now, as she was examining Helena's photos, he rang her again.

'I'm sorry, sir, I was going to return your call.'

'DI Talantire, I'm not happy. Where are the results? Where is our suspect?'

'I'm working as hard as I can—'

'Yes, you seem to spend most of your time exonerating people,' he said. 'First the adopted son Rustam, then the disgruntled former employee Luka Horvat, then the lowlife who fraudulently used the commissioner's bank cards. All of these are plausible candidates for the killings.'

'That's not quite true.'

'And now, Jan, when the NCA hands us a suspect on a plate, John Rice, who we've already established was in the house soon after the murders, you seem to spend all your time telling us why it cannot be him.'

Talantire couldn't remember Ross losing his temper before. She knew it was no good charging somebody if the evidence didn't stack up. The CPS would see through it in a heartbeat, but Ross just didn't want to hear it.

'Jan, I've had the Home Secretary ringing me at home, yesterday evening. She simply cannot understand why such a gory crime hasn't produced enough evidence to charge somebody.'

'As you well know, sir, it is a painstaking process.'

'The public don't seem to understand that!'

'Well, sir, explaining it to them patiently is part of why you get paid so much more than I do.'

'DI Talantire, there's no call for insubordination!'

'I'm just saying we need to keep cool heads.'

'That's all very well for you to say,' Ross said. 'Look, Jan, I've just had a phone call from Greater Manchester

Police. They want Luka Horvat back for questioning, over a sexual assault.'

'What are the details?' she asked.

'A woman claims to have been tricked into a kinky sex session with him, and she was horrified to find that the scene was uploaded onto a pornographic website. She had been trying to persuade him to take the footage down for some months apparently.'

'Where did the incident take place?'

'Not here, don't worry. An address in their patch.'

'So that might explain why he was hotfooting it to the airport the other day.'

'Absolutely. But it backs up my hunch that he's a lowlife.'

'I never suggested otherwise. But he didn't kill the commissioner or his own brother.'

'Then who did, Jan? Who did?'

He hung up, leaving her staring at her phone. Annoyed, she closed the suitcase after putting the contents back inside. She then headed back into the incident room. There, she spotted a plastic tray of ordered-in sandwiches and made a beeline for it. She hadn't had any breakfast, let alone lunch, and joined the line of detectives who were queueing up to help themselves. She arrived at exactly the same time as Dave Nuttall did.

'Ham and mustard sarnies with granary bread,' he said in approval. 'DCS Ross must have a better budget than we imagined.'

'And a worse mood.'

'Ah, rumour has it he's on the war path,' Nuttall said.

Talantire smiled as she tucked into one of the sandwiches. Having swallowed the first bite, she grabbed another sarnie, put it on a paper plate, then said to Nuttall, 'Do you have a moment?'

'Yes,' he said, grabbing a couple more sandwiches before following her out of the door and down the wooden staircase off the back of the lorry.

'I want to run a radical scenario past you, and have you tell me what you think of it. I'm sure the CPS will have none of it, so we are going to have to do a lot more work. What do you know about ketamine?'

Mystified, he stood there while she laid out what was to him the most incredible and unbelievable story. He asked numerous questions, many of which she couldn't answer.

'I'm still waiting for two forensic tests, which should be back this evening. In the meantime, there's some research I'd like you to do for me. It will involve looking at some of the evidence we just got back from Paula Zucketort's apartment. It's in the evidence van.'

'Right, sounds like it will keep me busy for the rest of the day.'

'I'm sure it will. It's right up your street. And, Dave, not a word to anybody. Understand?'

'My lips are sealed.'

Chapter Fifteen

Nuttall was pleased that you couldn't type with your lips, so he could keep his promise to his boss. He immediately tapped out a message to Primrose, asking how she was. He felt it was the right thing to do after a night of passion, even if it was unlikely to be repeated.

She responded:

> Fine, thank you, Dave. Busy right now.

Fine? Fine? Is that all *she can say?* To say that he felt deflated was an understatement. He felt elated after last night and had nobody to share it with. He'd gone into the gents purely in order to smirk into the mirror at himself, which hadn't been quite as much fun as he'd hoped. He was in thrall to the promise of secrecy he'd made to Primrose, and now he was equally bound to one that he had given to his boss. He realised that being the repository of secrets wasn't quite as exciting as it seemed.

Slightly disappointed, Nuttall returned to his work. He'd already put aside the Betamax tape Talantire had told him about, but then found a second one, not in its case, but in a tatty brown envelope along with some film industry magazines. This was right up his street because he knew fellow jazz lover Stan Tufnell was also a collector of 1970s and 80s cult films, and that he still possessed a Betamax player. If anyone could get to the bottom of this, he could.

Primrose was certainly busy and happy to be so. Part of her was already regretting last night's events and wanted to bury herself in work. She trusted Dave, but she couldn't be sure that he wouldn't go bragging to his mates about having bedded her. If that happened, it would destroy her. She was smart enough to be aware that a woman's standing in a male-dominated office was at its highest when nobody knew who she was sleeping with. It hadn't been hard to maintain that mystique for the first two years since her appointment because she hadn't been in a relationship at all. Life had been solid work, and a very long commute, but garnished with the praise and respect of her colleagues, and particularly of her boss. Talantire had been her mentor and protector, the woman she had turned to when she had been subject to racist abuse in the office.

Today's workload had come from her too. A desktop personal computer and a laptop, seized by the Met police from the apartment of Paula Zucketort in central London, to be examined urgently, putting the rest of her workload aside. Primrose wasn't party to Talantire's thinking, and she felt rather left out of Barnstaple CID when the rest of the team were working from the mobile incident room at Little Bychecombe. But judging from the evidence she was being sent for examination, she had a feeling that the net was closing in around Paula Zucketort. The woman had been in the manor at the time of the attack and had apparently claimed to have slept through the whole thing.

Primrose had never believed that, and she'd seen on TV her attempts to garner publicity and attention for herself outside the police HQ at Middlemoor.

She started on the laptop, an up-to-date MacBook Pro. It was protected by a thumbprint on a Touch ID power button. The only way they could get into it was if the owner herself was persuaded to apply her thumbprint. She turned to the desktop, which was password protected. She then deployed a suite of software tools designed to crack it. Hashcat, Hydra and Ophcrack were the ones she had to hand, and using brute force quickly generated the eight-character password. Once she was in, Primrose discovered that this machine was used by several named employees as well as Zucketort, each having their own user ID. Documents that she saw gave the impression that all the fashion designs, clothing images and intellectual property were kept on the other device that she didn't have access to. This one had some security software, including cameras in the building, plus a folder marked 'personal', which only one user had access to. It didn't take Primrose long to find a way into it.

There seemed to be quite a lot of holiday photographs, as well as a subfolder labelled 'homunculi'. Primrose didn't know what this meant until she looked it up: a small humanoid. The photos within revealed they were dolls, like the one found hanging on the back of the door that led to the well chamber. These were individually made, somewhat spooky red-headed Gothic manikins. Right at the end there was a series of videos labelled 'Bychecombe Manor' with a numeral. She started at the first, which seemed to have been taken in the antechamber to the well room and lasted only twenty seconds. The doll was on a hook on the closed medieval wooden door.

Whoever was holding the phone went up to the door and turned the big metal key, then backed away. There was a shout in a woman's voice of 'ready', and the doll suddenly jiggled, its arms and legs kicking out. There was female laughter, then the video ended. The second was very similar. In the third, the doll fell to the floor, which produced more laughter. In none of these was it clear why or how the doll had been made to move. The fourth was different. It showed Helena, on her feet, working with something around the doll's neck. She then carefully positioned the doll on a hook, opened the wooden door, slipped through and closed it behind herself, with the cameraperson locking the door behind her. The fifth video was similar to the first two. The sixth was a little different. Whoever was holding the phone went up to the door and positioned a knife blade through the handle of the big metal key before retreating. On the shout of 'ready', the doll, hanging partially above the lock, jerked and fell about six inches and hit the knife, which then turned the key before clattering to the floor. The seventh video was almost exactly the same.

Primrose didn't know what to make of this performance, except one thing. She understood that Helena was confined to a wheelchair because of multiple sclerosis, but here she was, on her feet and able to walk apparently normally, at least for a few steps. She didn't have the experience to know whether that was common in multiple sclerosis or not. She was about to give her the benefit of the doubt, when she flicked through the holiday folder and saw a selfie of Zucketort and Helena sitting together in a snowscape. They were on a chairlift, high in mountains. Both wore woolly hats and tinted visors, and ski poles were visible.

She checked the date it was created. Two years ago.

She spent the next half hour googling MS symptoms and discovered that, yes, in some cases with rehabilitation and intense therapy, patients could walk again. Surely there was a big difference between being able to walk a few steps and coping with the exertions of skiing? Further googling led her to specialist websites offering harnesses and aids that allowed some MS patients to return to the slopes. So it wasn't impossible. But how likely was it? Now feeling thoroughly out of her depth, Primrose messaged Talantire to ask if they had Helena's medical records.

—

At three p.m., Talantire asked a PC to go to find Helena de Courchevel and bring her back to the drawing room. She was found in her bedroom and wheeled herself along on the ground floor. When she got there, she found Talantire sitting at the grand dining table, with Maddy Moran and Dave Nuttall to either side of her, along with a fourth man. A recording device sat on the table between them.

'Oh, this looks a bit formal,' Helena said. 'Shall I ask for some coffee?'

'Ms de Courchevel,' Talantire began. 'You are not obliged to say anything, but it may harm your defence if you do not mention when questioned something which you later rely on in court. Mr Davies here is the duty solicitor, to represent your interests.'

'What's this all about?'

'We believe you killed your husband, Lionel Hall-Hartington, and your former lover, Bassin Horvat, and then concocted an elaborate story in which you maintain you were beaten up and dragged downstairs to the well.

In fact, we have found evidence that your entire account is a tissue of lies.'

'This is utterly preposterous,' she retorted.

'It puzzled me that there wasn't enough time for any assailant to have done to you what you claimed. It took us a while, but we have discovered why. The chains were already lowered, weren't they? You weren't tied into them and lowered. You descended rapidly on an abseiling rope, something easy for a woman of your experience, which would only have taken a minute or two. We found your fingerprints on the belay and one of your hairs caught in it. You lowered yourself almost to the water, and with the belay brake applied then tied your ankles to the chain while you were safely suspended.'

The duty solicitor, a young man in an ill-fitting suit, was frowning at this explanation.

'At first, I thought you couldn't abseil down because the rope would still be hanging from whatever you had tied it to at the top. But then Sergeant Blakemore explained to me the technique for setting up a looped rope through a top ring so you can pull it down afterwards. You then threw it down the well from the ledge at the bottom, before tying yourself onto the chains.'

Helena folded her arms and leaned back in apparent amazement. 'In case you haven't noticed, I'm disabled and could not have done any of these things.'

'Not so. We have your medical records here and the tests for MS were inconclusive. Your GP notified you of this two years ago and has not prescribed any of the usual MS drugs.'

'I'm being treated by Dr Camilla Kerr-Wallace from Harley Street—'

'Yes, a personal friend, who I saw you with at the Forge in Great Bychecombe. Look, we have photographs of you skiing just two years ago, and a video of you walking with no apparent difficulty here in Bychecombe Manor.'

'I've worked very hard on my physio, so, yes, on a good day I can walk a little.'

'So it seems that the day of the murders was a very good day for you indeed,' Talantire said.

'You took pints of your own blood in advance so that you could drench your clothing with it to give the impression that you been stabbed. You did cut yourself, shallowly, and only after you'd taken ketamine, which being a powerful analgesic would have dulled the pain considerably. It showed up in your blood tests.'

She said nothing for a while, but then pointed a finger. 'You're not a very good detective, are you? You failed to find the man who attacked me and who murdered my husband, so now you're down to victim blaming. You should be ashamed of yourself. I'm a widow! I demand to be treated with respect.'

'Your fingerprints are on the murder weapon, Helena,' Maddy interjected.

'I told you, I wrestled with my assailant and grabbed the barrel of the gun. Don't you even read your own witness statements?'

'We've all read it,' Talantire said. 'Your fingerprints were found on the shotgun barrel *and* on the stock. You couldn't have reached that if the assailant was holding it, because his own hand would have been over it.'

'You're crazy! I was locked in the well room with the key still in the lock on the outside. How could I do that myself?'

Talantire smiled and passed across her iPad, on which she displayed the videos found in the suitcase, in which Helena disappeared into the well chamber and closed the door. The doll then jiggled and fell onto the knife that was jammed into the key handle.

'This was clever, I admit,' Talantire said. 'It fooled me for a long time. But having looked at this and the other videos, it's clear that you and your mate Ms Zucketort practised long and hard to find a way for you to lock yourself in while leaving the key on the outside. We have now established that you greased the lock pretty thoroughly to allow the key to turn easily, then wedged the knife you'd used to cut yourself through the oval key grip, so when the doll fell on the knife it twisted the key, locking it. The doll was hung up on a piece of nylon fishing line that you had threaded under the lintel through to the other side, where I believe you cut it to cause the doll to fall.'

'This is complete nonsense,' Helena said, then turned to the brief and asked: 'Don't you think so too?'

'They will have to make it all stand up in court,' the lawyer conceded.

'You weren't very happy in your marriage, were you?' Maddy asked. 'You were having an affair with Bassin Horvat, which we believe he broke off just a month or so ago. You were very lucky not to be found out, weren't you? Bassin's wife Tanya always assumed that it was Kelsey her husband was being unfaithful with. You, being in a wheelchair, more than a decade older, were not an obvious suspect. Indeed, your late husband fired the wrong Horvat, didn't he? Intercepting a Valentine's card in Slovenian, he naturally suspected the younger, handsome womaniser, not the diligent, quiet manager who he himself appointed to run the creamery.'

'Luka sent that card,' Helena said.

'He denies it,' Maddy said.

'Well, he would, wouldn't he?' She gave a twisted smile. 'My always jealous husband confronted me with the card and wouldn't accept my denials. Luka, unfortunately for him, had too much of a publicly known track record for his own denials to be accepted.'

'Handwriting on the Valentine's card matches Bassin's, not Luka's,' Maddy continued.

'What possible motive would I have for any of this?' Helena said. 'Lionel and I already lived largely apart, with separate bedrooms, different groups of friends. I was already the main beneficiary of the will, so whether he lived or died made no financial difference to me.'

Talantire had no answer to that. What the woman said was true. Yes, there was possibly a motive for killing Bassin, if he had recently ended the relationship and returned to his wife. Helena might have been so angry about that that she killed him. Everything they had on her spoke of extensive premeditation, a phenomenal level of planning. But Talantire knew that to convince a jury, you always needed more; some plausible motivation.

'Helena de Courchevel, we are arresting you in connection with these murders. You will be taken to Exeter Middlemoor Police Station and held in a cell.'

'Oh, this is absolutely preposterous!' Helena exclaimed.

Talantire called in a uniformed officer who had been waiting outside and told him to wheel the prisoner to the police van. The three detectives watched her departure, exchanging nervous glances.

'Have you told Ross yet?' Nuttall asked.

'No, I was leaving it as a surprise.'

Nuttall's glance at Maddy spoke volumes. 'I think I'm going to go and hide somewhere,' he said.

—

'Have you gone absolutely raving mad?' Ross bellowed at her. 'She's the commissioner's wheelchair-bound widow, for Christ's sake! She's the victim.'

Talantire, standing in the leafy surroundings of the Victorian walled garden, held her phone away from her and switched to speakerphone.

'I think if you see the evidence, sir, you will be convinced.'

'I doubt it, Talantire, I very much doubt it.'

'I haven't charged her yet, but we have twenty-four hours to get her to admit it.'

'How is that working so far?'

'She's denying everything and maintaining a position of total outrage.'

'Not bloody surprising.'

'We've got some additional leverage,' Talantire said. 'I've had Paula Zucketort arrested, with a view to charge her with conspiracy, along with possession of Class B drugs. Zucketort seems a more slapdash conspirator, indeed much of the evidence we found was in a suitcase at her apartment in London. I've got a hunch we'll easily get more incriminating information out of her.'

'Are you aware that the Home Secretary went to school with your suspect?' Ross said. 'They were friends at pony club, so she told me.'

'Why should that make any difference. My job is to follow the evidence.'

'The CPS isn't going to like it, Talantire, you know that. You better have a bloody good case to put together.'

'I'm already working on it, sir. We've got a virtual meeting for ten a.m.'

No sooner had Ross hung up than she was called by Moira Hallett from the press office, who sounded on the verge of panic.

'Jan, is this true? That you're thinking of charging the commissioner's widow with double murder?'

'Yes, we always felt it was an inside job. We just didn't know how deeply "inside" it happened to be.'

'Have you seen the media coverage so far, in which Helena is being portrayed as a heroine? *The Daily Mail* has interviewed her sister and done a double page spread headlined *Dangling in the Dark*, which is basically a hagiography of the woman, makes her sound like a cross between Anneka Rice and Mother Teresa. And I have to say it's been a narrative I've been more than happy to support. Only this afternoon I told Ross that I thought it would be good to let the media interview her now she is out of hospital.'

'I'm not responsible for the way that the press happens to spin the story,' Talantire said.

'Couldn't you even have given me a bit of a heads up, though?'

'I'm sorry, we've only just pieced together the evidence. Were you aware that we also had Paula Zucketort arrested?'

'Yes, a reporter from the *Daily Express* told me about ten minutes ago! I denied it because I didn't have the information. Damn, that's going to produce problems of its own. Right, firefight mode; I have to go.'

She hung up.

The CPS meeting turned out to be heated, just as Talantire expected. She was on Zoom from a meeting room in Barnstaple, and DCS Ross was speaking from his office at Middlemoor with press chief Moira Hallett by his side on her own laptop. Three CPS bigwigs were speaking from their respective homes in the London area. They listen carefully as Talantire outlined all the evidence that she had amassed against Helena de Courchevel, sharing images, videos and some of the fingerprints and DNA documents.

Kelvin Brunswick was the first to respond. 'I think, Detective Inspector, you should be complimented on the evidential diligence with which you've conducted this enquiry. This is quite an extraordinary collection of forensics, but I do have to say it's quite a complicated narrative to put across to a jury, and that worries me more than anything.'

Hermione Scott, Talantire's antagonist from the previous meeting, nodded vigorously. 'Can you just imagine the defence team wheeling in the accused to give evidence, helping her up on unsteady feet to the witness box, and describing the heroic bravery with which she survived being dangled hundreds of feet down a dark well? You need an awful lot of firm evidence to counter-balance the emotional power of that, yet it seems to me that there is no one element of this that is conclusive—'

'Certainly not beyond all reasonable doubt,' said Mark Kingswood, the final member of the CPS trio. 'The hair caught in the belay clip, fingerprints on the stock of the murder weapon – both of these could have been innocent.'

'I think not,' Talantire said. 'Particularly her prints on the gun could not be explained by her simply grappling with a man who she said was holding it.'

'But could those prints not have been from her own much earlier use of the weapon?' Brunswick said. 'We already have on record that she has used a shotgun to kill pheasants in the past.'

Talantire checked her notes. 'Not, I think, at Bychecombe Manor. Probably not that gun.'

'"Probably" isn't going to cut it, Detective Inspector,' Scott said. 'We need a smoking gun, not one that has clearly been the subject of a tug of war between two people.'

'I'll do my best to provide you with one,' Talantire said.

'On that subject, what about ballistic residues?' Brunswick asked.

'They were on her, yes, but by claiming to grab the barrel of the weapon, she's found an innocent explanation for them.'

'While you're at it, we're really looking for a clearer motive,' Kingswood said. 'There's no extra money in it for her for killing her husband, is there?'

'No, I think that the ending of the relationship with her by Bassin Horvat was the trigger. He may well have offered her a way out of the failing marriage, but then Helena may have felt betrayed when he returned to his wife.'

'Do we have any evidence of this?' Scott asked. Getting no immediate reply, she added: 'Then it's pure conjecture.'

'I'll be interviewing the suspect again today,' Talantire said. 'But first I want to see if we can get Paula Zucketort to incriminate her friend.'

Chapter Sixteen

It hadn't taken Paula Zucketort very long to get herself a famous barrister. When Talantire and Maddy Moran walked into the interview room in Middlemoor, they saw the bulky figure of Sir Hugh Dinsmore KC flanking their interviewee.

'I'm here to ask you to release my client on police bail, immediately. The minor drug charges so far preferred do not provide an adequate excuse to deprive her of her liberty,' he boomed.

'Those may not be the only charges, and in the light of what we are investigating we consider she may be a flight risk.'

'Detective Inspector, please,' Dinsmore said. 'The lady has offered to surrender her passport.' He used his rich chocolatey voice in a theatrical manner, projecting it for an audience that in this case wasn't present.

'That offer is noted,' Talantire said, as she prepped the tape.

The size disparity was such that Zucketort, in her faux schoolgirl outfit, and sitting on two cushions to boost her height, looked like the dummy to Dinsmore's adjacent ventriloquist. The preternaturally smooth and glossy left-hand side of her face, with its tightened eyelid, contrasted with the more normally lined but still heavily made-up right-hand side, all under a great cascade of dyed copper curls.

It was hard to look away.

Talantire began with one of her prepared questions. 'Ms Zucketort, you have already been shown the videos from your computer that show you and Helena de Courchevel moving one of your dolls on the back of the door into the Bychecombe Manor well chamber. Can you tell us what exactly you were doing?'

'We were just trying to arrange Suzie so she looked her best.'

'By Suzie, you mean the name of the doll; is that correct?'

'Yes, it's stitched onto her clothing.' She chuckled and looked to her barrister.

'It seems clear to us that you were trying to find a way to lock the door from the other side.'

'No, not at all.'

'That is clearly what the videos show.'

'It wasn't why we were there.'

'Ms Zucketort, we believe you conspired with your friend Helena to arrange a double murder. This is an extremely serious allegation, yet one you seem to be taking very lightly.'

'Naturally I am, because it's so, so utterly preposterous.' She began to giggle, which made her shoulders rock and made her look even more like a ventriloquist's dummy. 'I mean, why would she even bother. Old Bagpuss didn't have long to live anyway. He had cancer.'

Talantire tried to stifle her shock.

'Oh, didn't you know?' She laughed again. 'I thought everybody knew. He'd been diagnosed with cancer of the oesophagus.'

Talantire and Maddy looked at each other. They hadn't known. This certainly did muddy the motives even further.

'Another thing,' Zucketort continued. 'This nonsense about her having an affair with Bassin, it's just twaddle. He wasn't remotely in her league. Helena is a beautiful woman, so it must be immediately obvious to everybody that she wouldn't be interested in this squat, balding workman.'

'We have a Valentine's Day card bearing Bassin's handwriting,' Maddy said.

She gave a short bark of laughter. 'I could certainly get that he might be obsessed with her, but that doesn't prove she had feelings for him, does it?'

Talantire began to realise that this self-confident celebrity would be a huge thorn in their side at trial. She made everything sound so utterly reasonable.

'All right,' Talantire said, 'let us turn to some of the possessions that we found at your apartment in central London.'

'Yes, and what a grotesque violation of my rights and dignity that was!'

'Why did you have a suitcase of Helena's possessions under your bed?'

'She asked me to look after them for her. Old Bagpuss was very jealous of her past, especially after the Valentine's card incident. She could never even mention the name Yves in front of him.'

'Yves being her previous partner?'

'Yes, Yves Montagne, a handsome French scoundrel, stuntman and playboy. He tragically died in a skiing accident, not before time I have to say. Anyway, compared to him, old Bagpuss had all the charisma of a bent paperclip.'

'So why did she marry him?' Maddy asked, unable to resist getting the answer to a question she had often brought up to Talantire.

'Well, she *was* at a low ebb. And Bagpuss did have money. I think she soon regretted it. As I said before, she could have done better.'

The two detectives went backwards and forwards over Zucketort's movements and what Helena had told her without finding any significant discrepancy between the two women's accounts. After three hours, they decided they had gone as far as they could. They negotiated a police bail arrangement in which Zucketort would stay at the Westcombe Fields for another week, and while she could travel to London to get her workshop back in order, she would ring the police twice a day to give her location.

–

Primrose Chen sat at her desk studiously ignoring Dave Nuttall. She had heaps of work to do, which gave her every excuse. She did permit herself a couple of oblique glances in his direction, when he was on the phone or talking to somebody else. What she wanted to know, needed to know, was whether he was going to be professional about their one-night stand. The first glimpse of a smirk, or an overly jocular conversation with male colleagues, or – worst of all – him making puppyish eyes in her direction, would indicate that she had endured a lapse of judgement. She had this horrible feeling she was going to regret it.

So far, however, Nuttall seemed to be composed. Apart from a couple of uncharacteristic trips to visit Dr Crippen, he was doing everything he normally did.

She turned back to her screen. She ticked off all the phones that she had looked through, all the video and image evidence downloaded, either directly from the device or via the service provider. The commissioner, both his official and private phones, Bassin and Luka Horvat, Helena, Zucketort, Rustam. She had scanned through sent and received emails for both murder victims, for Helena and Zucketort.

What she hadn't done, she realised, was to look through attached documents and files. This kind of thing was generally of secondary importance, but seeing as the fraud people had been looking into the commissioner's finances and bank accounts, there might be some corresponding documents that would be useful to them. It would take hours, but it was the kind of mind-numbing task that she could do without really concentrating. For the next hour and a half, that's exactly what she did, until something pulled her up short.

Something astounding.

Tuesday was the last day for the mobile incident room. DCS Ross, believing the crime scene had no more to yield, had ordered the investigation be moved back to Middlemoor. Talantire wasn't consulted. Now she was finishing up, making sure that all the evidence was accounted for and that everything they needed from the crime scene had been taken. After much complaining, staff at Sleepy Monk Creameries could resume control of the premises in their entirety. But for the investigative team, the nagging worry remained that despite all the evidence secured, they were going to be unable to secure a conviction.

It was late afternoon when Talantire got a call from Primrose, who seemed quite excited.

'I've just found a new will drafted by the commissioner two days before he died,' she said.

'Where was it?' Talantire asked. 'I thought we'd been through everything.'

'There was an email in drafts, obviously one he hadn't yet sent, with Geoffrey Wheatcroft as a recipient, and the new will as an attachment. I subsequently discovered that the actual draft will attached had already been deleted from the commissioner's desktop at 11:17 a.m. on the day before his death. However, it survived as an attachment.'

Talantire could sense Primrose's excitement. 'Come on then, what was in it?'

'It's what *wasn't* in it. There was no provision for anything to go to his wife. Not a penny. Helena was cut out of the will completely.'

'Well, if she knew about it, there's our smoking gun. A motive for killing him, before he sent it to Wheatcroft.'

'Absolutely. There was no password on his personal PC, so she could have had access to it.'

'Can we tell who deleted it?'

'No, there's only the one user. It could have been anyone who used the PC.'

Talantire had an idea. 'We have a time for the deletion, yes? Was there much other activity on the computer then?'

'I can't really tell whether there were many other deletions, because the computer's trash bin was emptied at around the same time.'

'Hold on a second,' Talantire said. 'I'm just looking at the commissioner's work diary. Yes, he was at Middlemoor that morning, a meeting with the chief constable that didn't finish until noon. So it must've been somebody else who deleted the file.'

'Yes, even if he had remote access to his PC, he wouldn't be doing that in the middle of a meeting with the most senior police officer in the region.'

'We've still got a problem,' Talantire said. 'We need to have firm evidence to show that Helena was aware that she was being cut out of the will. If we can prove that, I think we're home and dry.'

'It's not a very easy thing to prove though, is it?'

'No, that's certainly true, Primrose.' Talantire asked her to forward the documents in question. Then she sat down to think.

—

Flicking back through interview statements, Talantire realised that Rustam had mentioned an argument between Helena and the commissioner on the Friday night when he arrived. Perhaps he could be persuaded to give more detail? The commissioner's decision to cut her out of the will might well have been the result of an argument about something else, but what? Zucketort was also present for the Friday night meal, but she might be more circumspect.

Rustam had been released on police bail yesterday, and in all likelihood had returned to London. He had previously been a nightmare to track down, but at least now Talantire had his current mobile number. She rang it, and somewhat surprisingly, he answered.

'What do you want?' he said gruffly.

'Just a bit of info.'

'I'm on a delivery, so make it quick.'

Talantire smiled to herself at this pugnacious response, swallowing the temptation to remind him that he could be called in at any time. 'In your statement, you said you attended a meal hosted by your adoptive parents at Bychecombe Manor on Friday, the day before the murders.'

'Yep, but I didn't stay long.'

'You mentioned that they were arguing.'

'They were *always* arguing.'

'What about?'

'Dunno, I always zoned out from it.'

'So you have no idea?'

'Yeah, I think it's always basically the same thing: he doesn't notice her and takes her for granted. She called him "an old soak". It's one of her favourite phrases.'

'What did he say?'

'He said the same old things too: "I've just about had it up to here with you. If you think you'd be better off somewhere else why not go? I wouldn't care." It was about that moment I decided to leave.'

'Was anyone else witness to this?'

He thought for a moment. 'I don't think so. Venus, you know, Paula, hadn't come down at that point. It seemed I was stuck in a long-running bout of bickering... Look, I'm sorry I really have to go now.'

'All right, thank you, it's been very helpful.'

'So you don't suspect me any more?'

'The focus of our investigation has changed,' Talantire said circumspectly. She could now hear him open a vehicle door and louder background traffic noise.

'You reckon Helena did it, don't you?' His footsteps crunched on gravel.

'What makes you say that?'

'Well, just as I was walking out, he said: "You think I wouldn't do it, don't you? Leave you high and dry. Well, wake up, madam, you can push a man just so far."'

'What did you take that to mean?' Talantire asked.

'It's about money, isn't it?'

Talantire heard a doorbell ring, and as a conversation involving Rustam began, she was cut off. What he'd overheard at Bychecombe Manor was fascinating, but he was hardly a disinterested party. Not only was he potentially a suspect in the killing but also a beneficiary of the will. The CPS would inevitably be fairly sceptical that his testimony could make much difference. They needed more.

But who would know more?

―

Soraya Hinton was on sick leave and now staying with her sister in Bideford, but she had left her mobile number. Talantire rang it. If anyone knew whether the commissioner and his wife argued regularly, it would be a member of the domestic staff. Talantire, having heard what a delicate mental state the cleaner was in, began gently by asking how she was. The woman was having nightmares and flashbacks, and she was clearly unwilling to spend long on the phone.

'Can I just ask you one thing, Soraya? Did Helena and her husband argue a lot?'

'Oh, yes. There were raised voices many times. They always stopped when I walked into the room, but it was clear from the tone of their voices.'

'Do you know what they argued about?'

'Phew! Almost everything.'

'Money?'

'Yes, I think so. But I do recall a really massive row, more than a year ago, in which unusually it was Lionel who was doing the shouting. He was really furious and made her cry.'

'What was that about?'

'He found something and accused her of lying. I remember it because it was on Valentine's Day, and she'd asked for a special meal to be prepared.'

Talantire was pretty sure what the argument was about, but she needed to find out what was said more recently. 'Were you about last Friday, the day before the murders?'

'No. That's my day off. But I can tell you that there was a big argument the day before, on the Thursday.'

'Were you close enough to know what it was about?'

'I heard breaking glass. I think she'd thrown a bottle of wine at him.'

'Was that unusual?'

'God, yes! Usually in the arguments it was her voice more than his. She used to push the door closed so we couldn't hear. Making trouble in front of the servants isn't considered good form.'

'Is there anyone else who might have heard more than you?'

'Not Mrs Stotfold, certainly. She is notoriously deaf and generally stays in the kitchen. Tanya maybe. You could ask her. She'd have been on duty on Thursday.'

—

Talantire made her way up the lane towards the cottage where Tanya Horvat lived with her children Adam and Nikola. Talantire rang the doorbell and waited, hearing the children thundering downstairs. The door was opened by a slim, dark-haired lad of about nine, his brother hiding behind him. 'Mum, I think it's the fuzz!' he called out.

Talantire laughed. 'It's a long time since I've been called that!'

Tanya followed downstairs. She was an exhausted-looking woman, clearly pregnant despite the baggy clothes.

'Do you have a moment?'

She nodded and led her into the dining room, closing the door to keep the boys out. Talantire guessed that the liaison officer must have gone home for the day, and when she asked, Tanya confirmed it.

'I understand you did some work in the manor, Tanya. Could you tell me about it?'

'Yeah.' She sighed and pulled her hair back into a ponytail, which she rapidly secured with a scrunchie. 'I did some cooking and the odd bit of cleaning. A little bit of waitressing when they had people around.'

'Were you working last Friday?'

'Yes. In the afternoon I made the engagement cake for the party, and later on I made the evening meal, which was just a light tea.'

'That meal was for how many?'

'Four. Lionel and Helena, Rustam, and that strange woman from London.'

'Paula Zucketort?'

'Yes.'

'Did you hear an argument?'

'Well, it was hard not to hear. I had a plate of sandwiches in my hand but retreated back into the kitchen. I thought I'd give it another five minutes for them to calm down. That's what I normally do.'

'Can you remember what exactly was said?'

'Unusually, it was his voice I could hear. Normally when they rowed, she'd go on and on. This time she was quite quiet. He certainly threatened something about leaving "her high and dry". I didn't really get it. He'd said it before, but this time he definitely invited her to leave, which I assumed meant going back up to London. She spent a lot of time away.'

'Did she ever threaten him?'

'Threaten, how?'

'Violence?'

'She was in a wheelchair,' she said, as if somehow Talantire hadn't noticed. 'I mean, she could look after herself in an argument. Soraya said she threw thing sometimes, but I never saw it.'

Talantire realised they were straying into hearsay now. There were useful hints that Helena knew she was going to be cut out of the will, but she had a gut feeling it still wasn't enough. Rowing couples threaten each other with things the whole time without ever meaning to follow through. Actions, not words; that's what mattered.

'You think she killed him, don't you?' Tanya asked.

'It's certainly one line of enquiry that we are looking at,' Talantire responded. 'And I would ask you not to disclose it to anybody else.'

Talantire could almost see the cogs turning in Tanya's brain. 'If she killed her husband, who killed Bassin?' she asked. 'He was working upstairs in the barn.'

'That's something we're still looking into.'

'She was in a *wheelchair*. There's no lift in the barn.' The turning of mental gears continued.

'I know.'

'So who killed him then?'

'That's something we're still looking into.' Talantire hated stonewalling, but she had to do it.

'I'm not happy. Me and my boys, our new baby, we need closure.' Tanya rested a hand on her bump for emphasis.

'Mrs Horvat, I promise you that everyone on this investigation appreciates the terrible grief and suffering you have endured. We are working night and day, literally, to bring the killer to justice.'

'So why haven't you got him yet?' She picked up a copy of Tuesday's *Daily Mail* from the sideboard and flung it in front of Talantire. The headline was *The Killer in Black*, and it fleshed out Helena's story in lurid detail.

'Don't take the papers as gospel.'

'What else do I have to believe in? My husband is dead, snatched away from me.' She began to cry. Talantire realised that she wasn't cut out to be a family liaison officer. She apologised and backed out as gracefully as she could, leaving Tanya to a miserable evening and a ruined life. That was even before the poor woman discovered, as she eventually would, that her husband had been having an affair with the murderer. It was a bloody brutal business, that was for sure.

–

Talantire had wanted a CPS conference call the next morning, and it was her bad luck that she drew the short straw. Hermione Scott, it turned out, would be the barrister taking on the case for the Crown. The most sceptical of the three lawyers involved in the case, she was the only one available for the 9:15 call. If anyone embodied the standing joke about the CPS, that it stood for Can't

Prosecute Sorry, it was Scott. She was driven, meticulous and sceptical, and she'd spent years as a King's Counsel, on the receiving end of withering remarks from judges about the quality of evidence. While Talantire was going through her papers and evidence sharing plan in the small conference room in Barnstaple, DCS Ross had already logged into the video call from Exeter.

Talantire had a surprise for them both, something that had come through quite late last night from the Met Police, as a postscript to the evidence that they had found at Paula Zucketort's apartment. She thought if anything could change a jury's mind about the poor, long-suffering, disabled Helena, it was this.

Once Scott had appeared on screen and they had exchanged greetings, Talantire said, 'I'd like you to take a look at this security footage from the internal cameras at the building in London. As you can see from the date stamp, it's from a week before the murders.'

She enlarged the video app and hit play. It showed an external view of the apartments from a couple of floors above. A London black cab arrived, having crossed Carnaby Street. The cab door opened and a woman emerged, wearing a summer dress and a broad-brimmed hat. The cabbie helped move two suitcases to the kerb, from where, after paying him, she took over. One of the cases was modern and wheeled, the other much larger, old-fashioned and clearly heavy. She lugged them down towards the bottom of the picture, at which point she disappeared from view into the building. The next camera on a staircase showed her making her way up the steep stairs, with one of the bags in each hand, rounding the corner, and continuing up the next flight of stairs. The final camera, a fisheye lens, showed the final ascent of another fifteen or more steps, with sound, at which point her familiar face became visible. Talantire paused the video.

It was Helena.

'She's supposed to have MS!' Ross exclaimed.

'As you can hear, she's not even out of breath,' Talantire said, hitting play. The doorbell could be heard, and Helena's distinctive cultured tones rang out. 'Hi, Paula, it's me.'

The door was opened. The video didn't show who was there, but there was an embrace and the sound of air-kissing.

'How was your journey?' Paula Zucketort's voice could be heard to ask.

'Not too bad.' She slid the suitcases forward, and said: 'This is all the stuff I mentioned that needs to be out of sight.'

'Blimey, that's heavy. I can't even lift it.'

Helena laughed. 'We cripples are stronger than you think!'

Zucketort was laughing too. 'Still, never mind, eight days to freedom, eh?' At this point, Helena disappeared into the apartment and the door closed. There was no further sound. Talantire clicked off the media player.

Scott leaned forward and said: 'Well done, Detective Inspector. This massively buttresses the quality of the evidence, particularly the allusion to conspiracy. "Eight days to freedom" is open to multiple interpretations, of course, and the defence team will surely dig up some innocuous ones, but as evidence of a premeditation, it's quite compelling. Particularly in combination with the pretence of disability. What do her medical records say?'

'She's not formally been diagnosed with MS. She's certainly been active in visiting her GP and NHS specialists. Blood tests, MRI scans and lumbar tests have been inconclusive. She didn't meet the McDonald criteria. I've been reading up on this, and it doesn't automatically exclude her from being diagnosed with MS, particularly if it's of the relapsing–remitting type. She is seeing a private practitioner in Harley Street, who says it *is* MS and is prescribing alternative therapies.'

'So what you're saying,' Scott said, 'is that she is likely to claim that she was having a good day when she carried the luggage, and bad days when she is in the wheelchair?'

'That's what I would expect, yes,' Talantire said.

'Well, we can blow a hole in that, can't we? If all the bad days were in front of her husband when she was at her home in Devon, yet all the good days were when she was somewhere else with her friends, we'll know that statistically it's very unlikely, won't we?'

'It's not just that,' Talantire said. 'Ms Zucketort failed to say the obvious thing when greeting her at the top of the stairs, which would to my mind be: "My God, look at you! What a recovery!" The fact she never said anything of the kind shows that she wasn't surprised to see her carrying her own luggage up all those flights of stairs.'

'That's a very good point,' Scott said. 'We'll need a medical expert witness, but I think we have easily enough to proceed now.'

Talantire was jubilant. Ross, initially hesitant, was now firmly behind her too.

Chapter Seventeen

One Year Later

The trial took place at the Old Bailey in London, in front of the notoriously old school judge Sir Anthony King-Sholton. Helena de Courchevel and Paula Zucketort were charged with conspiracy to murder, and Helena alone with the actual killings. Maddy Moran and Dave Nuttall were in the public gallery, while Talantire, due to give evidence, waited in the witness room. Right from the start, the jury seemed astonished to see a wheelchair-bound woman, apparently frail, being helped to her seat in the dock.

'She's affecting a stoop now, and she's dyed her hair grey,' Maddy muttered to Nuttall.

'Aiming for an Oscar,' he replied. 'She's added ten years to her appearance.'

The jury looked even more bemused to hear the prosecution case, laid out by Hermione Scott KC, which alleged that this woman, fearing being cut out of her husband's will, had murdered both him and her former lover with a shotgun, minutes apart, on a day in which, because of an engagement party nearby, there would be no witnesses. 'Her original plan, we believe, was to steal the Bychecombe Brooch, a valuable Anglo-Saxon item of jewellery, which was in the safe. This would have added substance to her story of having been attacked by a masked intruder. However, the fact that the combination code on the safe had been changed recently foiled that. Nevertheless, it was an ingenious plot, brilliantly executed.'

Scott continued: 'Members of the jury, do not be deceived by the apparent disability exhibited by the defendant. She is acting, for your benefit and indeed her own. It's been quite a habit. We will show that this devious and intelligent woman was quite capable of spending years pretending to have the symptoms of multiple sclerosis in front of her husband, firstly in order to depart the marital bedroom, then later to lay the groundwork for this cold-hearted killing.'

She gestured towards the dock. 'I'm sure many of you will find it rather hard to believe that the somewhat shrunken woman before you, after shooting both men, gave herself a series of superficial injuries with a knife. She then drenched herself in her own blood – which she had collected gradually over the previous week – locked herself in the well chamber of Bychecombe Manor, abseiled fifty metres down into the abysmal darkness of a medieval well, and tied herself to chains she had already lowered on a previous occasion. She then waited for help, which she knew would not be long in coming. The prosecution will show that this woman, an experienced mountaineer, a sometime film stuntwoman who lived a life of adventure until her second marriage, was easily capable of this ingenious and breathtaking act of murder.'

Sir Hugh Dinsmore KC, in his opening remarks for the defence, took in the entire court with a gaze of incredulity. 'Ladies and gentlemen of the jury. Well! In my forty years practising at the bar, I have never before come across a more preposterous set of allegations. It is almost as if my learned colleague has been watching too many James Bond films.' He gestured at Hermione Scott with his reading glasses.

'Let's be clear, right from the beginning, it was obvious that a terrible crime had taken place, perpetrated by a determined and wicked assailant. My client gave an extremely clear description of a terrifying ordeal that she endured at the hands of this vicious man. Yet Devon and Cornwall Police, for all the considerable resources that they have poured into this enquiry, have been unable to identify let alone catch the culprit, someone who was clearly very strong, having hurled my client down a set of stairs in her wheelchair, someone who wore size ten boots – we know from hundreds of bloody footprints he left behind – and who was practised enough with a shotgun to have killed two men in quick succession. This man tortured my client in order to extract from her the combination code to the safe, in which valuable Anglo-Saxon artefacts were kept.'

He gazed at the jury and rotated his glasses in one hand. 'I can only imagine the Honourable Lionel Hall-Hartington would be spinning in his grave if he knew that his own police force would conclude that it is his recently widowed wife, a disabled lady of advancing years, and if I may say, of considerable grace and poise, who is responsible. That they have charged her is absurd. I trust in your common sense to reject, out of hand, the unsubstantiated nonsense peddled by the prosecution.'

It took three days for Hermione Scott to cover all the evidence that Talantire had painstakingly assembled. The videos of Helena trying to lock herself in the well chamber and carrying her luggage upstairs to Paula Zucketort's flat certainly raised eyebrows amongst the jurors. It was only when Talantire herself was called to give evidence that Dinsmore, in cross-examination, began his process of ridicule.

'Detective Inspector, what forensic DNA and fingerprint evidence have you to link my client to the killings?'

'We have hundreds of samples of her across the crime scene, most of which, because of her residence in that very building, may have an innocent explanation. However, we did find her fingerprints on the murder weapon, a shotgun that was recovered from the bottom of the well—'

'Did she not say that she had grappled with the assailant and grabbed the barrel of the gun?'

'She did. We also found fingerprints on the stock, in a place she is unlikely to have reached unless she was actually wielding the weapon.'

'In the melee, would it not have been possible for her to do that?'

'Unlikely.'

'But possible, Detective Inspector, would you say?'

'I suppose so.'

'Well, that was a *very* grudging concession,' Dinsmore said to the court. 'So you have literally tens of thousands of forensic samples, and this wobbling uncertainty is the best you can do?'

'We found her fingerprints and her hair on a belay clip, again recovered from the well.'

'Which is how you came to assume that she had abseiled?'

'One of the reasons, yes. We found the rope too.'

'But as we have heard, my client has some mountaineering experience in the past. Could this simply have been one of her own clips, from the time when she was active in this hobby?'

'It was a modern design, less than five years old.'

'As it is not disputed that Ms de Courchevel was dangling in the well, one can assume, surely, that she may have lost hair during this terrifying ordeal, and when the clip was recovered from the water, they became entangled, yes?'

'But the fingerprints?' Talantire asked.

'Detective Inspector, you are here to answer questions not to ask them. Now, I ask again, could her hair have become entangled in the belay clip, which was apparently underwater before being recovered?'

'I suppose it is possible.'

'Thank you, we got there in the end. Now, onto the bloody footprints. We have been told that these were made with a size ten Caterpillar work boot. Did you measure the defendant's feet, and would you care to share with the court her shoe size?'

'A five.'

'Yes, more specifically a ladies' size five, which is smaller, is it not, than a man's equivalent?'

'Yes.'

'So in your account, this elderly disabled lady, stumbling about in massive male boots, was able to kill two men in quick succession without tripping over her own feet?'

'I didn't say disabled or elderly. She's only sixty-one.'

Scott interrupted at this point and objected to the phrasing. 'My Lord, as the witness says, my learned colleague is putting words into her mouth.'

The judge agreed, and Dinsmore rephrased the question.

'I believe it's entirely possible,' Talantire said in answer, 'for a woman to wear much larger boots in order to mislead. I take a size six and found that two pairs of socks were quite sufficient to allow me to walk and even climb stairs without difficulty in size ten boots.'

'Well, Detective Inspector, I can only suggest you must have experience as a clown,' he said with a grin. 'Certainly, the evidence presented so far would indicate a circus was in town.'

There was considerable laughter in the public gallery, earning a rebuke from the judge who ordered Dinsmore to be less flippant. Nonetheless, the defence counsel continued to chip away at every part of the evidence, sowing doubt in the jury's minds.

The prosecution rested its case after two days, Scott looking quite glum about the chances of conviction. The defence case rested almost entirely on the testimony of Helena, who was called as a witness immediately. Talantire watched from the public gallery as she made her way over with agonising slowness, using two sticks, and needing help from an usher to climb the final two steps to the witness box. For the defence it had a mute eloquence: what were they doing persecuting this poor widow?

While Helena was there, Dinsmore guided her through her life history, giving her the opportunity to play down her life of adventure.

'Ms de Courchevel, I have to say I am deeply sorry that we have to put you here in the witness box when you should by rights be allowed to grieve privately over the death of your husband, and to continue to fight against the debilitating ailment with which we can all see that you are afflicted. I for my part will endeavour to keep this ordeal as short as possible for you.'

The judge intervened at this point and asked her to let him know if she felt tired or unable to continue. Talantire realised that that in itself was a boon for the defence. His concern for health and safety in the court left the impression that the judge himself believed in her disability.

Dinsmore then asked her to describe her marriage, and she obliged.

'It was basically very happy. I adored him, really. He wasn't by any stretch of the imagination a glamorous or handsome man, but he had an endearing scruffiness, and he was devoted to me.' At this point, she began to cry. The judge gave her a minute to compose herself before Dinsmore continued.

'The prosecution has described, with various witness, a series of overheard arguments between you. Would you describe your marriage as tempestuous?'

'No, not at all. Everybody argues from time to time, don't they?'

Dinsmore turned to the court and amplified her response. 'Yes, indeed, Ms de Courchevel. I'm sure there is no one in this court who has never argued with a partner.' He turned back to her and said: 'I understand you had a pet name for your husband. What was it?'

'Bagpuss,' she whispered, and after Dinsmore repeated it, there was a gentle wave of sympathetic laughter around the court.

'He could get red in the face and did look a little bit like the cartoon cat,' she said.

They are crucifying us, Talantire thought. *The court loves her.*

'I'm sorry to have to ask you this but, since your marriage to your beloved Bagpuss, did you ever have an affair?'

'Of course not.'

There was some kind of noise from the dock. Zuck-etort had her hand over her mouth, but her shaking shoulders indicated she was laughing at some private joke.

Helena, briefly distracted, continued more volubly. 'I did once receive a Valentine's card from one of the employees at Sleepy Monk Creamery, which my husband rather misinterpreted. It was, apparently, a joke. Though it did, I have to admit, cause my husband and I to argue.'

'My learned colleague has alluded to a revised will on your husband's computer, attached to an email draft ready to send to his lawyer. This draft apparently excludes you from any benefit from his inheritance. Were you aware of this?'

'Not at all. When we argued, it was always his standard joke that he would cut me out of the will. He had said it so many times that I never took it seriously, and we usually ended up laughing about it afterwards when we made up. I don't think he would have gone through with it.'

'Did you go onto his computer and delete the draft will?'

She laughed. 'No. We both used the computer, and I had my own folders and storage. I didn't go poking about in his part of the PC. I'm not very good with computers.'

The barrister, having apparently successfully portrayed Helena as a loving wife beset by grief, turned to under-mining the prosecution case over her capacity to plan and commit two murders.

'Now, Ms de Courchevel, the defence seems anxious to portray you as some kind of action woman, with this photograph of you abseiling in your youth, and another apparently recent picture of you on a ski lift with Ms

Zucketort. Would you care to explain the background to these?'

'Yes, it's true that I did a little rock climbing in my twenties, and I did go abseiling once, which was terrifying. I'm actually quite scared of heights, and it got worse as I got older. It's true that I have enjoyed skiing up until recent years when my mobility has been restricted by my multiple sclerosis. I am still able to ski a little, with the help of special orthopaedic leg supports, and was keen to try these out last year, with mixed success.'

Talantire was amazed at the effrontery of these lies, but she also had to admit that they were plausible.

'What about your history as a "stunt girl" as portrayed by the prosecution?' Dinsmore asked.

'I was a model in my teens, and I auditioned for a part as a Bond girl in the 1981 production of *For Your Eyes Only*. I was a bit young and inexperienced, and in the end I only got three seconds on screen by a swimming pool in the trailer. They did shoot a scene with me skiing, alongside the bobsleigh, but it got cut. You can hardly call them "stunts". Certainly, my first husband, Yves, who was a genuine stuntman, didn't think so.'

Dinsmore was clever too, asking for frequent adjournments because the witness was tired, giving multiple opportunities for Helena to parade her apparent disability in front of the jury as she made her way awkwardly up to and back from the witness box, often leaning on the usher. It reinforced the impression that this poor widow, still bereft at the death of her husband, was being hounded by a police force too dim to find the real criminal. The jury had myriad opportunities to forget any of the thousands of facts fired at them by the prosecution, but every one of them would remember Helena's physical difficulties and the convincing look of pain on her face. Actions, as everyone knew, spoke louder than words.

Eventually, Dinsmore sat down and offered the witness to the Crown for cross-examination. Maddy Moran, sitting next to Talantire in the public gallery, whispered to her: 'He's made her look like Mother Teresa.'

'We're toast, Maddy.'

—

While the trial continued and the prosecution's hopes faded, Dave Nuttall used his weekend to restart the search for new evidence. He needed something, anything, that would prove Helena had carefully planned the murders.

There was a glimmer of hope. Stan Tufnell, one of Nuttall's jazz fanatic friends, was also a horror film buff. On the Friday night at the Coach and Horses, Stan had brought up the subject of a woman suspended down a well in an obscure horror film. Nuttall said that they had found a copy of *The Well*, an Italian production that had come out in 2021.

'No, I don't mean that one. I recall there was an earlier version, a Hammer film, I think, late seventies, filmed in Germany at some gothic castle or other.'

'I don't think so, Stan. Hammer Films stopped in 1979. I looked through the filmography and there's nothing.' He'd spent weeks here and there, all in his own time, chasing down every film.

Stan did a bit of googling, failed to find what he was looking for, then said: 'I know somebody who would know for certain. Derek Nugent.' He made a call and put it on speaker in the pub.

'Derek, I'm here with my friend Dave in the Coach and Horses. I want to tap into your unique knowledge of horror films.'

'Okay,' Derek said.

'It was a film from the late seventies, I think, involving a woman dangling down a well.'

'Are you thinking of *Secrets of the Abyss*? That wasn't a Hammer production, and it was never finished.'

'Oh, that's a disappointment,' Stan said.

'Is there any footage knocking about?' Nuttall asked.

'I doubt it. Some of the producers used by Hammer made it but ran out of cash,' Nugent said. 'They never secured a distributor. However, I do recall they shot a scene in Königstein Fortress near Dresden, in which a woman was lowered down a very deep well. It's one of the deepest in the whole of Europe. They were very pleased with the footage of that, according to the director in his autobiography.'

'Is the director still alive?'

'Charles Lovelace? No, he died in 2015. Let's have a look if there's anyone else. Ah, the cinematographer died in April. Harry Cotton-Douglas. You know, I think all of them must be dead by now.'

'That's a shame,' Stan said.

'You could try the various film museums. They all have stuff left to them. A lot of it takes years to catalogue.'

'Where do we start?' Nuttall asked.

'The BFI probably,' Nugent said. 'The British Film Institute is a mine of information. I'll snoop around.'

'As fast as you can, Derek,' Stan said. 'Dave needs it before the trial finishes.'

Chapter Eighteen

Hermione Scott began her cross-examination on the Monday by asking about Helena's medical history.

'Ms de Courchevel, when did you first start experiencing the symptoms of multiple sclerosis?'

'About five years ago, but it was almost a year later before I went to the doctors, when I began to have trouble with my balance and with stairs.'

'And how long have you been using a wheelchair?'

'Just over two years.'

'I see. Now you will have heard from our expert witness, whose analysis of your MRI scans and various other tests show that you do not reach the so-called McDonald criteria for a definitive diagnosis of MS.'

'Yes, but others disagree.'

'Evidently, as we have heard from your own expert witness. However, the NHS does not believe you have MS.'

'They think I have something closely related, a degenerative syndrome. That's also what Dr Kerr-Wallace says.'

'Yes, your Harley Street specialist, Dr Camilla Kerr-Wallace.'

'That's right.'

'You are friends with Dr Kerr-Wallace, are you not?'

'We have become friends, yes.'

'And I believe you had lunch together in the Forge pub in Great Bychecombe just the day before the murders?'

'Yes, as I say, she is a friend.'

'Did you not go to the same private school as Dr Kerr-Wallace?'

'Apparently, yes, but I didn't really know her then.'

'So you say, but she is clearly a good friend, and apparently willing to tell you what you want to hear, in exchange for a fee.'

'It's her professional opinion I pay for.'

'So you say.' The barrister then turned to another subject. Helena's friendship with the co-accused, Paula Zucketort. She briefly asked her to outline the start of her friendship.

'And you are still a regular visitor to her home in London?'

'Yes.'

Scott again showed the jury the CCTV of Helena climbing stairs with heavy suitcases at Paula Zucketort's apartment.

'Ms de Courchevel, in your statement to Devon and Cornwall Police, you said your ability to carry such heavy luggage up five flights of stairs was because you were, and I quote, "having a good day". Is that right?'

'Yes.'

'We can see from the ticket you bought that you booked assistance to get on and off the train. CCTV at Tiverton Parkway station, already shown to the jury, shows you being pushed in a wheelchair by a member of staff, who then helped you settle in your seat. It wasn't a good day then, was it? Your heavy luggage was lifted on and off for you. However, at the other end in London Paddington, the internal carriage camera shows you lifting down the same evidently heavy suitcases from the overhead luggage rack yourself, and walking off the train without assistance.'

'I had requested assistance, but they didn't show up.'

'It doesn't look like you needed it. Indeed, once you got onto the platform, as the CCTV showed, you walked a considerable distance from your carriage to the ticket barrier at a similar hurried pace to that of the other passengers.'

'As I said, I was having a good day.'

'Indeed, you were, Ms de Courchevel, a prodigiously splendid one. In your previous visit to London two months earlier, you seemed to have an equally good day. In each case, an almost miraculous recovery in your mobility seems to occur the moment you set foot in London.'

'I wouldn't say that. I still get very tired.'

'Yet on the other hand, Ms de Courchevel, not one of the witnesses who work for you at Bychecombe Manor can recall you being able to walk more than a few steps in their presence. Isn't that so?'

'I do have good days at home, but there may not always be somebody around to witness it.'

'How convenient.' She turned to the jury. 'How very convenient that these good days arrive just when you need them.'

'That's not true. It's quite random.'

'Really? You seem to be having quite a bad day today, for the benefit of the jury and of your case. You wouldn't want to risk having a good one, like you had in London when you sprinted up those stairs with that heavy luggage. That wouldn't suit your narrative at all, would it?'

Dinsmore objected, and the judge agreed. 'A little less sarcasm, please, Ms Scott,' he said.

The barrister acknowledged the rebuke and then continued: 'When you climbed the stairs to see your friend Paula Zucketort, she didn't seem at all surprised that you were capable of carrying such heavy luggage up the stairs. This magnificently Herculean feat went entirely unremarked, as the court has heard.'

'I'd already told her by phone that I was having one of my better days.'

'Again, how very convenient. Isn't it the truth, Ms de Courchevel, that this entire disability of yours is a charade; a years' long preparation for a murder that you had long intended to commit? You laid the groundwork well in advance to make it appear to the casual observer that you would not be capable of the killings.'

'That's not true—'

'Isn't it also the case that you and Ms Zucketort conspired together to make this plot work, leading to this rather incriminating comment from her as she opens the door to you: "Eight days to freedom, eh?"'

'No. She is referring to the engagement party.'

'Do you expect the jury to believe that? Engagement is many things: happiness, commitment, but freedom surely is not one of them. Besides, the comment is couched as if it refers to you, not some third person.'

'Then you will have to ask her,' Helena said.

'I will, don't worry.'

The cross-examination continued for two hours, interrupted by a further two breaks for Helena. Talantire could certainly see some quizzical looks from jurors who had previously warmed to the defendant. There was doubt, plenty of it, but could they get to a position beyond all reasonable doubt? It seemed in the balance.

Paula Zucketort was called from the dock to the witness box. She was dressed simply in a knee-length blue dress with her trademark T-bar sandals. Sir Hugh Dinsmore took her through her background and friendship with the defendant, and her knowledge of the disability of the accused. He asked her if Helena had ever disclosed an affair to her, to which she replied: 'No.'

'Were you not surprised to see Ms de Courchevel carry her luggage up the stairs to your apartment?'

'Not really. She'd already told me she was having a good day, and I do know that she sometimes has these exuberant moments when she is able to come up to London. I sometimes think she finds Devon stultifying.'

'The prosecution has brought up your comment about "eight days to freedom". Can you tell us what you meant by it?'

'It was about the engagement party.'

'The party?'

'Yes, that took place on the Saturday. She had complained about all the arrangements that she was expected to make, things that her husband had promised to do and had fallen to her because he hadn't done them or had forgotten.'

Talantire and Maddy looked at each other. They knew it was a lie, but it was plausible enough. 'The jury will give her the benefit of the doubt,' Talantire whispered. 'On every single damn thing.'

–

Hermione Scott began her cross-examination of Paula Zucketort with a simple query. 'When Helena arrived at your flat, you referred to "eight days to freedom". That was, let me remind the court, eight days before the murder of the Honourable Lionel Hall-Hartington. That's what you were referring to, wasn't it?'

'No. It was about the arrangements for the engagement party that we were both going to.'

'Do you really expect the court to believe that?'

'I'm sure the court always believes the truth,' Zucketort said.

'Well, they will not find it in your testimony. The truth is that you were complicit in the murder, were you not?'

'No, I knew nothing about it.'

'You and Helena cooked up the plot between you, as we have seen from the videos that show practice sessions of your co-accused trying to lock herself into the well chamber, with the aid of one of your dolls.'

'It wasn't that at all.'

'What was it then?' the barrister asked.

'We were trying to get the doll to hang right.'

'And what purpose did the knife through the shank of the key have, except to act as a lever to lock the door?'

She hesitated. 'I don't know.'

'You don't know,' Scott repeated to the court. 'Well, actually, I think you do but just cannot think of any other plausible idea.'

'Not true,' Zucketort said, more as a whisper for her own benefit.

'Ms Zucketort. When I asked your friend Helena whether she'd ever had an affair, you were seen in the dock to be laughing. Why was that?'

'It was simply the humourless way you ask your questions,' she said with a smirk. 'It's funny.'

'Well, considering you are here on a charge of conspiracy to murder, I think the court might find your levity a little inappropriate, wouldn't you say?'

She simply shrugged, like an aged schoolgirl caught smoking behind the bike sheds.

'Answer the question, please.'

She rolled her eyes. 'I just find this whole charade absurd.'

'Evidently. Now back to the question, and let me remind you that you are under oath. Has Helena to your knowledge ever had an affair?'

Helena was leaning forward in the dock, grim-faced, eyes laser-focused on her friend.

Zucketort eyed her friend nervously before answering, 'Well, yes, obviously. In the past. I mean, she's an extremely beautiful woman. Men were drawn to her like bees to a pot of honey.'

Helena mouthed something, the final word easy to discern: bitch.

'Helena, darling, there's no point denying it,' Zucketort called across to the dock. 'The papers were full of the rumours in the run-up to the trial—'

'The witness must not communicate with the co-accused,' the judge thundered. 'You are here to tell the truth in answer to questions.'

She turned to the judge. 'Oh, darling, now please don't throw your toys out of the pram.' A ripple of laughter swept around the court, terminated by a furious response from the judge who threatened to clear the court if there was any disorder. Zucketort endured a two-minute lecture from Sir Anthony King-Sholton, which ended with: 'Finally, madam, the correct way to address a judge in the Old Bailey is My Lord.'

'Oh my Lord,' she said, rolling her eyes towards the jury, from whom she received several sympathetic grins.

When the court was adjourned, the two detectives were invited into the barrister's chambers, where Ms Scott was not in the best of moods.

'The trouble is the jury like both defendants: Helena, of course, because she's had years of practice pretending to be disabled and is hamming it up brilliantly. And Zuck-etort, well… She's famous for a start and treating the whole thing with characteristic disdain. She even made the judge look a fool. The defence are going to wrap up their case tomorrow, so we'll just have to keep our fingers crossed.'

Talantire stepped outside to take a phone call, and when she came back in she was beaming. 'I think we've got something, if we can get the judge to let us reopen our case.'

—

The next day, the judge warily allowed the prosecution to admit one more witness. Derek Nugent was a large shambling man with long unkempt dark hair, wearing a black T-shirt with ill-fitting jeans. He waddled his way to the witness box. After he'd taken the oath, Hermione Scott flicked through a pile of papers in front of her and asked: 'Mr Nugent, would you care to tell us about your area of expertise?'

'I'm a fan of horror films, and the author of a series of books, guides and magazines on the subject.'

Scott then spent a few minutes listing the various publications Nugent had produced over the last thirty years, and then asked: 'Would it be fair to describe your knowledge of the horror genre as encyclopaedic?'

'Well, I would in all modesty say so.'

'And I believe you have managed to secure a rare piece of film footage from a horror film that was never released. Is that right?'

'Yes, it's an extremely obscure production called *Secrets of the Abyss*. It was slated to be produced by Hammer Films originally in 1974 based on an old script by Milton Subotsky, and to star Peter Cushing, Christopher Lee and, crucially, a young starlet named Veronica Courtney.'

'And why was it in doubt?' Scott asked.

'Well, by the late 1970s, the gothic horror genre was in terminal decline, and Hammer Films was close to collapse. They failed to bring the project forward due to funding troubles. However, the producer Max Rosenberg, who was behind the 1965 Amicus production *The Skull*, took it over and after years of delay hired the crew. He was convinced the project should go ahead, particularly because he had found a wonderful location. Königstein Fortress near Dresden in Germany was so well suited that he believed very little studio work would be required. Rosenberg secured funding and planned for shooting to begin in 1980.'

At this point, Sir Hugh Dinsmore stood to interrupt. 'My Lord, this is no doubt a fascinating niche of popular entertainment, but can I ask where all this is leading?'

'I was thinking the same myself,' the judge said. 'Can you elucidate, Ms Scott?'

'M'lud, if you would bear with me for just a couple of minutes more, all will be revealed.'

'Very well. Proceed,' the judge said.

'Mr Nugent, perhaps you can tell us why this particular production might be of interest here?' Scott asked.

Nugent responded: 'Quite simply because it features one of the deepest medieval wells in Europe, over 150 metres. The plot was that our hero, Lord Felsham, played by Peter Cushing, was being held prisoner in a Transylvanian castle with his beautiful daughter Francesca, to be played by Veronica Courtney. In order to persuade the noble lord to give up the combination to the family's bullion safe, the evil count, who was played by Christopher Lee, ordered his henchman to lower Felsham's daughter hundreds of feet down the well into the monster-infested lake beneath. The screaming Francesca was to be tied by her wrists to the chains, which were unwound from the windlass into the depths below.'

'I think the court can see why there may be a parallel to the current case,' Scott said. There were mutterings of assent from the public gallery. In the jury box, several individuals were leaning forward with apparent interest.

'Now, Mr Nugent, what happened next?'

'To save money, director Charles Lovelace and cinematographer Harry Cotton-Douglas decided in April 1980 to film on location with just a skeleton crew, although Ms Courtney was flown in for the crucial well descent scene. This was detailed on page 143 of his autobiography. However, she took one look at the dark and forbidding abyss that she was to be lowered down and refused point-blank to be part of it. With money running down rapidly, Lovelace turned in desperation to one of the film's runners, a sixteen-year-old girl who had only been taken on two weeks previously. According to his account, she eagerly volunteered for the role. And they filmed quite a successful scene.'

'And who was this plucky wannabe actress?'

Nugent pointed at the dock. 'She's right there. Helena Kirchner became her stage name – that's how it appeared in his biography. But her real name was Helena de Courchevel.'

There was a gasp in the court. Several members of the jury were staring open-mouthed.

'Thanks to some sterling work on film restoration at the BFI, we are now able to see a short fragment from this abortive film,' Scott said. She gave the signal to a technician, and it began to play on a large screen that was visible from the public gallery as well as the jury box.

The crackly black and white footage showed a young Helena, sitting on the edge of the well wearing a revealing white lacy dress and smoking a cigarette, while technicians rushed about in the background. Even at sixteen, she was poised and radiated a hauteur like a young Lauren Bacall. She looked archly at the camera, which was clearly handheld. At the director's call, she lay back while a group of technicians attached the safety harness to her, and then chains padded with foam rubber were wound and padlocked around her wrists. 'Action!' was called, and she was carefully lowered over the edge into the darkness, while the sound of clanking chains dominated in the background. There was a rapid shot of the camera descending into the darkness, as if it was falling.

Nugent interjected at this point: 'Cotton-Douglas rigged up an innovative vertical camera dolly to get this unusual shot.'

There was a clumsy edit, then a few seconds of Helena being winched up and brought over the lip of the well back to safety. She was grinning, and there was a round of applause from the production crew.

The screen went blank. Dinsmore had no questions for the witness, and after Nugent was dismissed, the defendant was again called to the dock. This time, a few members of the jury rolled their eyes as they watched Helena make her faltering way up to the witness box. That to Talantire was an encouraging sign; scepticism of her disability had taken root.

The judge reminded Helena that she was still under oath. Hermione Scott resumed her questions. 'Have you ever seen that film clip before?'

'I don't think so.'

'Do you agree that it's you?'

'Yes.'

'In your previous testimony, when asked about your film experience, you made no mention of this. Why was that?'

'Well, the film was never made.'

'So you didn't think it was relevant?'

'No.'

'You played a part that was an exact prototype of your supposed ordeal at the time of the murders, and you didn't think it was relevant?'

Helena looked down and didn't answer. It was the first time Talantire could see that there was any element of shame on display.

'Would you answer the question, please?' Scott asked.

'It was so long ago,' Helena whispered.

'Yes, indeed, Ms de Courchevel, a very long time ago. What it does show the court, I think, is that when you said being lowered down the well at Bychecombe Manor was the most terrifying experience of your life, you were lying, weren't you?'

'No, I wasn't.'

302

'We can see from this film clip that you enjoyed the process as a youngster. According to the account in the director's autobiography, you "eagerly volunteered" for this role.'

'I didn't.'

'So why did you do it?'

'I just wanted desperately to get into films.'

'But you took the opportunity for something that had so terrified the original actress that she refused to do it?'

'That was the only chance I had.'

'Now, Ms de Courchevel, perhaps we can return to the day of the crime, a full forty-four years later. According to your testimony, the assailant who attacked you prepared the very same ordeal to get the bank vault code from you in almost every detail as had been done in the making of the *Secrets of the Abyss* all those years previously?'

'Not exactly the same. He suspended me by my ankles, not my wrists,' she said.

'Nonetheless, what are the chances, would you say, that a robber breaking into Bychecombe Manor to steal a rare artefact from the safe would use precisely the same method as had appeared in that obscure film?'

'Perhaps he was aware of it. Maybe he was a film buff.'

Hermione Scott leaned on her lectern with a smile on her face. 'Well, ladies and gentlemen of the jury, the defendant has provided an interesting piece of conjecture. Let us suppose for a moment that her suggestion is correct. That this putative murderer was one of the vanishingly small number of people still alive who were aware of the film and the defendant's role in the stunt. If so, then he would also know that she appeared to enjoy it. So as an attempt to scare her into giving the code to the safe, it would simply not work, would it?'

She turned back to the defendant: 'Would it, Ms de Courchevel?'

Helena stared down, unable to look her interrogator in the eye.

'I put it to you, Ms de Courchevel, that you dreamed up this entire scenario precisely because for most people it would be terrifying, but you knew that you were capable of enduring it with equanimity. No one would imagine that you could have done these awful things to yourself. No one would imagine that you could throw your own wheelchair down the stairs, drag a blood-soaked dress along the corridor, then lock yourself in the well chamber. Most of all, no one would imagine that you could voluntarily abseil hundreds of feet down into this chill dark well. Sympathy with you because of your supposed disability and the horrific ordeal you underwent would be a natural reaction, and so for much of this trial it has been so.'

Helena shook her head.

'You lied about almost everything, did you not? You lied about loving your husband, you lied about not having an affair with Bassin Horvat, you lied about your experiences on the day of the murder?'

Helena's shoulders had begun to tremble, and she slumped in the witness box.

'My Lord,' Dinsmore interrupted. 'I think my client would benefit from a short recess at this point.'

'I'm sure she would.' The judge said, with a noticeable hint of sarcasm. 'However, I'm minded to let the questioning continue for another few minutes.'

A box of tissues was handed to the witness by an usher and, after she blew her nose and regained her composure, the questioning resumed.

'Ms de Courchevel, I think it's quite clear now that your testimony has been a confection of lies from start to finish. You had been planning to kill your husband for some time and replace him in your affections with your lover Bassin Horvat. However, when Mr Horvat ditched you to return to his wife, you decided in a cold fury to kill him as well. It was then that you offered to arrange and pay for your god-daughter's engagement party at a nearby pub, inviting almost every employee of Sleepy Monk Creamery to be there. That would give you the opportunity to commit both murders with no witnesses about and very little chance of being discovered. You might, I suppose, have had doubts about going through with your plot as the event approached, but the discovery just a day or so before the party that your husband finally intended to go through with his oft-repeated threat to cut you from his will put you into a towering rage, steadying your wicked resolve.'

'It's not true.'

Talantire glanced across to the dock and was amazed to see Paula Zucketort nodding her head in agreement with the prosecuting barrister's summary. It did not go unnoticed amongst the jury either.

Hermione Scott was not finished with her yet. 'In all this evidence, I have to thank the diligence of Detective Inspector Jan Talantire and her team at Devon and Cornwall Police. It was she who noticed that there simply wasn't time for an assailant to do all the things that the defendant claimed had happened. It was also she who noticed and pointed out why that one small discrepancy between the film and the defendant's experience at Bychecombe Manor mattered.'

She gestured to the public gallery, where Talantire was sitting. 'In the film clip we've seen, Ms de Courchevel was suspended by her wrists. But when she was rescued by Detective Talantire here, she was upside down suspended by her ankles. The simple reason for that difference was that the defendant, after rapidly abseiling down the well, needed her hands free to tie her ankles to the chain that she had already lowered some hours or days earlier.'

Scott rested the prosecution case.

After summaries from both sides and the judge, the jury filed out to deliberate.

There was no verdict that day, but on the morning of the next day, a note was sent to the judge indicating that the jury was split. He said that he would accept a majority verdict, with at least ten in agreement.

Late that afternoon, the jury announced it had reached a verdict. Two of the four jurors who had originally wavered changed their minds, leaving only two who would not convict. By a 10–2 majority, Helena de Courchevel was found guilty of both murders. She was acquitted of conspiracy, on which no verdict was reached by a sufficient majority. Paula Zucketort likewise was acquitted of conspiracy, enough of the jury being unpersuaded that she really knew in advance what Helena had in mind. When the judge allowed her to be freed from the dock, the two women embraced and held each other for a full minute before being separated by custody officers.

Helena was sentenced to life with a minimum term of twenty-five years, a verdict that she took stolidly.

Epilogue

It took a year to untangle the will of Lionel Hall-Hartington. After debts were settled, the ownership of Sleepy Monk Creameries and the estate passed back to Ted and Elizabeth Beauchamp – the sister and brother in-law of his late wife Gillian – who held it in trust for their children. Rustam inherited enough for him to buy a small terraced house in Devon, but he wasn't interested in staying in the region, instead returning to London with his boyfriend, Chris Tolworth, who had worked as a chef at the Griffon. There was, as yet, no replacement for the post of Devon and Cornwall Police crime commissioner.

Chief Constable Hamid Sharif had both Superintendent Paul Shortland and Detective Superintendent Timothy Weaver sacked for gross misconduct, based on the incriminating conversation recorded on the phone that Nuttall had anonymously sent him. No charges were made, but the council planning committee resigned, and the housing development that they had corruptly attempted to build was never begun. The portion of land to be used, which adjoined Bychecombe Manor estates, remained in agricultural use.

Caroline Cheetham continued to work for the police force, her role as a spy for Paula Zucketort undiscovered. Gavin Stone, who was arrested after the Immingham raid, was convicted of the theft of quadbikes from Bychecombe

Manor. His DNA was found not only on the shipping container of stolen parts, but on one of the padlocks that had secured the barn at the manor where the stolen vehicles were kept. He was sentenced to eight years. Luka Horvat was charged with rape over the pornographic sex scene but absconded while on police bail. He was believed to be abroad.

-

It was a week after the verdict against Helena when Jan Talantire and Adam Tuppen finally took possession of Honeysuckle Cottage in the village of South Buckland, a fifteen-minute drive east of Barnstaple. The village had a shop and a pub, and it was just five minutes west of the town of South Molton. The two-bedroom honeystone Victorian dwelling oozed charm as well as damp, which explained the somewhat knock-down price. Low ceilings, original sash windows, a flagstone kitchen floor and two open coal fireplaces gave it a homely feel. There was half an acre of land behind it, rough pasture that fell towards a brook adjoining a field full of cows. The place was cold, but there were two large sheds, which Adam wasted no time in filling with his windsurfer, his motorcycle and various other accumulated possessions.

It was no doubt going to be a lengthy renovation project, one that Talantire herself was looking forward to. As the more practical member of the couple, she had very clear plans about installing solar panels, an air source heat pump, and replacing at least one of the fireplaces with a wood-burning stove. Adam had promised to help. She relished the idea of the two of them working together to make a home.

It was a few days after the verdict when Tanya Horvat laid a spray of fresh roses on the grave of her husband in Little Bychecombe cemetery. He was buried in a secluded spot halfway between the lichgate and the west entrance to the church, and some way from the rather grander grave of Lionel Hall-Hartington. She knelt down in front of the newly installed headstone and wiped down the surface. The boys were at school today, and at these times she often took a moment to come down here and talk to her deceased partner. It gave her comfort and allowed her to tell him about her day. She was pleased she never had to look at that woman again, now she was in prison serving a life sentence.

Just yesterday, Tanya had been clearing out the garage, selling some of Bassin's tools, his chainsaw and electric power saw. She opened one of his toolboxes, an old wooden one that must have come from Slovenia years ago. In the bottom was a large brown envelope, creased from much handling. A sheaf of cards and letters were stashed within it. Inside one, dated in a neat hand, 'Valentine's Day 2023', was simply a crimson lipsticked mouth impression, and below it the one word: 'Later!' The most recent letter was dated the very same day that she had revealed her pregnancy to Bassin. It was brief and anguished.

> Don't do this to me, Bassin. We have something special. You care about me, you listen to what I have to say, you have nurtured me.
> I cried after your phone call today, and I couldn't believe it. Tanya is just using emotional blackmail to get you back, don't you see? Having

a child just to keep a relationship together never
actually works. Please ring me. We can work this
out. All my love.
　　Helena XXX

She had heard of the affair at the trial and refused to accept
it. But here was the proof, in black and white. Not Kelsey,
but Helena. Tanya had it wrong the whole time. Not the
young, curvy barmaid, but a supposedly disabled woman
almost fifteen years his senior. She could still hardly believe
it.

But now Bassin was dead, the affair died with him.
She could bury all her emotions and anxieties under the
crushing weight of her grief. She would remember all the
good times, the happiness, and erase the last two years for
the sake of her children. She thought about it for a few
days, then decided. She took all the letters and cards and
burned them. There: done and dusted.

The affair never existed.

But her love rival still did.

She had seen the tabloid coverage of the imprisonment, including in the *Daily Mirror*, where insiders
at the women's prison she was being held at said that
the woman was walking normally and showed that no
signs of disability. The article claimed that Helena de
Courchevel was ascribing her recovery to an infection
with a rare bacterium, one only found in the darkness
of the deepest wells. 'It's a miracle,' she apparently told
her fellow inmates. One of the final secrets of the abyss, it
seemed.

Tanya finished arranging the flowers and stood up.
Behind her, the baby was beginning to cry. She returned
to the pram and picked up the girl, now four months old,

rocking her gently. She walked with the gurgling infant in her arms and knelt by the headstone.

'Say hello to Daddy, *kochanie*. He's gone to heaven and sits with the angels, but he still loves you, darling.'

She put her fingers on the child's wet, rosy lips, and then pressed them onto the stone. 'Goodbye, Daddy. See you another day.'

She replaced the child in the pram and arranged the blankets. The girl opened her eyes and smiled at her, the most beautiful thing in the world. Tanya could already see she had her father's brown eyes. *Right at the end, he made the right decision and came back to us. For that I forgive him, even though it cost him his life. And you are his last and most precious gift.*

She turned the pram around and walked slowly back along the carefully mown path, back into the village.

Afterword

I would like to thank Hester Russell, Head of Crime at GWBHarthills solicitors in Sheffield for her expert guidance on the court scenes. Thanks are also due to Dr Neil Rushton, my long-time sources Home Office forensic pathologist Dr Stuart Hamilton, and retired detective Kim Booth. I'm also grateful to my beta readers Jo Joseph, Valerie Richardson and Tim Cary. Any remaining errors are my own.

I'd like to thank Louise Cullen, Alicia Pountney, and all the editorial staff at Canelo, plus freelance editors Bonny McLeod and Millie Godwin. Craig Thomson and Julian Holmes at WF Howes continue to be massively supportive of the audiobooks, superbly voiced by Mandy Weston. Thanks also to Julie Davenport, Helen Jennings, Murray and Dani Sharpe, plus Bill Allen and Sarah Milden for friendship and support during my research and publicity trips to Devon and Cornwall.

Last but not least, I'd like to thank my wife Louise, as always, for her patience and support.

canelo
CRIME

Do you love crime fiction and are always on the lookout for brilliant authors?

Canelo Crime is home to some of the most exciting novels around. Thousands of readers are already enjoying our compulsive stories. Are you ready to find your new favourite writer?

Find out more and sign up to our newsletter at canelocrime.com